I0558857

Fishtown

Adam Mayle

Orphan House Books

Fishtown. Copyright © 2013 by Adam Mayle
All rights reserved. No part of this book may be reproduced in any form
without written permission by Adam Mayle.

Cover Design by Allison Meierding

For more information: www.adammayle.com.

ISBN-13: 978-0-9882630-4-8
ISBN-10: 0-9882630-4-1

Published by Orphan House Books

O Lord, how long shall I cry, and thou wilt not hear! even cry out unto thee of violence, and thou wilt not save!

Book of Habakkuk

All art is quite useless.

Oscar Wilde

Chapter One: The Altar Boy

The intersection was empty that day. From where Bobby Bright sat on the concrete steps in front of St. Stephen's, he could see all the way down Belgrade Street. The ranks and files of row homes were huddled together in their obligatory intimacy. Parked cars clogged the narrow road. Aside from a solitary breeze that puffed up an American flag adorning the occasional door front, nothing stirred. Fishtown seemed abandoned.

This was very unusual. During his tenure as an altar boy, Bobby had maintained a dedicated vigil from this very church step every Sunday morning for as long as he could remember. He had never seen it so empty. He didn't know what time it was exactly, but judging from the way the sun bore down, he knew the morning was getting on. Bobby looked up at the sky with a pained squint. The great stone church behind him, for all its size and symbolic stature, provided nothing as useful as a stripe of shade and he was baking on the step like a particularly pale and thin-crusted pizza. Wiping beads of sweat from his prominent forehead, Bobby looked down to his feet where his oversized black socks had slipped down to his ankles. With the prompt compulsion of a practiced Catholic, he pulled up one of the adult-sized socks and began to fidget with it, muttering and running its hem through his fingers like a fetish.

It must have been almost ten – nearly time for Mass. Bobby had never been kept waiting so long outside the church. And he never, *ever* arrived before Father Landy. One Sunday the previous fall, the old priest had not heard Bobby knock when he first arrived. That morning Bobby had waited on the steps for fifteen minutes, shivering in the November air. But this only happened once! And on that occasion, when Father Landy eventually opened the door, it was well before ten and the start of services.

1

Today, for all of Bobby's rapping, there was no noise in the church. There was no answer at the door. There was no sign of the Father.

Even stranger than the absence of Father Landy, however, was the desertion of the neighborhood itself. For all the moral failings of its blue collar inhabitants – their constant cursing, prevailing alcoholism, and regular meditations on un-Christian things – there was a righteous compass in the wives and mothers of Fishtown. Encouraging a modicum of respectability in husbands and sons (at least on Sundays) these women would hound them out of bed and into St. Stephen's, regardless of the severity of the weather or their hangovers. That there was not a stream of congregants marching up to the church on such a sunny spring day as that day was inconceivable. It was a riddle that, despite the volume of his preternaturally large brow, Bobby couldn't wrap his head around. Wincing with mental exertion, he returned his attentions to his second-hand socks, which had once again sunk around his ankles.

If there was to be no Mass, Bobby did not want to wait around. He looked down the street at his house. It was a brown, two-story row home that was nearly identical in size and style to every other house in the neighborhood. Bobby longed to get out of the sun, run into his house, and jump onto his bed where he would lose himself in one of his many well-worn novels: thrillers, slashers, and mysteries of the pulpiest sort. From the baking step where he stood, he envisioned picking through his tattered stacks of thoroughly-thumbed books and mentally selecting a copy of the most recent Stephen King offering called *IT*.

Bobby fantasized about the horrors buried within its pages. His eyes fell to a gutter on Belgrade and, like the illustration on the book jacket, he envisioned a claw groping through the grate, grabbing at rats, small pets, or the ankles of passersby. Bobby peered through the grate into the blackness running under the street and imagined that there was something

2

lurking beneath Fishtown, cruising its sewers, biding its insidious time, and preparing to embark on mayhem. The thought of such an evil exhilarated Bobby. In a rush of giddiness, he grabbed his own ankles, once again bare above his slack socks. He could almost feel the monster's hand upon him. But this sensation of awful wonder passed as reality gradually asserted itself. The idea of something exciting happening in Fishtown was as crazy as the notion that Bobby would have the opportunity to go home and read. Although his house was just up the street, it might as well have been in another country – or across the bridge in New Jersey, which was weirder than any foreign land that Bobby could conceive. No, Bobby would not read that morning. Pop Pop would see to that.

To say that Bobby's Pop Pop was a strict disciplinarian was like calling Genghis Khan an uppity goatherd, or cancer a minor medical hiccup. Pop Pop had fought in World War II and preserved a warrior spirit for the rest of his curmudgeonly existence. Although cataracts had compromised his vision, infirmity had taken none of the fight out of him and the only thing shorter than his diminished sight was his temper. If he saw his grandson at home on a Sunday morning, Bobby would not have time to explain the situation before Pop Pop (coming to the severest conclusions about his grandson's truancy) would lob some heavy object with sharp corners at him. There was no sympathetic presence of a mother in Bobby's life. Nor was there the conciliatory factor of a father. Only the discipline of an unforgiving grandfather. If Pop Pop found out that Bobby had skipped Mass, his punishment would be far more severe than heat stroke.

Bobby slouched over and wagged his head from side to side, searching the street for some sign about what to do. It was then that Bobby noticed that he was no longer alone. A solitary figure walked up Belgrade, strutting like a cock of the walk.

3

Ronnie Delco was a neighborhood kid about Bobby's age. Like Bobby, Ronnie loved the Eagles, hated school, and thought about rubbing himself against girls every other minute of the day. But apart from these characteristics, which virtually every other healthy, heterosexual boy in Philadelphia shared, the similarities ended. Whereas Bobby was rapidly wilting in the hand-me-downs that passed for his Sunday best, Ronnie was at ease in black jeans and a gruesome Iron Maiden T-shirt. He had a jaunty athletic strut that suggested school sports and pubescent sex romps. But despite these critical differences in athletic and erotic potential, Bobby and Ryan were friends. They'd been born on the same street and had known each other as long as either remembered. There was an affinity, rooted in shared place and shared adolescence, indescribable to the uninitiated. When Ronnie saw the beleaguered altar boy, he laughed and trotted across the street to join him. Bobby raised his hand in a limp greeting. They smiled at one another. For a moment, Bobby felt the fuzzy buzz of friendship.

But this moment quickly passed. In the special intimacy of boys, natural affection is balanced with a compulsive cruelty. And cruelty was strong in Ronnie. He strolled up to Bobby, smirked and proclaimed to an imagined audience, "Look at this, gomer! Father Landy been chasing you around the chapel again?"

Bobby's smile disappeared. Sitting on the stone step, upraised on a pedestal like some sacrificial lamb, he was the perfect target for the insults that Ronnie conjured in his demented brain. Ronnie ran his eyes from Bobby's broad forehead to his scuffed leather shoes and an impish grin tugged at the corners of his lips. Ronnie cackled. As his chest shook the half-cannibalized zombie on his t-shirt chuckled in happy conspiracy.

"You look like he really worked you over. Where'd you get it? The confession box? The altar? Eh?" Ronnie hypothesized with gleeful heresy.

4

Bobby did not respond and wearily wiped a trickle of sweat from his cheek.

Ronnie slapped him on the neck. "It looks like you've been splashing in the holy water. A little hot under that polyester collar, retard?"

Smarting from the love tap, Bobby rose to Ronnie's provocation. "You're one to talk... you... you goon," he muttered. "That shirt's really something. Don't you know that Halloween is, like, six months away?"

Bobby was obviously not a master of the verbal joust.

Ronnie shook his head at the pitiful comeback. "This shirt? I love this shirt. This shirt is fierce. Iron Maiden is awesome. Number of the Beast, baby!" He howled and pumped his fist at the church. Concluding this display of adolescent apostasy, he returned his attention to Bobby. "Seriously, what are you doing out here? Don't you have a god to worship or something?"

Bobby shrugged. "I can't get in. I don't think anyone is here."

Ronnie looked around, only then noticing that they were alone. His shoulders slouched a bit, disappointed that his performance was wasted on a single altar boy.

"Did you try knocking?" he asked.

Before Bobby could reply, Ronnie stepped over him (although it would have been far easier to walk around) and pounded on the door.

"No one is answering," he announced as if he was the first to reach this conclusion.

"No kidding," Bobby said.

"So there is no one here?"

"Not unless they're invisible."

Ronnie paused. His faced reverted into a taught, naughty grin. "Well, when the congregation is away . . ." He reached into his pockets, removing a lighter and a crumpled soft pack of Winstons.

5

"What are you doing?" Bobby asked nervously.

"What?" Ronnie mumbled ingenuously as he lit a cigarette.

"You can't smoke here!"

"Why not?"

"Because you'll get me in trouble. That's why."

"Get you in trouble with who? There's no one here to get in trouble with."

Bobby considered this fact. Grudgingly, he conceded the logic.

"You need to loosen up," Ronnie said, puffing out a smoke ring. "Relax." He extended the cigarettes to Bobby.

Bobby literally turned up his nose at the gesture, but Ronnie didn't retract his arm or his offer. He shook the soft pack like one would rattle a ring of keys for a baby. Bobby looked from Ronnie to the Winstons. He glanced over his left shoulder and then his right. He snatched a cigarette and lit it. He inhaled tentatively. He coughed violently.

Ronnie nodded with approval. "There you go. Tastes good. Like a cigarette should."

"Where did you get these?" Bobby gagged.

"My Mom."

"Your Mom did not give you these."

"Did I say she gave them to me? They were on her dresser this morning. With this," Ronnie added rakishly and withdrew a crumpled $20 bill.

Bobby surveyed the note warily. "You are so screwed, dude," he said. "When she finds out that they're gone, she's going to crack you."

"She isn't going to find out nothing. She came back last night blot-toed. She'll just think she smoked it, or spent it, or something."

Bobby looked at his delinquent friend with a mixture of disbelief and jealousy. It must be wonderful to have a mother.

6

"So what are you doing out here?" Ronnie asked as he drew a slow, insolent drag from his cigarette. "Waiting for the second coming?"

"Har, har. What else am I supposed to do? I can't go home."

"Why not? They got you on a leash?" Ronnie inquired with limited interest. He was surveying the street, considering the possibilities the empty neighborhood presented.

"If I go home, my Pop Pop will kill me."

Bill nodded with a yawn. "Oh, yeah. I forgot about the hard ass."

"Damn right he's a hard ass. He fought in the war," Bobby said, simultaneously indicating the respect that the scion of his very exclusive family unit deserved while justifying his fear of the man.

"Whatever. World War II was a hundred years ago. It's ancient history. Your Pop Pop is a fossil."

"He's no fossil. He'd still beat your ass."

"He couldn't beat his own…" Ronnie began, but was interrupted by a thunderous squeal that shattered the morning silence. The boys jerked their heads around, their cigarettes dangling from their mouths, and saw a black blur of a car streak through an intersection a few blocks away. The peeling tires echoed through Fishtown and diminished into the distance.

"What the hell was that?" Ronnie asked.

"I don't know." Bobby responded, now on his feet.

They both hesitated, listening for some report of the car. When none came, they resumed their conversation.

"Anyway. Forget Pop Pop," Ronnie said. "You're just going to wait out here? Sitting in the sun like some jerk-off?"

Bobby groaned. He plucked his cigarette from his lips and threw it away in disgust. But the combination of a bandy-armed throwing technique and a cross breeze caused it to falter in mid-flight and fall inches from his feet. "I don't have a lot of choice here. I can't go home," Bobby sulked.

7

Ronnie frowned at the throw. "You know, for someone with a really big head, you're pretty dense." He pulled a mighty drag on his cigarette and flicked the butt. It cleared the median and skipped fantastically to the opposite curb. "There is a world of possibilities out there," he philosophized.

"What do you mean?" Bobby asked, pouting at the difference in the length of their flicks.

"Staying here and going home aren't your only choices."

"Yeah? What are my choices then?"

Ronnie regarded Bobby with dwindling patience. "We are healthy, resourceful young men in the prime of our youth. Between the two of us, we have half a pack of cigarettes, twenty bucks, and a whole morning to burn. The world is our oyster."

Bobby considered Ronnie's delinquent optimism. "Go on…" he said.

"Have some imagination!" Ronnie cried. "How about this? We'll go to the movies at the Pavilion. They're doing a double feature of *The Thing* and *Escape from New York*. We'll hit the first show. Throw some popcorn around. Rub one out in the back. You know, see where the afternoon takes us."

Bobby shook his head as if a swarm of horse flies had appeared and started to sting his face. There were several pertinent points in Ronnie's proposal that he objected to. But one consideration dominated. "No way, Ronnie. If Pop Pop found out I skipped Mass, he'd kill me."

"Grow a pair, gomer," Ronnie encouraged. "Gramps doesn't talk to anyone and he hasn't been out of the house in years. He'll never know. Besides, look around! There's no one here. Mass has been suspended. God's taken the day off."

"God doesn't take a day off, man."

8

"Of course he does. Doesn't the Bible say that on Sunday, God had a beer and watched football?"

"I don't think that it does."

"Of course it does," Ronnie insisted. "Now, come on. Let's go. It's practically a commandment."

Bobby fidgeted, torn between two irreconcilable camps. He didn't want to stay, but he was afraid to go. His role as an altar boy was a minor one, but vital. If he left, he'd be letting down his grandfather, Father Landy, the congregation he represented, and, in a vague but altogether more vital sense, God himself. (Or herself. Bobby was no sexist!) He gazed up at the church and felt this responsibility weigh upon him like the hundreds of tons of slate, limestone, and timber from which it was constructed.

But also pressing was Ronnie Delco, who stood above Bobby, arms crossed upon his Iron Maiden shirt, daring the altar boy into action. Although he lacked Father Landy's wisdom, the church's physical volume, and the infinite mystery of God, Ronnie did have a certain something. Like most awkward and unsure boys, peer pressure had a powerful effect on the Bobby. Despite his better judgment, Ronnie's demands won out over the other abstract arguments of accountability, responsibility, and eternity. Bobby stood up and committed himself to the path of idleness, Winston cigarettes, and matinees.

The boys walked up Belgrade. As the church sank behind the receding roof tops, Bobby relaxed, settling into his sinful course. He removed his tie and undid the top button of his shirt. The sun still burned overhead, but be breathed more easily. He was no longer withering in the heat. He was basking in it.

"So when does the movies start?" Bobby asked. His head was tilted back and the sunshine gleamed off his wide brow.

9

"I don't know. Eleven, I think," Ronnie said absently, concentrating on his rakish swagger. "Maybe."

Bobby shot an unhappy glance at Ronnie. He hated uncertainty and unsettled things. But Bobby controlled himself. On a strange day like this, it was best to go with the flow.

"Oh," he said with restraint. "What are we going to do 'til then?"

"Who knows?" Ronnie declared with happy indifference. "The world is full of possibilities. Don't be so hung about the details. You never know what's coming anyway."

Bobby looked up the street away and considered his friend's words with no small skepticism. Belgrade Street was, like every street radiating off of it in regular intervals, rutted and faded to a chalky gray. Uncollected garbage sat on sidewalk corners. Bobby observed the row homes on his left and right. Their two-story facades echoed one another like beats of an architectural metronome ticking away until eternity. In his adolescent mind, he could not conceive of anything that would interrupt their persistent monotony.

But just as Bobby concluded that his first twelve years of life would provide the template for all the years that would follow, and things would remain as they were forever, circumstances intervened to undermine this premature confidence.

At that moment, a figure in black emerged from a side street, making haste.

Although this figure was some distance away, Bobby recognized him immediately. It was Father Landy. His head hung low and his short legs pumped and scissored anxiously in the direction of St. Stephen's. The usually even-tempered priest exuded a palpable unease. A sense of foreboding filled Bobby. This foreboding was quickly followed by panic as Bobby realized that he would be caught playing hooky from Mass.

10

An unrepeatable curse issued from Bobby's lips that gave even Ronnie Delco pause.

"You kiss your mother with that mouth? Oh, wait. You don't have a mother."

"Shut up, dude. It's Father Landy!" Bobby peeped as he clumsily buttoned his shirt. "If he sees me, he'll know that I'm skipping Mass."

"So what? He's skipping Mass too. What's the big deal?"

Bobby didn't have time to argue. He whipped his tie out of his pocket and nearly choked himself as he cinched it around his neck. "I'm screwed," he gasped.

Bobby wanted to bolt back to the church, but it was too late. He watched the priest's approach with the grim inevitability of a driver who stalled on the railroad tracks and was watching an oncoming train.

Father Landy didn't see the boys until he nearly bumped into them. As he lifted his eyes from the sidewalk, the priest's round face, which was so often composed in a comforting smile, was red and jowly. He looked between the boys distractedly. His confusion was exacerbated by the gruesome corpse printed on Ronnie's chest. For a moment it seemed like Father Landy wanted to chastise Ronnie for wearing such a hellish shirt on the holiest of days. But he said nothing. Father Landy had more pressing matters at hand and some souls were not worth the effort.

Regaining his composure, the priest addressed Bobby. "What are you doing on the street, my son?" he asked with more concern than censure.

"I'm sorry, Father. I know I should be at the church…But, you see, I was on the steps waiting for Mass for a really long time… and then Ronnie here came along and…" the altar boy muttered.

"Mass? Is anyone else at the church?" Father Landy asked.

"No, Father. No one. That's what I was saying. I was sitting on the steps by myself and Ronnie came along . . ." Bobby swallowed nervously. "He made me leave." His eyes darted accusingly at Ronnie.

Father Landy paid no mind to Bobby's attempted betrayal. "No one? You're sure, my boy?"

"Uh-huh," Bobby said.

"Thank our Mother Mary in Heaven," Father Landy proclaimed. "Now Bobby, you ... you and your *friend* (his tone oozed with disapproval) must get off the street. You need to go home." He placed his hands on their shoulders and guided them back in the direction of St. Stephen's.

"What's the matter, Father?" Bobby asked.

"Yeah, what's with the hands, Pops?" Ronnie said, flinching from the clergyman's touch.

"It's not safe for you boys to be outside."

"But why?" Bobby was alarmed by the priest's behavior.

"Sweet Mary in the manger," Father Landy declared. "You're in mortal danger, my son. It's the Grauwickels. Gus Grauwickel and his boys are out for blood."

"Gus Grauwickel? Who'd be stupid enough to set him off?" Ronnie asked with happy misanthropy.

The Grauwickels were a large, broken family that lived in a little, broken house on Susquehanna. The family drove down property values for blocks in any given direction. Gus was a well-recognized bastard whose calculated meanness had only been sharpened since being laid-off from the Westinghouse plant. Although his four boys could never match the pitch of his pure, unadulterated son-of-a-bitchery, they more than made up for this shortcoming with undiscriminating violence. Everyone in Fishtown knew about the Grauwickels and everyone avoided them. Only a fool would step on their toes.

12

Father Landy had a pained look on his face. If he hadn't been urging the boys along with both hands, he would have made the sign of the cross on his chest. "Ed Flood," he exasperated. "Poor, foolish Ed Flood."

"*Ed Flood*?" Ronnie guffawed. He couldn't help laughing when he thought of the pockmarked and awkward Ed Flood, a high school flunky who graduated to bag boy at the IGA.

"What did Ed do?" Bobby asked.

Father Landy considered his words carefully. "He wasn't keeping his Temple Holy," he said vaguely.

"What do you mean by that?" Ronnie grumbled. Euphemism and subtlety irritated him.

"He got friendly with young Ellie Grauwickel and he didn't treat her in the most honorable way," Father Landy elaborated.

"Huh?" Bobby said. Innuendo was also lost on him.

The priest rolled his eyes. "Jumping Jehosephat. I know what filthy imaginations you boys have. Use them. He wasn't keeping his steeple in his pants, do you follow?"

Comprehension flashed across the boys' faces. Ronnie smiled widely. A grin tugged at the corners of Bobby's lips.

"That's right," the priest said. "Now you're on the trolley. Ed Flood messed around in sin. He did things he shouldn't have done. Now he has set off Gus Grauwickel and his brood like a hive of inbred bees. Oh, there will be hell to pay for this."

"But what are they going to do? What do they want?" Bobby asked.

Father Landy paused, giving his reply a mortal gravity. "They want blood," he said.

The economy of the priest's words sent a shiver down Bobby's spine.

Sensing Bobby's alarm, Father Landy adopted a more heartening tone. "Now, Bobby, there's no need to worry. Nothing is going to happen to you. Even Ed Flood, the poor wretch, will be fine. He is well and hidden. But in the meantime, we need to get you off the street until the Grauwickels wear themselves out."

Father Landy ushered the boys along the street. When St. Stephen's came into view, it had a calming effect on the priest. Reminding him of his duty as a man of the cloth to guide and educate his flock, the churched encouraged him to take a more didactic view of the morning's events. "Let this mess with Ed Flood be an example to you," the priest sermonized. "This whole situation could have been avoided if he hadn't strayed from the righteous path. Our Holy Father wants the best for you and this sort of trouble won't happen if you follow his commandments."

"Never forget that sin doesn't only affect you," he pointed out with sudden severity and shook the boys' shoulders for emphasis. "Your evil deeds also hurt others. Now I know what dirty minds and sordid inclinations boys have, but you shouldn't encourage it in young girls. Do you think any of this would have happened if Ed Flood hadn't goaded that Grauwickel girl into sin? You don't want to ruin some poor girl's life because you can't keep your passion in your pants, do you?"

Bobby shook his head, indicating vigorously that he did not. Ronnie, however, lifted his chin defiantly, suggesting that he could think of worse things. Father Landy frowned at the boy. But he was prevented from addressing Ronnie's prideful display by an explosion up the street.

The priest and the two boys turned and saw an ungainly young man burst onto Belgrade from Marlborough Street, scrambling in their direction. The flailing sprint and pimpled panic at once marked the young man as Ed Flood. Another boom shattered the silence, which was followed by the muddled reports of agitated human voices.

14

"Oh, Peter, Paul and Mary," Father Landy murmured. He swallowed deeply and his Adam's apple rose and fell like a buoy on a troubled sea. "They found him. My God, they found him." He turned to Bobby and Ronnie. "You two must run home. Now!"

"What are you going to do?" Bobby asked, quaking in his loafers.

"Don't worry about me," the priest said. "Just go home."

Contrary to his command, the boys stayed in place: Bobby out of fear; Ronnie out of morbid curiosity.

"Go, I said," the priest repeated and shoved them up the sidewalk. "Run!" he commanded, before starting back down Belgrade.

Ronnie and Bobby half-obeyed. They ran, but they didn't run home. Once they turned the corner at St. Stephen's, they stopped and peeked back around the building.

Father Landy walked towards Ed Flood. Ed Flood ran full bore in the priest's direction, his arms flapping with each step as though they were only loosely tethered to his body. As the young man approached, the priest called out to him. Ed Flood did not stop. He ran past the priest.

Father Landy turned after Ed Flood. Bobby saw irritation on the priest's face. He wasn't accustomed to having his heavenly-dispensed authority ignored. But before he could reproach the fleeing Ed Flood, he saw another opportunity to exercise his clerical clout and mediate the crisis. Huffing up Belgrade in the priest's direction was the stocky, red-faced giant that was Gus Grauwickel. He was flanked by his four sons, all armed with bats, stones, bricks, and other bits of debris repurposed for violent ends. Gus carried a twelve-gauge shotgun in his hands.

Chapter Two: A Very Meager Vanity

Bobby Bright awoke with a terrible start. While asleep he had the sensation of being smothered, of having a great weight upon his chest, suffocating him. He tried to sit up, but an uncertain mass pressed down on him. Bobby struggled to escape from the twists of bedding, but like some linen quicksand, the more he strained to get free, the more the covers clung to him. With all the might he could summon, he finally jerked himself free and stumbled onto the carpet.

Covered in sweat and his heart trembling, Bobby looked back at the bed. It took a moment for his eyes to adjust to the darkness. When they finally did, his fear was replaced by a cozy familiarity. Visible in the nest of bedding was an arm, thigh, and ample backside, all of which belonged to his girlfriend, Suzie. She murmured in her sleep and then, like a beluga whale rolling on the ocean, twisted onto her back, dragging the bedding with her and disappearing entirely beneath the comforter.

Bobby shivered out a sigh. So it was that he met his Friday – naked, fully-grown, and trembling on a dark September morning.

He shuffled to the bathroom and locked the door behind him. He was not worried that Suzie would bother him. She was taking a light course load this semester after nearly failing last term and rarely got up before ten. No, Bobby locked the door simply because morning was one of the few times of day that he was alone. He relished his privacy. When he locked the door, the bathroom became a cocoon, a private sanctuary, a place where he could revel in "Bobby time."

Greeting his reflection with a mighty yawn, Bobby looked into the mirror. Although he was not old – or even middle aged, really – the man looking back at him was no longer young. His cheeks were stubbled. His eyes had dark circles. He ran his fingers through his thinning hair, which seemed more recessed than it actually was because of his oversized forehead. In sum, Bobby belonged to the hazy demographic where twenties give way to thirties and the accumulated effects of three decades of a life more or less lived start to show.

But while his bloom of youth had lost its proverbial petals, traces of the boy were yet evident in him. Bobby still had the thin sloping shoulders of his gangly adolescence. He turned his head in profile to better inspect his face. He was pleased to note that his eyes and cheeks were smooth and unwrinkled. Even his enormous forehead, a feature that generally did him no favors, hinted at youth, as though it was still something to grow into, some physical expression of expectation and promise.

"Not so bad," he thought, indulging a very meager vanity. *"Not so bad at all."*

Bobby thought about his appearance often. By considering his physical features, he felt as though he gained greater control of himself. This meticulous inspection of his person was evident in every step of his morning routine. From scrubbing each armpit exactly twenty times in the shower to the precision detailing he applied to brushing his teeth and counting from one to one-hundred while rinsing his mouth with Listerine. Each of his ablutions was also an act of self-possession.

Emerging from the steaming bathroom, dressed in khakis and a button-down shirt, Bobby peeked back into the bedroom. Suzie was still in bed, splayed on her back, her long blonde hair fanned radially across her pillow. Her large and unmanageable breasts rose and fell beneath an over-sized Eagles t-shirt. Bobby looked on her and the uncomplicated pleasures she represented. As she slept, she crinkled her button nose and sniffled out a little glottal snore, which, to his ears, sounded like a purr. He smiled and with no small reluctance left her to her dreams.

17

The sky was still dark gray when Bobby stepped outside. The sun had not yet risen over Fishtown and the street was empty except for a swarthy man carrying some lumber into a dilapidated row home across the street. A vaguely Slavic personage, the man had been fixing up the house for the better part of the month and, for the better part of a month, Bobby had done his best every morning to avoid making eye contact.

As Bobby looked down at his feet, trying to prevent any accidental engagement, he tried to recall where he had parked his car. When he remembered, he cursed. He had parked up Belgrade, around the corner from St. Stephen's.

Deliberately watching his feet progress along the sidewalk, Bobby tried to ignore the old church. But it was impossible not glance up at it as he passed. Although St. Stephen's had closed years before, the church loomed large over the block. In some ways, its abandonment and cumulative decay made it even more imposing. The stained glass windows were secured behind a layer of protective steel mesh. Its stone face was disfigured by the weather and the application of graffiti. Bobby noticed an enormous new tag – "69 Squad" – scrawled across the side of the church in dribbled, red spray paint. St. Stephen's great oak doors were locked and barred with the finality of a tomb. Being so close to the church sent a shiver down his spine. He thrust his hands into his jacket pockets and assumed a severely pinched expression that could be best described as constipated.

But once Bobby turned the corner and the church disappeared from view, St. Stephen's solemn spell was broken and he relaxed again. Lifting his head a little higher, walking a little more upright, Bobby could once again enjoy the neighborhood, at least as far as one could.

In all its history Fishtown had never been a bright spot on Philadelphia's map. Located in the northern stretches of the city bordering the Delaware River, this musky spit of society got its name in the fabled

18

past from the fishermen who comprised its population and potpourried its streets with their noisome trade. Although Fishtown changed along with the rest of the city in the following generations – as Swedish settlers were supplanted by English colonists who were themselves replaced by an uneasy mélange of Germans, Italians, and Irish – the essence of its character, its quintessential fishy funk, remained more or less the same. A little dirty, a lot low brow, and very working class, Fishtown had always been in spirit, if not in the strictest sense of geography, a curious slice of Appalachia snuggled between Frankford Avenue and York Street.

The worried houses and buildings sagged and faded. Some of the row homes, which had never presented their best faces to the street, no longer had facades at all: their front exteriors, windows, doors and brick, were gone and covered over by plywood. The streets that were always rutted now saw their manhole covers and grates disappear as they were stolen and sold for scrap across the river in New Jersey. Although the residents were still the same people – Fishtowners, by and large, missed the memo on white flight – they had changed. Those that lived there seemed older. A little slower. While the world had grown richer, they had grown poor.

But Bobby was an exception to this. Unlike the rest of the neighborhood, he was happy and almost proud, alive with a self-satisfaction that would not have been possible if not for an uncommonly low denominator. His was the dignity of a small fish in a very depressed pond.

Bobby saw his car, an unremarkable Taurus station wagon that was already a decade old when he bought it, wedged tightly between two other cars. As Bobby got behind the wheel, the sun was just cresting over Fishtown, filling the deserted streets with a faint gold light.

Bobby started his car and looked at the side mirror. He made sure there was no oncoming traffic. But he needn't have bothered. There was no traffic at that time of the morning. As he put the car in drive, its transmission whinnied like an abused pony. He inched his wagon forward and tapped the car in front of him. He inched his wagon back. He inched his wagon forward, maneuvering its nose into the empty street.

Chapter Three: Bobby Bright and the Free Market

"Everyone on this forum must be insane. A Dango is the worst stroller that I have ever used. DEFINITELY!!! ABSOLUTELY!!! WITHOUT A DOUBT!!! It's bulky. The wheels wobble like a shopping cart's. And even the optional cup holder is a disaster! Yesterday, my iced coffee spilled all over my little boy. Ermahrgod!!! Thank goodness, it wasn't hot!!! I am finished with this Dango. That's what I get for buying Japanese junk. This is an abortion. If you love your children, don't buy a Dango. I'm going back to BumbleRide. – Joonbug69.

Bobby rubbed his fingers over his forehead like he was polishing a bowling ball and read what he wrote. It wasn't perfect. But it read well enough. The capitalization of sentences three through five was a nice touch. (Upper-case always GRABBED the online consumer's ATTENTION.) The punctuation bothered him though. Would a mother who was incensed about the hypothetical scalding of her child fire off exclamation points in bursts of three – !!! – with such consistency?

He pondered this question for a moment, but then, like the professional that he was, batted away his uncertainty. Bobby always had some doubts about his copy. But what artist is completely secure in their creative process? After five years on the job, he had learned to trust his instincts, go with his gut, and let the character speak through him. He didn't know everything about *Joonbug69,* but he imagined her with enough detail – some college, mid-30's, an avid eBayer, and committed watcher of *Glee* – to be confident about her punctuation. Reassured, he logged out of the site and entered a new profile name and password. The profile page of another one of his alter egos, *SuperSingleDad2000,* appeared.

As part of his work, Bobby maintained more than two dozen email addresses linked to profiles on a variety of commerce sites: Amazon,

Overstock.com, Yelp. If you could rate products or write reviews on the site, he was there. He had real estate on all of them.

Bobby worked at an obscure business named InfoCon. Although his company billed itself as a full-service communications firm specializing in a wide range of customized marketing solutions, it was really more of a one-trick pony. Most charitably, it could be said that InfoCon was in the reputation management business, but that description missed the point. The company was in fact a purveyor of the dark arts of public relations, a specialist in the online smear, a hired gun firing negative reviews across the blogosphere. And of all the dark knights of the spin at InfoCon, few were as committed, or as capable, as Bobby.

Our protagonist observed the other dozen employees in the dingy, low-ceilinged office. Bent over their desks, some tapped out perfunctory copy. Others diddled on the Internet. A few simply stared at the dull white walls. Bobby allowed himself a superior smirk, relishing his position as top dog at InfoCon. But this exercise of self-satisfaction was brief. Bobby, who was fully aware that his competitive edge was solely due to effort, would not rest on his accomplishments. Feeling the full weight of a reputation to be maintained, he returned to his assignment. He rested his fingers on the keypad, leaned towards the computer screen, and prepared to channel the spirit of *SuperSingleDad2000*. But before he could dig deep and channel one of his professional alter egos, his concentration was broken.

"How's it going, Kafka?" Marco asked as he crashed into his chair across the table from Bobby.

The nickname was spot on. Hunched over his computer with his receding hair disheveled and a startled look in his buggy eyes, there was something definitely entomorphic about Bobby. It would not be hard to imagine him feeling quite at home with the some beetles lurking beneath a punky log.

22

"How flow the words?" the tanned young man continued, his face half-hidden behind a large pair of aviators.

Bobby glanced at the clock on his computer's status bar. It was 11 a.m. He looked back at Marco. "You're in early," he said.

"Yeah," Marco yawned, lounging as much as humanly possible on his swivel chair. "I'm just having one of those crazy, industrious days. It must be this brisk autumn air."

"Your Dad made you come in?"

"Yup. The old man asked me to be in by noon. Which is totally ridiculous. I was at a show last night, you know?

"We all have to make sacrifices."

"You said it, brother," Marco removed his sunglasses, revealing two bloodshot eyes that looked on the verge of hemorrhaging. "Oh, man, it's bright in here." He looked frantically around the room as though he were suffocating. "I need to go get some coffee. Want to come?"

"No, I'm working."

"I guess someone has to," Marco said philosophically. He replaced his sunglasses and stumbled to the door.

There were certain advantages to being the boss's son. They include a guaranteed income, complete job security, and a totally flexible schedule, which was helpful because Marco was in a band. InfoCon was his livelihood, but a uniquely psychedelic brand of alt-country was his love. Given the irregular hours that his musical mistress demanded, Marco always came in late and usually left early. Being the boss's son was an enviable position, but Bobby tried not to be jealous. He had his own reasons to be proud.

After all, Bobby was one of the most widely read writers in America. His work was never published under his own name, but he published thousands of words a day, holding forth on a variety of subjects

23

that ranged from airlines to zip drives, vacuums to dish soaps, and all the baby strollers in between. Virtually anyone who had ever bought something online had read Bobby's prose. If a universal readership wasn't a measure of success, Bobby did not know what was.

Concentrating again on *SuperSingleDad2000*, Bobby narrowed his eyes and conceived an identity for his pseudonym. The contours were hazy at first, but eventually congealed into a back story. *"I agree with Joonbug,"* he typed, *"as a single father and an elementary school educator, I can say with no small authority that the Dango is a poor excuse for a stroller..."*

Bobby smiled. He was the best writer at InfoCon. And since InfoCon was the only company that he knew of that engaged in this particular brand of communications, Bobby was the best in his own little world, as limited and precisely defined as it might be.

The morning passed unremarkably. Bobby continued to toil. Back crooked, his eyes so close to the screen that his hairline bristled with the static from the old monitor, he dispatched scores of negative user reviews, impacting consumer opinion and damning the Dango brand. While he wrote, Marco sat at his computer, sipping a very vente latte, making no pretense of working. When he wasn't making personal calls or tinkering on his website, Marco interrupted Bobby with pieces of Internet trivia: Eastern European brides, cryptozoology, celebrity gossip, etc. Whether he did this out of a sincere enthusiasm for triviality, or a naughty pleasure in seeing Bobby fluster at each disturbance, no one could be sure. But one thing was certain. The distractions began to take their toll on Bobby. After a very productive morning, he came down with a sudden and severe case of writer's block.

At noon, Gretchen, the thickset accountant headed for the exit, informally inaugurating lunchtime. The rest of the staff followed her like lemmings, vacating their desks and racing to the elevator. As was often the case, Bobby was the last to leave and sat alone at his desk. Today there would be no lunch though. There were deadlines to be met and Bobby wanted to make the most of an empty office free from distractions.

Operating under the pseudonym *CatLady42*, Bobby began, *"When I bought the Dango, I had no idea that I was buying the biggest piece of trash on four wheels since the Gremlin..."* Bobby stopped. Realizing that a reference to an obscure 1970's automobile would be irrelevant to a mostly female stroller-buying public, he started again.

"The Dango is the Dang-dest..." he typed and promptly deleted.

"The Dango is a Ding-dong..." crossed his mind, but he dismissed it as well.

Seeking inspiration, Bobby navigated to Dango's website. But this offered no special insights into some dark heart or market weakness in the brand. Besides listing product models and specifications, there were only pictures of smiling Asian children, wrapped in what appeared to be giant dumplings. The website was not helpful.

Bobby tapped on his desk and huffed with growing agitation. Pecking the keys like a starving crow, he typed, *"The Dango ate my baby!"*

No, this would not do.

Bobby pursed his lips and stared at the word "Dango," hoping to see something new in the letters, some heretofore hidden aspect that he could seize upon. But this inspection achieved nothing except for the realization that Dango was a palindrome for "gonad."

He leaned back in his seat and crossed his arms, defeated by the brand. Had he sulked there long enough, he might have considered that no one bats .1000. No winning streak lasts forever and any life, followed to its inevitable conclusion, ends on a fairly dismal note. This simple truth might have consoled him. But Bobby never quite got there. His brain was still

25

humming with the riddles of commercial copy when his telephone rang. His boss's extension flashed on the caller ID.

Bobby did not immediately take the call. He regarded the telephone warily. It was unusual to receive a call from Mr. Dominico in the afternoon. It was unusual to receive a call from him ever. For better or worse, his boss had a laissez-faire management approach, preferring email communication to the telephone and maintaining a closed-door policy with his employees. This call was unusual. Bobby did not like the unusual.

When the ringing could no longer be ignored, Bobby picked up the phone and spoke.

There was a pause on the line. "Hello, Bobby," a voice with a Latin accent said. "This is Mr. Dominico. How are you?"

"I'm fine," Bobby replied, returning the question like a wobbly lob of a tennis ball. "How are you?"

"Oh, I am good. I am fine…" his boss trailed off.

The conversation was a meeting of managerial remove and menial unease. Only because he talked more when he was nervous, Bobby spurred it along. "Is there something you need, Mr. Dominoco?"

Another pause. "Yes. When you get a chance, would you please to come by my office?"

The request sent goose bumps up Bobby's neck. "Sure, I'll be right over."

"But only if it's a good time," Mr. Dominico said.

"Now is fine."

"Oh. Okay then. See you soon," the boss said and hung up the phone.

Bobby looked across the work room. Mr. Dominico's door was inscrutably closed. Whatever the reason for the meeting, the door offered no clues.

26

As he approached the office, Bobby assured himself of the quality of his work and his contribution at Infocon. Despite internal pep talk, however, his chest felt tight and his ears tingled. With each step, his arms grew heavier. His fingers felt like swollen sausages as he twisted the door knob and opened the door.

"You wanted to see me?" Bobby asked, teetering on the threshold of the boss's office.

Mr. Dominico looked up from his desk. He was two eyes and a large, pale forehead peeking into his office. "Come in, Bobby. Take a seat."

Bobby sat in a seat in front of his boss's desk. Marco wore an agreeable, if impenetrable, expression.

"So, Bobby. You are working on the Bumbleride account?"

"That's right, Mr. Dominico."

"And everything is going well?"

"Yes, it's not bad."

"Not bad?" his boss asked, raising an eyebrow that begged for more detail.

"Well, better than 'not bad.' It's good. I've been writing copy all week for the campaign."

"That's good. And how is the campaign?"

Bobby cleared his throat and breathed deeply, struggling to maintain his poise in front of the man who signed his paychecks. "It's good. We've been panning every other standard, umbrella, and twin stroller in the same class as Bumbleride's sport utility pram. We're working on Dango now, which is the last competitor we're targeting. Dango, along with the rest of the campaign, should be finished up by the end of the day."

"Very good," Mr. Dominico said. "And what else is on your plate?"

Bobby thought for a moment, tilting his head to the side as though the answer was stuck to a bit of gray matter in his brain that he couldn't quite dislodge. "Odds and ends," he said at last. "Writing some emails. Revising copy. Filing a few invoices. Not *too* much. It is the end of the quarter and things are a little slow right now."

Mr. Dominico nodded vaguely. Bobby realized that his reply might not have been the best response to the question. Worried that it reflected poorly on his efforts, he quickly added, "But when things pick up next quarter, like they always do, I'm sure I'll be very busy. I'll be ready to dive in."

This show of gung-ho, however forced, won a smile from Mr. Dominico. "That's good, Bobby. I'm glad to hear your enthusiasm. Not many young people seem to have that spirit anymore. It is refreshing to see it in you. You'll go far with it."

Bobby flushed at the complement. "Thank you, Mr. Dominico," he chirped. He started to relax, daring to hope that this meeting might not be so dreadful after all. From the way the conversation was going, it might involve a promotion. Or even a raise! Bobby clenched his jaw to keep from grinning at the thought.

"How long have you worked here at InfoCon, Bobby?"

"Almost five years, sir."

"Five years. That's a long time. You've done a lot of good work for us. You've enjoyed it here?" Mr. Dominico asked with the peculiar intonation of a foreign speaker that blurs whether a sentence is a statement or a question.

Despite this tonal ambiguity, Bobby replied without hesitation. "This is the best job that I've ever had. I love it here."

Mr. Dominico smiled again, but added awkwardly. "And we were very lucky to have you."

Bobby was so delighted by his boss's praise that he failed to notice the strikingly past tense of the preceding participle. "I feel lucky to be here," he said.

Mr. Dominico rubbed his chin. He was by nature a subtle man, rabbit-like in his evasions. Like any fluffy rodent, he was most at home in the underbrush of hint and allegation, avoiding the open fields of directness whenever possible. But now, regrettably, was not an occasion when candor could be avoided.

"Bobby, you are one of InfoCon's oldest and most-valued employees," he prefaced uneasily. (Despite the conversation's change in tenor, Bobby brightened.) "Your hard work hasn't gone unnoticed. I don't believe that the company would be where it is today without your individual contribution. (Bobby sat up a little straighter.) I can say with complete honesty that you are one of the best employees that I have. Maybe even the best. (A simpering grin tugged at Bobby's lips.) Because of what you mean to the InfoCon family, and I really do think of my company as a family, I wanted to be the first to tell you this, before anyone else. (Bobby nodded eagerly.) I am going to have to let you go."

For lack of a better word, Bobby crumpled. But "crumpled" doesn't do justice to the complete and total deflation he experienced. His legs became jelly and his shoulders slumped forward. His back bowed like a question mark. Even his cheeks went limp as his smile melted into a flaccid frown. "I'm being fired?" he hiccuped in disbelief.

Doing his best to maintain a baseline of dignity and avoid an employee freakout, Mr. Dominico adopted a more formal posture and commanding tone. "No, you aren't being fired, Bobby. But I'm going to have to let you go. I'm sure you can appreciate the economic climate that we are facing. After going over the numbers, I have decided to make some strategic changes at InfoCon."

"But I'm your best writer," Bobby defended pathetically.

"You are one of our strongest employees. There is no doubt. But the fact of the matter is that I've decided to eliminate the entire editorial department."

Startled from his own self-pity, Bobby declared, "But InfoCon produces content. It's what we do!"

"It's what we *did*," Mr. Dominico said, never breaking his professional equanimity. "I promise you this wasn't an easy decision. I don't want to bore you with figures, but we're just not making a profit. We've decided to outsource some of our departments. This includes the editorial department."

"Outsource? To where?"

"India, Bobby. We're outsourcing editorial to an office in Bangalore."

"Bangalore? India? But do they even speak English there?"

"Yes. I'm afraid they speak awfully good English. They're excellent writers. Fantastic grammarians. Plus," he added with ill-concealed enthusiasm, "I can pay them a fraction of what I pay a worker here."

As though the news was too heavy for his neck to support, Bobby's head fell forward and his chin rebounded off his collarbone. "I'm being fired," he repeated.

"Yes, I'm afraid so," his former boss said.

Bobby remembered little of the conversation that followed. Thanks for a job well done were followed by promises of a good reference. Before he knew it, Bobby was leaving the office with a severance check for two weeks pay.

The other workers were still finishing their lunches. No one noticed him slouch back to his desk. Not even Marco, who was prattling away on the phone as Bobby sank into his seat. With a sigh that ended into

30

a whimper, Bobby opened his desk drawer. As he surveyed its cluttered contents, he was amazed by how much a person can accumulate in five years.

Chapter Four: A Crasher at the TV Party

"It's real life, Bobby!"

These were the first words he heard when he stepped through the front door with a box of his personal effects from the office. The curtains were drawn and he squinted into the dark living room, which was lit only by the television. Sitting in the flickering light as she painted her toenails, Suzie was an unlikely oracle in gym shorts and a Brian Westbrook jersey. But her exclamation uncannily divined Bobby's cruel experience with the world that afternoon.

"How's that?" he muttered, taken aback.

Suzie looked up from her freshly lacquered toes. "It's real life, babe," she repeated brightly and chomped her gum. "Real life is coming to Philadelphia!"

"What do you mean?"

"I mean MTV's *Real Life* is filming this season in Philadelphia! They said it in the *City Paper*!" She gestured to a newspaper beside her on the couch. "What do you think I'm talking about?" She smiled an undiscriminating smile and shook her head in gentle disbelief that someone in this day and age would not grasp such an obvious reference. "How was your day, honey?" she asked, rocking forward to blow on her wet toenails.

"It's been better," Bobby said and dropped the box in the corner.

"Why's that?" She failed to notice anything peculiar in Bobby coming home with a cardboard packing box. She was much more interested in her nail polish and extended a stubby leg to inspect her work. From where Bobby stood, her toes resembled a row of closely-packed gnocchi. He sat next to Suzie and watched as she wiggled her digits, making them do the higgly-piggly.

"What were you saying?" she asked, at last satisfied with her grooming.

"Nothing, Snooze," he said. "What was that about the *Real Life*?"

Suzie's eye's brightened. She loved to talk. Especially when she knew what she was talking about. She tore open the *City Paper* and proceeded to read aloud.

"It was reported that *MTV* producers were in the city last week, finalizing an agreement to lease a large historic property in Center City. According to an undisclosed source close to the negotiation, this building will be the site of the next *Real Life!*" she concluded with a trill. "Isn't that great?"

"What's so great about it?"

"MTV will be filming a reality show in Philadelphia! That's so neat!"

"I guess. It could be. I'm sure it will be…" he trailed off.

Suzie tilted her head, smacked her gum, and regarded him curiously. If someone couldn't appreciate such an inaugural event in Philadelphia's cinematic history, something must be amiss. Inquiry etched itself across her face in an expression that was at once concerned and just a tad bovine. "Baby, what's wrong?" she asked, batting her big brown eyes.

Bobby opened his mouth to speak. But no words came. His chin trembled and puckered into a prune.

Convinced that something must be very wrong, Suzie slid her ample person towards him and began to rub his knee. "What's wrong, babe?"

With her touch, Bobby overflowed with emotion and vented like an antique fan. "I lost my job, Suzie. I've been…let…go!" his words whirled.

Suzie's face was a portrait of compassion, like a Rubenesque cherub borrowed from a painting of the Passion. Her eyes wide and worried, she plumped her lips to a size more commensurate with her chubby

33

cheeks. "Oh, poor baby," she soothed, wrapping her arm around his shoulders and guiding his head to her soft, pink thigh.

Bobby took to her lap with a mighty sigh, rubbing his cheek against her leg and nestling towards her crotch. When he was appropriately burrowed into her embrace, he looked up. Beyond the massive arc of breast and knit jersey that sheltered him from the troubles of the world, there was a consoling smile.

No longer experiencing such an urgent need to weep, Bobby breathed more easily. He let Suzie run her fingers over his smooth scalp.

"I've been downsized. Outsourced. Five years at a company and they just give my job to an Indian," he explained, more defeated than angry.

"An Indian?" she asked. "Like a Native American?"

"Not that kind of Indian. An Indian from the country, India."

Suzie slowly digested the information. "Why would they do that? Do they even speak English?"

"Apparently they speak very good English,"

"Really?"

"Sure. They're apparently excellent grammarians too."

Suzie pouted. "I'm so sorry, Bobby." She bent and kissed him on the forehead, enveloping him in a cocoon of bosom and damp hair, which smelled enticingly of Herbal Essences and Cheeze-Its. "What are you going to do?"

"I don't know…" Bobby said distantly, blinkered by the prospect of finding new work. "I don't even want to think about."

"Then don't think about it, honey," she said, rocking him in her arms. "Don't think about anything. Let me take care of you. Do you want anything?"

He shook his head. "Just stay here. Keep on doing that with you fingers. Yeah … that …ooh … Just keep talking."

34

"What about?" she asked, tickling his hairline with one hand and kneading his ear lobe with the other.

"I don't know. Tell me about your day."

"I didn't do anything today. I never do anything. You know that."

"Then tell me about *Real Life*."

"No kidding?"

"Why not? I didn't even know it was still on the air."

"But it is!" she confirmed enthusiastically. "Last year was in Phoenix. I had heard they were going to do it in Cleveland this year, but now the newspaper said it will be Philadelphia!" she declared. In her exhilaration she tugged on his ear a bit too roughly.

"Ouch, Snooze!" Bobby yelped.

"I'm sorry, babe," Suzie cooed and moderated her touch. "Is that better?"

He grumbled that it was and snuggled against her tummy. "Phoenix? Cleveland? Really? They're scraping the barrel a bit, aren't they? Why don't they do New York something?"

"They've already done New York twice. Brooklyn once. Los Angeles and San Francisco. Miami. Boston. Hawaii. . ."

"And now they're here?" he interrupted, wearied by the list of American municipalities. "I can't wait."

"Don't be so negative, Bobby," she admonished good-naturedly. "It's exciting. It will be fun to see our city on TV."

"But Philadelphia is always on TV. Every day. Just watch the news. The cops are always shooting someone."

"Oh, Bobby," she purred. "I mean the *real* TV. *Cable* TV."

"Well, I just hope I don't run into them around here. I don't need the excitement."

"Don't worry. I'm sure they won't bother you in Fishtown. No one ever comes to Fishtown. So just settle down, grumpy boy. Lay back and take it easy."

Bobby did as he was told and submitted to Suzie's petting.

"What's on tv, Snooze?" he asked. If he was fired, Bobby would make the best of it. Daytime television was a minor consolation, one of the luxuries that the sick and chronically unemployed had over their happier, healthier, and more productive counterparts.

"What time is it?"

"3:30."

"Well, it depends," she said as she accessed her encyclopedic knowledge of the channel guide. "There's Maury. Ellen. General Hospital. I'm pretty sure we could find a *Law & Order* without too much trouble."

Bobby frowned at his options.

Noting his dissatisfaction, Suzie offered another choice in the sing-song manner that a mother uses to entice a difficult child. "I think that *Night Court* is on TV Land," she added, dangling the suggestion as though it were a bright red lollipop.

"I like *Night Court*," he said.

"I know you do," she replied, already changing the channel.

The television screen flashed the opening credits that Bobby knew so well. He had watched *Night Court* during its original run, sticking with it through the curse of the dying bailiffs, the golden age of Markie Post, John Larroquette's three Emmys, and the cringing Soviet era humor of Yakov Smirnoff. The re-run brightened his day. The numbness that had beset him all afternoon fell away and by the first commercial break, he had remembered how to smile again.

And with this smile other feelings returned too. Bobby shifted onto his back and gazed up at his girlfriend. Suzie continued to stroke his head as

36

she stared at the television screen. Ever so delicately, he snaked his hand up her shorts and began to massage her rump. She looked down on him with a surprised, but not unhappy, expression.

"What's this?" she giggled.

"What's what?" he said naughtily.

Suzie grinned and returned the favor. She slipped her hand down his shirt collar and began to rub his chest. One of her fingers glanced his nipple. He shook with an erotic jolt, flopped on his belly and buried his face into her lap, groping and pressing into her.

"Tee-hee! That tickles!" she said and lifted Bobby's chin from between her legs. His face was twisted with an almost adolescent desperation. Her lips formed a more measured smile. It was not as eager, but it was kind and in every way obliging. "Come here," she whispered and tapped her lips with her forefinger.

Bobby wrapped his arms around her waist. Utilizing every muscle on his willowy frame, he clambered up Suzie as though he were scaling a mountain whose summit was a pair of puckering lips. Shoulder to shoulder, eye to eye, he paused just to gaze into her big brown irises. Then, without further ado, he plunged into her, enveloped by her capacious embrace, lost in a wonderland of soft curves and dense flesh. Her body was like one magnificent bosom whose contours flowed so seamlessly into each other that it was difficult to tell where the cleavage stopped and the rest of Suzie began.

Bobby squirmed in her arms, his limbs twitching in anticipation of what was to follow. But just as passions built to a pitch and zippers were fumbled by anxious fingers, there were three heavy raps on the front door. He turned and saw the door swing open. Standing in the doorway was a tall, lean man with a prominent scar above his left eye. "Sky rockets in flight," he crooned to the lovers. "Afternoon delight!"

"Ronnie! What are you doing here!" Bobby flustered and removed his hands from beneath Suzie's Brian Westbrook jersey.

"Thought I'd drop by and say hello to my old pal," he said and continued to gawk, showing no shame at his intrusion.

"Don't you know how to knock?" Suzie snapped.

"Don't you know how to lock the door?" Ronnie barked back. "Besides, I did knock. No one answered."

"Shouldn't that have told you something?" she suggested as she straightened her jersey.

"It absolutely did. There was no answer and the door was unlocked. Violent crime happens every day in Killadelphia. I was worried about dear, old Bobby. Now what kind of friend would I have been had I not come inside?"

Suzie groaned and got to her feet. She was noticeably unsteady after spending all the day on the couch. After working out the pins and needles, she stomped up the stairs. Her overstuffed gym shorts rubbed together with swishy indignation.

"Hey, Suzie, wait!" Bobby called after her.

"Yeah, Suzie, wait," Ronnie mimicked sarcastically.

Suzie made no reply. The bedroom door slammed shut and the television inside turned on.

"What are you doing?" Bobby grumbled, frustrated in more ways than one.

"I told you," Ronnie said, falling into a lumpy recliner. "I'm stopping by to say hello to my old buddy."

"I mean what are you doing with Suzie? Why do you have to rile her up like that?"

"I don't have to. I just like to. But don't worry about Suzie. She'll get over it. She has to. You support her, and I'm your best friend."

38

Bobby frowned and leaned back on the couch. Ronnie's views on Suzie, like that of all women, were well-known and not worth addressing. "So what do you want?" Bobby asked, changing the subject.

"Want to hit the bar for Happy Hour? See where the night takes us?"

"I don't think so," he said, buttoning his shirt. "I've had a bad day."

"What is alcohol for if not for bad days?"

"I'd really rather not."

"What do you mean *you'd really rather not*?"

"I don't want to talk about it."

"Sure you do. You love to talk about your problems."

Bobby nearly denied this statement, but it was true. He did like to talk about his problems. "I got laid off. I lost my job," he confessed.

"Oh, man. I'm sorry." Ronnie hung his head mournfully. After a moment of silence, he looked up. His face was bright again. He was eager to help Bobby begin the healing process. "Well that settles it. Let's go have a drink!"

"Did you hear what I just said? I got fired. I don't want to go to the bar right now."

"Are you kidding me? You just got fired. Now is the perfect time for the bar. This is why bars exist. For unemployed drips like you."

"No, Ronnie. Seriously. I just want to sit here and watch television. Reflect on my situation. Collect my thoughts. Consider my options. Maybe catch a *Law & Order*."

"Do you know who watches *Law & Order*, Bobby? Women. Women with dirty minds and fantasies of victimization. Do you know what men do when they have problems? They drink. So let's drink. It's not like you have anything better to do."

39

"Yeah, you definitely saw to that," Bobby frowned, recalling the soft promise of Suzie's thighs.

"Don't be such a puss-puss," Ronnie said. "Tell you what. Drinks are on me."

Bobby regarded his friend doubtfully. "You never pay."

"That may be true. But this is a very special occasion. You are in pain, and I'm here for you." Ronnie placed his hands on Bobby's knee and began to rub.

Bobby jerked away.

"Don't fight the love," Ronnie seduced, pressing forward and batting his weasel eyes.

Bobby sank back into the couch, raising his hands and feet into the air like a kitten assuming a defensive position. Ronnie hovered above his friend, prepared to test his feline defenses. The friends stared at one another, their eyes locked in a battle of wills, a battle that Bobby was destined to lose.

"Alright, I'll go," he said. "Just don't touch me. Sheesh. Let me say goodbye to Suzie."

"Forget Suzie. She'll be fine. She has the TV. She loves the TV."

"I'm sure she'll be fine," Bobby said as he walked to the stairs. "But I *want* to say goodbye. Hello and goodbye goes a long way in a healthy relationship. Not that you would understand."

"Whatever," Ronnie shrugged as he flipped through the television channels. "Take all the time you need, killer."

Bobby shuddered to a stop on the landing. "Don't call me that," he said, his voice almost a whisper.

Ronnie swung his feet onto the coffee table. "Live with it," he said.

Bobby opened the bedroom door. Suzie was in bed with the lights off. The covers were pulled up to her neck and the television was tuned to

HGTV. Without looking away from the screen, she asked, "Why are you friends with him?"

"I've known him since I was a kid." Bobby said.

"He's not a good person."

"But he's a friend."

Suzie rolled onto her side away from Bobby. "You're going out with him?" she asked the wall.

"We're going to get a drink. I won't be out late."

"Whatever. Stay out all night."

"Hey, Snooze. Don't be mad," he implored and sat on the bed.

"I'm not mad," she said. "I'm fine."

Bobby reached out and touched the mound of blanket that marked her hip. She did not respond. He regarded her broad curves beneath the blanket. He would have preferred to stay at home with her than go out with Ronnie. But this was impossible now. With no small regret he left the bedroom, closing the door behind him.

Chapter Five: Bobby Gets Drunk. Very, very Drunk

"Don't feel bad, Bobby."

"I didn't feel bad. Not until you came."

"Oh, you're breaking my heart."

"Like you have one."

Bobby sat with Ronnie inside a drab barroom called the Silhouette. It was just after 5pm on a Friday, but not one would call this hour "happy." The place was empty except for the regulars huddled around the bar drinking "City Wides," which were a Jim Beam shot and a can of Pabst. Ferrying his patrons on their journey to cirrhosis was the ancient proprietor Mitch Smutnik, who had spent the last forty years maintaining an increasingly senile watch over his establishment. The Silhouette was a quintessential dive. An unmanned karaoke machine playing a bouncy Nancy Sinatra tune threw the bar's dismal atmosphere into absurd relief. Bobby was only on his second beer. As he looked around the bar and its defeated clientele, he had the unwelcome apprehension that, as a new member of the jobless ranks, he had more in common with them than he would care to admit.

"Bull. Like you were all smiles before," Ronnie said and swigged his Kenzinger beer. "You were a sad sack when I found you. What were you going to do? Lay around with your girlfriend all night and feel sorry for yourself?"

"I could imagine worse things."

"Dude, that's so gay," Ronnie said, so stigmatizing his friend's heterosexuality without a trace of irony. "Seriously," he continued, "Suzie has her, well, *womanly qualities*. But stay at home with her on a Friday night to watch TV? That's just sad. Girlfriends are strictly weekday affairs. On the weekend guys need to expand their horizons. Taste a little freedom."

"Why are you such a misogynist?" Bobby asked.

"I'm not a misogynist," Ronnie said and lifted his beer. He paused with the bottle before his lips and waxed philosophically. "I'm just a pessimist who happens to think about women a lot." Pleased with his answer, he guzzled the rest of his beer.

Bobby could only smirk at Ronnie's nonsense. "God, I don't know how Julia puts up with you. She must be a saint."

Ronnie smiled cruelly. "Well, Julia is no saint. And she doesn't put up with me anymore. We broke up today."

"Come again?"

"I said we broke up. I ended it last night. We're finished," Ronnie related without any remorse before calling to Mitch for another round. The old bartender did not respond. He teetered slightly as he watched the news on a flickering television at the end of the bar.

In contrast to Ronnie's nonchalance about the subject, Bobby was shocked. "But you've been together since you got back from the Navy. I knew you two had problems. You two have always had problems. I mean, she had to put up with you. But I didn't know it was that bad."

Ronnie shrugged with all the concern of someone who has forgotten a loaf of bread at the store. "It wasn't working for me. I told her to shove off. Case closed." Once again, Ronnie called for a drink. Mitch responded by waving his hand at them as though he was shooing a fly.

"You're cold," Bobby said. Even though he had known Ronnie forever, he could still be amazed by his friend's dazzling lack of human kindness.

"It isn't worth talking about," Ronnie said, changing the subject. "This isn't about me tonight. This is about you, buddy."

"Still, it's kind of a big deal, isn't it?"

"Not to me." Ronnie wrapped his arm around Bobby and shook him playfully, but not without a certain violence. "Tonight is all about you. You're the one that got fired. Remember?" he added with an acid grin.

Bobby shook off his friend's embrace. He didn't appreciate the reminder and turned his attention towards the end of the bar where a lush staggered to the karaoke machine. Ronnie called to Mitch again and finally tore the old bartender away from the news. Muttering under his breath, Mitch got two beers from the cooler and poured two shots of Jim Beam. He took the money from the counter and doddered back to the television.

"I wasn't fired. I was let go," Bobby said.

"Fired? Let go? What's the difference?" Ronnie asked, drinking with increasing momentum.

"There's a difference."

"Maybe. But it doesn't matter. Either way you don't have a job anymore."

"You really know how to cheer a guy up."

"I do what I can. Now let's do this shot."

The shot was done.

Ronnie leaned against the bar and swigged his beer as a chaser, surveying the bar with an uncertain smile. Then, with the emotional contortion of a particularly unstable schizophrenic, his mood changed. His cheer melted away. Ronnie looked around, grimacing as though everything disgusted him. The lush by the karaoke machine, clumsily fingering the remote, aroused his ire most.

"I don't know where this is going, but I don't like it," he scowled.

"What do you mean?" Bobby asked and knuckled some Chex Mix from a nearby bowl.

"This bar. This scene. What are we doing here exactly?"

"Having a drink," Bobby replied through a mouthful of pretzels and cereal bits.

"This is beat," Ronnie said and squeezed his bottle as if he were intent on choking it.

"How can you say that? This bar is a Fishtown institution."

"So is Finnegan's Funeral Home, which is where most of these gomers are headed. Let's get out of here."

"Go where?"

"Anywhere."

"Anywhere isn't a place."

"How about the Tap?"

Bobby shook his head in disbelief. "Julia's bar? Seriously? You want to go to her bar right after you break up with her?"

"Yeah, I'm serious. She doesn't work tonight. And I doubt she'll be out on the town. She was pretty messed up when I left her this afternoon."

"This afternoon? I thought you said you broke up last night."

"Last night. This afternoon. What difference does it make?"

Bobby frowned. "It sounds like a bad idea."

"It sounds like a great idea," Ronnie said. "There will be girls, which I like, and those Wasabi peas on the bar, which you like. So there's something for both of us. Anyway, we need to go somewhere. If that jacko by the karaoke machine starts to sing, I won't be able to control myself. I could be provoked to violence."

Bobby took a long drink and looked around the pub. Except for the old man by the karaoke machine, swaying in rhythm to the muzak, the bar patrons were engaged in a great communal slouch, leaning over their drinks, absorbed in the punctilia of their dissipation. It was true. It was a dismal scene. And it was also true that Bobby did like Wasabi peas.

45

"Okay," Bobby said with a little burp. "Let's go. How are we going to get there?"

"How about your car?"

"No good. I'm already starting to feel buzzed."

"That's cool," Ronnie said and finished his beer. "I'll drive."

The friends stood up from their chairs. Ronnie tossed some bunched singles onto the bar. Bobby called out "thank you" to Mitch, who ignored them both as he watched the television. They staggered to the door. As the door closed behind them, the lush began to slur a verse from a Louis Prima song.

When Bobby and Ronnie drove up to the Tap, the street was so crowded that it took several turns around the block to find a space big enough for Bobby's station wagon. After edging onto the sidewalk beneath an overpass several blocks away, they walked to the entrance and pushed through the front door, immersing themselves in Friday night life.

Unlike the Silhouette, there were no karaoke machines, no ancient bartenders, and no ugly aspects of long-term alcohol use on display. A jukebox played vintage soul and the young and lively clientele made a persuasive show of having a good time. The place was clean and its dark wood décor had such a smooth sheen that the staff might have polished it with vaseline. Ronnie sidled up to the bar. Bobby, not so drunk as to be ignorant to the risk of running into Ronnie's ex, stood beside him warily.

"Rich, two stouts, my brother!" Ronnie called out, waving his hands like a politician at a rally. To Bobby's relief, the slim, bearded bartender smiled at Ronnie. News of the break-up had not seemed to have reached Julia's co-workers at least. While Ronnie and the bartender engaged in some conversation, Bobby took an empty seat.

"Rich, you remember my friend Bobby, right?" Ronnie said by way of introduction.

46

The bartender nodded without any recognition. "How's it going?" he asked impersonally.

"It's not going well," Ronnie answered for Bobby. "He got fired today. Five years on a job and they just pitched him out like a piece of trash. Can you believe that?"

"I'm sorry to hear that," the bartender condoled with the mildest interest.

"Actually, I was let go. Downsized," Bobby said.

"Either way, that's rough, fella," Rich said, already having forgotten Bobby's name.

"Yeah, it is rough," Ronnie continued. "It's been really hard on him. I'm taking him out tonight to cheer him up. Care to contribute a little charity to the cause?"

The bartender considered for a moment. "How about a Rusty Nail? It's a little sweet. A little bitter. It's good for somber occasions."

"Sounds perfect. Let's do it," Ronnie said.

As the bartender worked on their drinks, Bobby hissed to Ronnie, "I wish you wouldn't tell people that I was fired. It's embarrassing."

"Get over it," Ronnie said. "You don't get fired every day. Take advantage of it. Get a few drinks out of it."

Rich returned with a cocktail shaker and poured a copper brown concoction into three shot glasses. "Here's to Bobby," Ronnie toasted. "I've never known a better guy with worse luck."

"Ching, ching," the bartender concurred.

Bobby frowned at the toast, threw back his drink and gagged. "That's awful!"

"I've had worse," Ronnie said, smacking his lips.

"I've had better. A lot better," Bobby said. "Who drinks that stuff?"

47

"Only the most desperate souls," the bartender said as he herded the shot glasses. "Now, gentlemen, if you'll excuse me."

Rich went to the other end of the bar where some dudes in skinny jeans and Pendleton shirts clambered for service. The Tap was fully in swing. Every seat at the bar was occupied and customers collected on its outer fringe. At the high tables along the walls, clucks of women, chatty and buzzed, shook off their weekday worries, swaying to the rhythms of James Brown. One girl with tattooed arms and hips that filled her miniskirt to capacity was turning the room into a one-woman dance floor, thrusting and pumping her thick frame in determined cadence with the beat. Ronnie took a long drink of his stout and leered, getting high on her curves.

Bobby did not rise to his friend's carnal enthusiasm. Munching a bunch of Wasabi peas, he sulked, "I can't get the taste of that drink out of my mouth."

Ronnie threw his head back and roared with boozy disapproval. "Brighten up, dude! You are bringing me down. You got fired. That sucks. But guess what? It happens to lots of people. Man up."

"I only said I didn't like the drink."

"This isn't about the drink," Ronnie said. "This is about your attitude. Your perspective. You must take stock. Listen, you've got some savings, right?"

"Well, yeah."

"And you can get unemployment?"

"I guess."

"Savings? Unemployment?" Ronnie swished the last of his stout through his teeth. "You're fine. You're not going to be homeless. In my opinion, you're sitting pretty. It's better than what I'm doing."

"You're doing well enough," Bobby scoffed. "At least you have a job."

Ronnie gave his friend a chilly stare. "I'm a nurse, Bobby," he said. "Do you know what I did today? I emptied bed pans. Do you know who uses bed pans?" he asked and carried on without waiting for an answer. "Dying people. Incontinent people. Fat bastards who can't get out of bed. I don't mind touching dead people. I can deal with dead people. But I never, ever, like touching fat flesh. Shoving my hands wrist-deep between someone's thighs for the privilege of watching them poop into a plastic tray. That's just not civilized. So tell me, how many people did you have to poop today?"

"Well, none…" Bobby admitted.

"And how many people will you have to poop tomorrow?"

"None that I'm aware of."

"Then you don't have it that bad! Stop being such a busted out asshole and look around you. We are surrounded by totally doable chicks." Gesturing to the dancing girl, Ronnie flashed a lascivious grin. "The night is full of possibilities."

Bobby shook his head and fought a naughty smile. "You're crazy. I've got a girlfriend."

Ronnie arched his brows, flared his nostrils, and leveled an almost threatening gaze at Bobby. "I repeat. The night is full of possibilities."

Just then, as if the universe had decided to provide support for Ronnie's promiscuous philosophy, two men next to Bobby left their seats. They were replaced by two young ladies. Although one was plain and had a leg cast and crutches, the other was cute and not at all gimpy. Bouncing onto the bar stool, the cute friend flipped her garnet hair back and tossed an amorous glance to the general public.

Ronnie nodded in approval at her undiscriminating flirtation. He leaned across Bobby towards the girls.

"Can I trade you a shot of chartreuse for a codeine?" he asked, flashing a toothy smile.

The girls looked back at him without comprehension.

Adopting a more forward approach, Ronnie motioned at the crutches. "It's not every day you see crutches in a bar. I like your dedication. Drinking through the pain."

The plain girl, unaccustomed to the attention of strangers, blushed. But it was the redhead who spoke. "That's what kind of girls we are. We take drinking very seriously," she said, her natural confidence inflated by alcohol.

"I support your cause," Ronnie said. "Can I get you ladies something to drink?"

The two girls exchanged smiles. "Why not?" the plucky redhead peeped. "We'll have two vodka and cranberries."

Ronnie ordered another round of stouts and two vodka and cranberries. He returned his attention to the redhead and the two made enthusiastic conversation across Bobby who was uncomfortable amidst the pitching woo.

"My name is Ronnie. My friend sulking on the bar is Bobby."

"I'm Beth," the redhead said. "This is Sarah." She indicated to the plain girl. She smiled a hopeful, crooked smile.

"So tell me," Beth said, looking over Bobby and quickly returning her focus to Ronnie, "Do you always charm the ladies by pointing out their crutches?"

"Not at all. But when I see a lower leg fracture, I can't help but noticing. What is it? The tibia? The fibia?" he asked, somehow imbuing the words with loaded sexuality.

"It's the tibia," Sarah squeaked.

50

"Tibia? Fibia?" Beth purred. "What are you? Some kind of doctor?"

"Doctor, no. I'm a nurse," Ronnie said, as though there was nothing in the world he'd rather be.

"A nurse?" Beth said, somewhat disappointed. "That's interesting, too, I guess."

"It is interesting," Ronnie boasted and added, entirely without truth, "It's great work for a guy like me. I'm a real people person. I'm very caring. I like to know that I make a difference. I like to feel that what I do is important. Nurses touch lives everyday."

Bobby nearly choked on his stout, but Beth and Sarah hung on his every word. Feeling a full bladder coupled by the urgent need to vomit, he excused himself to the restroom.

When Bobby returned, Ronnie continued to hold court, expounding on his career, his passions and, above all, his modesty. A subtle shift had occurred. Specifically, the girls had each shifted one stool over and taken Bobby's seat, relegating him to the fringes of the group. Exiled from Ronnie, he was compelled to strike up a conversation with the gimpy friend, who grinned at him with desperate good nature.

"Your friend told us that you lost your job," Sarah drawled.

"He told you that?" Bobby asked.

"Yep. He said that you feel bad and that I should try to cheer you up. So here I am. Cheering you up," she hiccupped.

"Thanks."

Sarah chewed on the ice from her drink and stared. Her eyes were like a doll's: glassy, dull, and devoid of human intelligence. "So what do you do?" she asked.

"I was a writer."

"A writer, huh? That's neat. What did you write?"

51

"It's kind of hard to explain."

"Try me. I'm a very, *very* good listener," she stressed with misplaced eroticism.

Bobby rubbed the bridge of his nose. His brain began to throb. "I'm sorry, but I'd rather not go into it."

"That's alright. You don't need to say anything. A lot of people lose their jobs. I haven't. But I've heard of it. It definitely happens. It's totally a thing."

"Really, I'd rather not talk about," Bobby interrupted, getting fed up with the forced conversation.

Bobby was a tad snippy, but Sarah's drunkenness magnified the insult. Her mouth opened wide with incoherent offense. Rolling her eyes in wobbly orbits, she muttered, "Alright. If you don't want to talk, you don't have to be an ass."

Their conversation went into deep freeze. Sensing that things were not moving forward at a drunk and horny clip, Ronnie called over to them in order to effect a thaw in their relations.

"Anyone up for some shots?" he asked.

The call for alcohol had an immediate, salutary effect on Sarah. Forgetting her indignation, she indicated with a nod that she was ready for a drink. Beth, also enthusiastic about the suggestion, bounced on her stool, squeezing Ronnie's arm. Only Bobby was not excited by the prospect. At the edge of the group, he was the odd man out.

"What is this?" Bobby asked, staring into one of four shot glass filled with bright green liquor.

"Chartreuse," Ronnie said.

"Isn't that a color?"

Ronnie did not answer.

52

Bobby picked up the glass and recoiled as the liquor's vapor singed his nose. But he followed the other's example and drank. He was assaulted by an overpowering herbal flavor that was like a mosh of clove, citrus, cinnamon, and a very aggressive anise. The room began to spin and Bobby had to steady himself on the bar. With one tipple he had stumbled out of a harmless buzz into the more critical arena of full-blown intoxication.

Seized by the need for a little Bobby time, he stood up from his stool and staggered to the bathroom. His arms and legs were heavy. His head felt like a rag doll's, mushy with sawdust and stuffing. Just as he reached the bathroom door, Bobby felt a clap on his back. He turned and saw Ronnie, whose face was flushed with mischief and alcohol.

"How's my favorite boy?" he asked and wrapped his arm around Bobby.

"Not so good," Bobby said, wiping sweat away from his brow.

"Things aren't going well with you and Sarah?"

"Things aren't going anywhere with me and Sarah. But that isn't the problem." As Bobby spoke, hot nausea bubbled up from his gut. He leaned back against the wall. "I think I need to go home," he said.

"You can't go home," Ronnie objected. "We're just getting started!"

Bobby shook his head to the contrary. "You're just getting started. I'm just getting done."

"But what about the girls? You can't leave me here alone."

"I'm sure that you can handle them both just fine."

"Well, so am I. But I still need a wingman. Girls don't like single guys."

"I think you're past that point. Besides, I'm no good at this stuff."

"No way. You're an indispensable part of this social equation," Ronnie said and pulled his friend close. "I need you to keep Sarah busy. I don't want her uglying up a good thing. Come on, take one for the team."

Bobby was about to refuse in the strongest terms when the conversation suddenly turned. Ronnie uttered a consonant curse and jumped behind the wall.

"What are you…?" Bobby began before Ronnie yanked him out of sight as well.

"It's Julia!" Ronnie hissed, peeking into the main room.

Bobby crept to the edge of the wall and looked. Standing at a table by the front door, chatting with a group of girls, was Julia, Ronnie's ex-girlfriend.

"Oh. That's a pickle," Bobby understated.

"You have no idea," Ronnie replied, his voice tinged with devilish glee. "We're drinking on her tab."

Bobby stared at his friend with horror. "Are you serious?"

"Would I be hiding if I was joking?"

"Why does every night have to end with you screwing someone?"

"Tonight is by no means over," Ronnie said. "I still have plenty of screwing ahead of me. But that's not the issue. Right now we have to get out of here."

"For the first time tonight, I completely agree with you. The back door is right there. Let's go."

Bobby stepped towards a metal door by the kitchen, but Ronnie pulled him back.

"We have to get out of here," he said and pointed to Sarah and Beth. "*With the girls.*"

"With those girls? You must be joking. They're not worth it."

54

"I never joke about women," Ronnie said. "I'll get them out of here. You just have to run interference with Julia."

Bobby looked at Ronnie with disbelief. "You want me to distract your ex-girlfriend, whose tab you've been drinking on, while you escape with two floozies? Did I get that right?"

"I haven't been drinking on her tab," Ronnie corrected. "*We've* been drinking on her tab. We're in this together. Now go on. Take one for the team!"

"Why do I always have to take one for the team?" he asked as Ronnie thrust into the main room.

Bobby swore under his breath. He wanted nothing to do with this mess. Acting on his own initiative, he decided to leave – with or without Ronnie. Doing his best to be inconspicuous, he soft-shoed it to the front door. His skin tingled as he neared the exit, titillated by his imminent freedom. But steps from the door, Julia looked up from her cackling friends and spotted him.

"Bobby Bright!" she declared, instantly recognizing his broad brow and nervous prance. "You have a lot of nerve coming into my bar."

Bobby froze and his face pinched as though he'd bitten into a lemon. "Julia? Hey? What's going on?"

"Where is he?" she growled and marched towards him.

As she approached, Bobby had the opportunity to inspect her more closely. In addition to be being very angry, Julia was also very drunk.

"Where is who?" Bobby replied lamely.

"Your boyfriend is 'who.' Where's Ronnie?"

"Ronnie's not here. I am. Alone." As he spoke, he saw Ronnie creep across the bar to Beth and Sarah.

"Don't lie to me!" she exclaimed, stabbing him in the chest with her finger. "You never come out of your hole unless that rat drags you out. Tell me where he's hiding. I've got some cheese for that rat."

"Yow!" Bobby squeaked. "What's with you?"

"What's with me? Don't play dumb. Ronnie broke up with me. After all I did for that bastard. He dumped me!"

"I'm so sorry to hear that. I didn't, err, know." Bobby glanced over Julia's shoulder. Ronnie was at the bar with his arms around the girls. They squirmed on their stools, giggling as he slid his hands up their shirts.

"Then what are you doing here?" Julia asked.

Bobby snapped back to the conversation and blurted out in *non sequitur* fashion, "I was fired today!"

Bobby's exclamation caught Julia off-guard. She narrowed her eyes and observed him with the uncertainty of a cat without depth perception judging relative distances.

"I was fired today," Bobby repeated and elaborated. "Let go, if you must know. I needed a drink so I came in here because I thought I might bump into Ronnie. If I knew that I'd only end up drinking by myself and then getting harassed by you, I wouldn't have left the house," he said and punctuated his moaning with a genuine pout.

The daggers in Julia's eyes remained fixed on Bobby, but her tone mellowed. "Well, I didn't know," she said. "Maybe I was out of line."

"Well maybe you were," he said. He breathed more easily and felt that he might get out of the bar after all. Then, without thinking, Bobby conspicuously glanced at the bar. Julia saw him look. He cringed at his own stupidity.

Julia's lips twisted bitterly. "Well, if you're here by yourself . . ." She spun around and followed Bobby's line of sight to the bar where three stools stood empty.

56

Bobby exhaled with relief. "I should be going," he said.

"Maybe you should," Julia agreed, grinding her jaw as he dashed for the exit.

Bobby bounded out of The Tap and ran to his car. He was determined to go home and would have left Ronnie behind had his friend not been leaning against the car with Beth in one arm while Sarah teetered unsteadily on her crutches.

"Bravo, Bobby," Ronnie cried. "Good guy saves the day! Now let's keep this party going! What do you say ladies?"

"Let's go somewhere. It's cold out here," Beth cooed and nuzzled against his chest.

"You hear that? The girls are cold. I know just the place."

Bobby was happy to see them on their way and call it a night. He was driving home. But when he reached his hand into his pocket for his keys, they were empty.

"Don't worry, buddy," Ronnie laughed, dangling the missing keys from his fingers. "I'll drive."

Ronnie drove like he lived, recklessly and with little regard for social custom. Staying off the main roads and navigating the wrong way down one-way alleys, it would have been impossible for Bobby to tell where they were headed if he tried. But the volumes of alcohol had already taken effect and he couldn't be bothered with niceties like direction and location. When the Taurus wagon squealed to a stop and the transmission creaked into park, Bobby staggered out of the car and stumbled to an unassuming door on a deserted street. Then everything went very dark.

When he came to, Bobby sat in a dim booth with worn vinyl seats and a ragged laminate table top. Pressed between the ply-wood wall and Sarah, whose broken leg poked awkwardly out of the booth, he saw that the table was littered with glasses. Whether these belonged to his party or had been there when they arrived, he could not say. An untouched pint sat before him and he picked it up reflexively.

Bobby turned a bleary eye to the bar. Although music was blaring, the place was almost empty. With the exception of a few shadowy characters lurking on the outskirts of the room, Ronnie and Beth were the sole occupants of the dance floor and took full advantage of the situation to grope, grind, and bump into one another. The music hit a rhythmic crescendo and Beth, possessed by the beat, pulled up Ronnie's shirt, revealing a tattooed torso dominated by a shrieking skull that started at his sternum and descended to his navel. Bobby stared at the grotesque inking until Sarah broke his concentration.

"Looks like someone is having fun," she said, leering at Bobby.

Bobby inched back against the wall, repelled by the sloppy, wanting look in her eyes.

"Ronnie's a pretty fun guy," he said.

"I bet you're a pretty fun guy too," she hiccupped. "So what is it you do, fun guy?"

Bobby was far from thinking clearly, but he was certain this ground had been covered. "I'm a writer? Fired? Remember?"

From her expression, Sarah clearly did not. "Want to dance, fun guy?" she asked and reached under the table towards the sensitive space between his legs.

"You can't dance," Bobby stammered and brushed away her offending hand. "Your leg is broken."

"It only takes one leg to dance."

"Well, I can't dance. I have a girlfriend!"

"You have a girlfriend?" Sarah recoiled. "And you've been leading me on all night? What kind of girl do you think I am?"

Sarah struggled out of the booth and hobbled on her crutches to the rest of the party. Beth was now leeched to Ronnie's back and rubbing her palms over his hips. Already having forgotten about Bobby, Sarah dropped her crutches and proceeded to bounce on one leg like a hopped-up jack in the box.

Bobby returned to his beer. With every sip his eyes became heavier. His head balanced on his neck like a bowling ball. He continued to watch the others dance, gazing at the simulated threesome that their gyrations suggested. He was transfixed by Ronnie, who had his shirt off and was twisting it in the air, and the tattoo on his chest.

This gnarly tattoo, along with the other symbols and slurs that covered much of his body, was from Ronnie's Navy days. But Bobby's tired mind fancied that the tattoos had bled into his skin much earlier. He recalled Ronnie as a boy and imagined that the templates of the tattoos had been traced by the morbid images scrawled across the metal t-shirts – Iron Maiden, Metallica, Megadeth, etc. – that were the constant uniform of his youth. On the dance floor, Beth puckered out her rear and Ronnie lapped his crotch against her like the tide. The skull on his chest seemed to jitter and giggle with delight.

Bobby lost his hold on consciousness. When he awoke, he was shocked to see Ronnie next to him, shirtless, sweating, and manic. "Taking a nap there? This will wake you up!" He slammed two pint glasses on the table.

They were half filled with a dark liquid and Bobby stared at them with bloodshot eyes. "What are they?" he asked, stupid with alcohol.

"Car bombs!" Ronnie cried and produced two shot glasses, handing one to Bobby. In dumb mimicry, he followed Ronnie's example, dropped the shot into the glass, and threw back the foaming brew.

59

"Whoo!" Ronnie howled, his mouth covered in Guinness froth and resembling a rabid dog.

Bobby felt the drink like a punch to the stomach. He bent forward and his mouth lolled open. "I don't feel good," he said.

Ronnie laughter cruelly and turned a mean eye on his friend. "Oh, don't be a pansy," he cried and slapped Bobby across the cheek. "Come on, killer!"

A bitter chill shivered its way up from Bobby's toes to the top of his head. He looked into Ronnie's eyes, which twinkled with something sinister. Whether Ronnie repeated it or he imagined it, Bobby heard the word "killer" echo through his brain.

Ronnie stumbled back to the dance floor, leaving Bobby to cling to the table like a bit of debris on a turbulent sea. The room spun with queasy menace. The bar took on an ominous, funhouse character. Through his spinning Bobby perceived something evil in the shadows. The other patrons, obscured by dark, took on perverse inhuman forms. He looked back to the rest of the party. They were once again grinding on each other. His eyes were drawn to Ronnie's chest. The tattoo seemed to move of its own accord, cackling as it slapped against Sarah and Beth.

Unable to breathe, Bobby rushed out of the bar onto the sidewalk. The street was deserted and a thick fog had settled, washing out the street lights and discoloring the moon, which emitted a stale, dead light. Not a soul was around. But Bobby did not feel alone. Something seemed to be near, lurking. His eyes searched the alleys and the black windows of the bleak houses across the street. He saw nothing, but he was sure something was there, stalking him. With no direction in mind, he staggered forward. His vision constricted and reduced to a pin hole. There was a rustle behind him. As everything faded to black, he perceived some hot and fetid breath cut the cool autumn night.

Chapter Six: Double-Barreled Nightmares and Other Shotgun Shenanigans

Despite his anointed role as shepherd to his congregation, many sheep in Father Landy's flock did not particularly like him. A Jesuit by training and prickly by nature, he was cold, intellectual, and elusive. During his arcane and subtly accusatory Masses, there was no man who had at some point cursed under his breath during the liturgy or compulsively groaned during a psalm that seem to have no end. The women of Fishtown also resented Father Landy, disliking the way that he regarded them, as though the whole female race was a troubling calculus equation he had to solve without scrap paper. And this doesn't begin to address his relationship with children. Father Landy failed to grasp the children in his congregation were children at all. He seemed to look upon them as a strange species of fully-developed, if pygmy, adults. The priest would subject them to plodding inquisitions about lapsed faith, spiritual death, and eternal damnation. With the sole exception of Bobby Bright, who was fatherless and starved for any attention from an adult male, no other child lasted more than a month as an altar boy. So while they entrusted the care of their sacred souls to Father Landy on Sundays, the community religiously avoided him on every other occasion.

Fishtown's strained relationship with the clergy was nothing unusual of course. All the priests who had shuffled through St. Stephen's had their imperfections. From the short and senile Father Ward, to the red-nosed Father Collins, and the depressive Father Ignatius, it seemed like a certain antipathy between parish and priest was a job requirement, as though warm words and fraternity would undercut the flinty foundations of the church's moral education.

But although he had won few hearts during his years at St. Stephen's, Father Landy had earned respect for his sobriety, consistency and, above all else, his severe prosecution of ethical deviation. For Catholics liked their religion as Indians like their curry: fiery. As Bobby watched Father Landy approach the Grauwickels that summer day, he had no doubt that he would set them to task.

"That jerk is going to get himself killed," Ronnie Delco exclaimed cheerfully from behind the corner of the church.

Bobby did not reply. He had faith in his priest. Although the boy's hands trembled, he believed in Father Landy.

With his head held high, Father Landy strode towards the Grauwickel clan, raising his hands as though he were Moses parting the Red Sea. But this action performed no miracle on Gus Grauwickel. Grauwickel's appetite for revenge against Ed Flood was not sated. Without any regard for Father Landy or his heavenly mandate, Gus lifted the shotgun and fired at Ed Flood, who was still fleeing up Belgrade towards the church. Unfortunately for the priest, Gus had loaded his gun with scattershot, which was imprecise by design. The gun blast was accompanied by a howl of pain. Father Landy collapsed on the street, cradling a bloody hand in his lap.

Bobby's soul heaved at the violence. He stared at the scene with cracked belief. He had no idea if he screamed. His body was hot and sick with adrenaline, but he could not run. He could only watch.

Gus Grauwickel pumped his shotgun, ejecting a spent shell that oscillated wildly through the air before skidding across the concrete. Father Landy convulsed on the ground, tears roiling from his eyes and a stream of what passed for swearing issued from his lips. "Oh, Mother Mary!" he cried. "Joseph Jesus Jezebel!" Gus stood above the priest and hesitated for a moment, but only a moment, as he twisted his fluffy mustache in villainous fashion. If he felt any penitence, Bobby did not see it. Without another glance, Gus stepped over the blubbering priest and pursued his quarry.

Ed Flood reached St. Stephen's. With terror disfiguring his pimpled face, he frantically searched for an avenue of escape. Starting towards the corner where Bobby and Ronnie hid, he stumbled over the front step of the church and fell face down, splaying himself across the sidewalk. When Ed Flood looked up from the concrete, his nose and mouth were covered with blood. Gus raised his shotgun and took aim. But before he could fire, the peel of tires screeched onto Belgrade.

A black Camaro – the same car that Ronnie and Bobby had seen earlier that morning – skidded into the intersection, bringing with it smoke and the smell of burning rubber. Stunned by its arrival, the Grauwickels were doubly surprised when a man stuck a pistol out of the car window and began to fire at them. The man fired six shots, sending Gus Grauwickel's sons scrambling for cover. But old man Grauwickel was not cowed. Standing his ground, he lifted his shotgun and fired at where Ed Flood had been on the sidewalk. By then his prey was already on his feet, dashing towards the Black Camaro, and Grauwickel's scattershot missed and ricocheted off the concrete.

Ronnie shrieked. Bobby turned and saw his friend, who had been watching the scene with great satisfaction, fall to the ground amidst a cloud of dust and stone debris. "My eye!" the little sadist squealed. "They shot my freakin' eye out!"

It must be said that Ronnie was overstating things. He had not lost an eye. But there was a large gouge across his eyebrow streaming blood down his face and hands. Between streams of curses, Ronnie begged Bobby to get a doctor. Bobby could only look on helplessly at his friend, frozen in shock. As Ronnie lolled on his back and whimpered, Bobby pressed himself closer to the wall, watching the drama on the street.

Gus Grauwickel crouched behind a mailbox beside the church, swearing and shoving shells into his shotgun. The man who had fired from

63

the Camaro stood outside the car now, fumbling with a plastic case of twenty-two cartridges as he tried to reload. Ed Flood wrestled with the passenger seat and climbed into the back of the Camaro. The Grauwickel boys, who had regained their courage, rushed forward and pelted the car with sticks and chunks of concrete.

The barrage flustered the man with the revolver and he dropped his bullets, which bounced off the pavement and skipped into oblivion. He swore loudly and leapt into the car, firing twice without aiming as the Camaro jerked into reverse. But before Ed Flood and his would-be saviors could make their escape, Gus emerged from behind the mailbox and shot out their back wheel. The Camaro lurched and jumped the sidewalk, striking a telephone pole.

Bobby entered a state of mind beyond panic, descending from the nether realms of shock to the feather-walled world of catatonia. After the car crashed, everything went silent, as though some great vacuum pump had sucked all the sound out of the street. Steam and smoke from the Camaro filled the void. For a moment, it was eerily peaceful. Impossibly silent. The only interruption to this otherworldly ambience was Ronnie, who continued to moan at Bobby's side. He looked at his friend. But he could not help him. All he wanted to do was go home.

As though sleepwalking in a dream beyond danger, Bobby ventured into the exposed street. He went in the direction of home. But as he shuffled up Belgrade something made him look back. The Camaro's passenger door creaked open. The man with the revolver was on his hands and knees on the sidewalk. Beside him, staggering, bloodied, but not down, was Ed Flood. Emerging from the smoke that obscured the road, like some demon of vengeance that would not rest or be satisfied, was the shotgun-toting Grauwickel.

This horrible vision sent Bobby into flight. He sprinted in a beeline for home. He did not flinch when he heard the next shotgun blast. He did not blink when he heard the screams that followed. He had already stepped through his front door and slammed it behind him.

If Bobby expected sanctuary in his house, he was disappointed. He was greeted by the roar and flash of explosions, thundering from the television in the living room. Like a frightened dog, Bobby yelped and turned to the screen. He saw two-toned images of tanks burning and airplanes twisting and twirling as they plummeted to the ground. Above the documentary din, a gravelly voice that was as terrifying as Grauwickel's shotgun, yelled at Bobby.

"What in God's name are you slamming my damn door for?" Bobby's grandfather bellowed from his chair. His face was pinched into a prune of geriatric menace. "Why aren't you in church, boy?"

"It's Gus Grauwickel, Pop Pop," Bobby panted. "He's gone crazy. He's got a shotgun and he shot Father Landy." Chewing his lower lip, fighting back a whimper, he exclaimed, "He shot Ronnie!"

Bobby's grandfather composed his wrinkles into an ancient, unforgiving frown. "Gus Grauwickel? That trash should stay on his own filthy street," he said and returned his attention to the television.

Bobby, who had just seen his priest and friend peppered with scatter shot, was too discombobulated to speak. Before he could find his tongue, a muted report from a shotgun was followed by a shower of glass as the bay window sprayed into the living room.

Bobby's reaction was to cower on the floor. His grandfather, however, was made of sturdier stuff and responded to the interruption of his television program with great offense. With no small effort, he pulled himself to his feet and teetered as kept his weight off his game leg. "That son of a bitch shot out my window," Pop Pop swore. "Get up, boy. Follow me before you get killed!"

Bobby scampered up the stairs after the old man. His grandfather's bad leg could not bend and gave him much trouble. With each limp upwards, he cursed.

Once they reached the landing, they made their way to his grandfather's bedroom. The curtains were drawn and the room was dark. Bobby lingered by the door. The bedroom overlooked the street and he wanted to stay away from the windows, which experience has shown to be flimsy protection against a shotgun. Oblivious to this danger, his grandfather passed before the window on his way to the closet. He reached to the top shelf and searched under some blankets. His leathery forearms flexed as his hands found their object. He smiled. He removed a shotgun, a double-barreled break action model, and a box of shells.

With an efficiency that bespoke a man who knew how to keep cool under fire, the old man cracked the stock and slid shells into the twin barrels. Small arms continued to echo through the street.

"Grauwickel," Pop Pop muttered as he hobbled to the window. "Goddamn Germans. They're always causing trouble." He turned to Bobby, still cowering by the doorway. "Quit pussyfooting around and hold back this curtain for me."

Bobby, whose instinct for self-preservation was well-developed, shivered by the wall.

"Don't be a pansy. Get up, petunia. Get over here!" the old man said as he tried to swipe his drape aside with his gun barrel.

Bobby still did not move.

"I said now!" he growled. His grandfather gave his grandson a look that convinced him that the old man would shoot Bobby himself if he didn't do as he was told.

66

Bent over, Bobby crabwalked to the window. Leaning his back against the wall, he reached for the curtain as though he was grabbing hot coals, pulling it back with his fingertips, exposing as little of his hand as possible.

Bobby's grandfather looked at him with shame and lifted the shotgun to his shoulder. He tried to stick the barrel out of the window, but he could not maintain a good angle because of his bad leg. He stepped farther back and stared down the barrel. His pale, watery eyes blinked with futility. He cursed.

"Get up," he commanded. "I said get up!"

Bobby reluctantly complied.

"Take the gun."

"What do you want me to do with it?" Bobby asked.

"I want you to point it out the window and blow that German bastard's head off."

"But I don't know how to shoot a gun."

"Well, it's time you learned, boy. Just put it on your shoulder, point it at that son of a bitch's head, and pull the trigger. Now take it!" He thrust the shotgun into Bobby's hands.

The old man pulled back the curtain. Sucking down air as though he were having an asthma attack, Bobby inched forward and peeked out the window. Hiding behind their neighbor's steps, he saw Ed Flood and the man with the revolver. Back at the intersection by St. Stephen's, the Grauwickel boys were hunkered behind whatever they could find. But Gus Grauwickel was in full view, striding up the middle of the road with his shotgun.

His grandfather focused on the blurry smudge that he perceived in the middle of the street. "Is that Grauwickel?"

Bobby nodded weakly.

"Is that Grauwickel?" the old man repeated. "Answer me, boy!"

"Yes, it is," Bobby choked out.

"What are you waiting for then? He's right there. Shoot him."

Bobby swallowed and lifted gun to his shoulder. The gun was heavy and he had difficulty aiming it. He watched the barrel orbit erratically around Grauwickel's head.

"Go on, boy," his grandfather pressed.

Bobby's eyes were dry. He opened and closed them compulsively. He leveled the barrel on Gus. Somewhere in the neighborhood, he heard police sirens.

"Do it, Bobby!" Pop Pop exclaimed. "I said shoot him!"

His words reached the street. Gus looked up at the bedroom window. His red, thick face was dead in Bobby's sights.

Bobby's eyes clenched shut. He forgot to breathe.

"*Shoot him!*" his grandfather commanded.

Chapter Seven: A Great Day Starts with a Great Breakfast

The meat exploded on the grill, spitting and hissing, as the fat crisped into a crunchy, brown and cancerous crust.

Made from the inferior bits of pig that failed to pass the less than formidable standards of sausage, Scrapple could have only been devised by a German. Only a German mind, perverted by its madness for efficiency, would have collected these hooves, snouts, heart, and entrails and combined them into a mealy, livid loaf. With the texture of cornbread and slightly less market appeal than spam, scrapple was an acquired taste.

But that Wednesday morning, Bobby wouldn't have settled for anything else. The Denny's up the road was not a temptation. Nor were the bags of Fritos and Tasty pies lining the display racks just inches from his fingertips. With the residue of last night's liquor cottoning his mouth and a hangover looming, there was nothing like a scrapple sandwich to settle the brewing storm. And there was no better place to get a scrapple sandwich in all of Fishtown than the Exxon station across from the Port Richmond Shopping Center.

Bobby leaned over the counter and inhaled the peppery aroma of the mystery meat, seasoned with countless bacon slices, sausage patties, and fried onions that had come before it on the griddle. With stomach rumbling, he watched the woman behind the counter scraping the scrapple up with a spatula and plopping it, along with American cheese and two fried eggs, into half a loaf of Italian bread. The menu quaintly called this monstrosity a "Breakfast Pouch." But there was nothing quaint or pouchy about it. It was a breakfast sack. It was a bulge busting out of its translucent, wax paper wrapping.

After paying, Bobby drenched the sandwich with mayonnaise and ketchup at the fixings station, soaking it with every last ounce of condiment it could hold. Since he'd been fired the month before, Bobby had become an expert concerning the physics of this scrapple sandwich, learning the water proofing properties of its grease, the insulating capacity of its cheese, and the absorbency of the bread. Bobby had always liked these sandwiches, but he used to only have them on the weekends. Now that he had nowhere to be on weekdays, they had become an essential part of his routine, like his morning ablutions and the hours of daytime television.

With his sandwich just the way he liked it (wet, goopy), Bobby left the convenience store, excited by the two-thousand calorie cholesterol bomb tucked under his arm. It was a beautiful day: the last gasp of summer in early October. As he strolled past the gas pumps towards Aramingo, he stepped on the signal hose and the Milton bell let out a ding-ding like a tinny hello to the world.

There were many things that Bobby noticed now that he didn't have a day job. As a fellow daywalker, a term that he took to calling the diverse cast of characters that inhabited Fishtown during working hours, he saw his neighborhood in a brand new light. Specifically, daylight.

All the Fishtowners were taking advantage of the Indian summer. Single mothers were out in droves, smoking Virginia Slims and pushing their strollers. On every corner children splashed in plastic kiddy pools. Old men in speedos with skin the color of his scrapple sandwich sat in folding chairs, greasy and soaking up the sun.

For some time Bobby walked home contentedly, beholding the familiar, basking in the mediocrity of it all. But as he continued along, other things caught his attention as well. Slight changes in the urban fabric. Subtle shifts in the order of things that cumulatively threatened to disturb his good day.

The city, like the rest of the country, was in flux, undergoing a giddy boom in construction and commercial speculation. Philadelphia, like a diamond in the squalid rough, was relatively untouched compared to other places. It couldn't boast the swank of international business, high tech sectors, or falling crime rates of its happy cousins up and down the Eastern seaboard. Still it would have been impossible for none of the economic buzz to trickle in from the more vibrant conurbations of greater New York, Boston, and Washington.

A new office tower was going up in Center City. Veteran's Stadium had been torn down and replaced by Lincoln Financial Field. In the adjoining neighborhoods, what had been brown fields and vacant lots were rezoned into apartments and commercial retail space. Bobby had not expected any of these currents to affect his neighborhood. Fishtown had been as it always was and he fancied that it would stay that way forever.

But in his incarnation as a daywalker, he realized how wrong he was. Construction crews were out, taking advantage of the unseasonable warmth to work on a condominium development. On one block on Susquehanna alone, he saw three For Sale signs, symbols of the frothy bubbles of speculation and gentrification that wafted on the breeze from Center City. These unwelcome changes troubled Bobby in a personal, if difficult to describe way. As he passed this evolving urban landscape, he could only chew his scrapple sandwich with grave presentiment.

Bobby continued a bit faster, harried by his misgivings, until he reached his own street and was reassured by what he saw. Sitting on the stoop of a shuttered store, a grungy little man smoked a cigarette, flicking his ashes into a battered Folger's can. This man was a living, breathing blight on property values. This stalwart sentry against the advance of modernity set Bobby's conservative heart at ease.

His faith in its cozy decrepitude renewed, Bobby turned a happy eye on his street. There were no For Sale signs. There were no condos. Just the row homes that he had always known. As he walked up his stoop,

Bobby even ventured a smile at his Eastern European neighbor who ignored him as he installed a new front door.

When he stepped inside, Suzie was sitting on the couch. She looked at Bobby with disgust. "Not again!" she moaned.

"And hello to you," Bobby mumbled through a mouthful of animal by-product.

"You're going to kill yourself with those sandwiches. They're so unhealthy," she said with unconsidered hypocrisy. Although it was the middle of the day, Suzie was watching television in a full-body fleece blanket that made her look like a lazy wizard.

"What are you talking about?" he asked and lifted the half-eaten breakfast pouch. "This sandwich is the best thing that has ever happened to me."

"Do you know what they put in scrapple?" She crinkled up her nose with disgust. "It's like an abortion in a hoagie roll. It's just awful."

"It isn't awful." Bobby took a large bite of the sandwich. "It's offal!" he muttered through the meat.

Refusing to encourage his pork puns, Suzie returned her attention to the television. Bobby chewed his food happily and sat beside her.

"What are you up to today?" he asked.

"Knitting," she said and gestured to the recliner where a collection of knit hats of various sizes and colors lay in a pile.

Bobby looked at the television. It was on commercial. Before he could ask what Suzie was watching, she said, "*Law & Order.*"

"Ahh," he said with ill-concealed disappointment. There are many benefits of not having a job. But there are also drawbacks. And for Bobby, who had a stay at home girlfriend, these drawbacks included sharing the television. Suzie was obsessed with crime drama in general and *Law & Order* in particular. Whether it was the original *Law & Order* or one of its spin-offs – Criminal Intent, Special Victims Unit, Major Rape Unit, Vice Squad, or Mod Squad – Suzie was hooked. This was unfortunate because these shows could be found at any time of the day on some network. Although Bobby had nothing against plodding police procedurals per se, at that moment, he was positive that The History Channel was broadcasting some enlightening documentary about the Nazis and the Occult, the Caesars and Space Travel or, at the very least, the Sex lives of Neanderthals. The southern fried indignations of Fred Thompson, the piercing eyes of Jerry Orbach, and the hissy-fits of Christopher Meloni were no substitute for these historical gems. As the television screen panned across a fresh crime scene, Bobby scarfed the rest of his sandwich to stifle a groan.

Suzie didn't need to hear a groan to know what he was thinking. "We don't have to watch this."

"What do you mean?" he said with his mouth full.

"I know you don't want to watch this."

"No, really . . ." He swallowed, contorting his face as though he were suffering a hemispheric stroke. "Leave it on."

"Just change it," she said impatiently. She tossed him the remote. "I don't want you pouting all morning."

Bobby needed no more urging. He tuned the television to the History Channel. The banter of the Caucasian detectives haranguing a minority criminal was replaced by another brand of black and white conflict as the screen filled with the grainy archival footage of a WWII battlefield.

"Why do you watch this stuff?" Suzie asked with a sigh.

"I like it," Bobby replied, transfixed by the sight of a Soviet T-34 tank brutalizing a platoon of Nazi infantry.

"It's morbid."

"It isn't morbid. It's, you know, history. It's educational. It's like going to school. But I can do it on the couch."

73

"And what are you learning exactly?"

A flash lit up the room. An explosion crackled from the television. Bobby smiled. "Never be the guy that carries the flame thrower."

"I mean what do you learn that's useful?"

"That could be a very useful piece of information. Given the right circumstances."

Suzie pulled her blanket up to her chubby chin and turned a critical eye on her boyfriend. Illuminated by the warm glow of the television, he could have been a little boy on a Saturday morning watching his cartoons. He was not a little boy though. And it was not a Saturday morning.

"I'm worried about you," she said.

"You're worried about me?"

"Yes, I think you need a hobby."

"Why's that?"

"Since you've stopped working, you don't do anything anymore. You just sit around all day. It isn't healthy."

Coming from Suzie, this appeal to productive pursuit was eyebrow-raising. Bobby couldn't help snickering. "You think *I* sit around the house too much?"

Suzie's soft cheeks stiffened. She glared at him severely from the folds of her fleece snuggy.

Bobby wiped away his grin and adopted a posture of damage control.

"Snooze. Baby," he soothed. "I don't think you sit around the house too much. I didn't mean that."

"Well, what did you mean?"

"I was just joking with you."

"And what was the joke about?"

"Oh, nothing," he stammered, his jaw inarticulately flapping to find the right words. "I don't know. Maybe…. It's just… Come on, baby," he said, punctuating his sentence with an unconvincing smile.

Suzie's snuggie sleeves flapped across her breasts as she harumphed. "If it was a joke, it wasn't funny," she said and rolled on her side.

"You're right. It wasn't funny. I didn't mean anything by it."

Bobby leaned towards Suzie and placed his hand on what he guessed was her thigh. From beneath the fleece folds, something struck him in the stomach.

"What's that for?" he yelped.

"I don't want you to touch me right now."

"But baby…" he cooed and reached out again towards her.

"I'm not in the mood. Just watch your war show."

Bobby deferred to Suzie and retreated to his side of the couch. He tried to watch the television, but he couldn't enjoy it with Suzie, swaddled in her slanket, making such a scene of ignoring him. It robbed even The History Channel of its heady pleasures. By the next commercial, which coincided with the Nazi defeat at Stalingrad, the best part of the war was over anyway. He'd had enough.

As footage showed a twitchy General Paulus sign the Nazi surrender, Bobby got up and grabbed his coat from the side table.

"Where are you going?" Suzie asked with surprise, as though she hadn't snubbed him for the previous ten minutes.

"I'm going for a walk," he said.

"That's a good idea. It'll be nice for you to get out of the house."

He didn't bother to ask for whom it would be nice.

Bobby stepped onto the sidewalk with no particular direction in mind. He knuckled his hands into his pockets and strolled north with the vague notion of taking the long way around the block. He had nowhere to go. The day spread out before him like a yawning blank and he consoled himself with the recognition that at least it was nice outside.

As he loped aimlessly around the corner, he heard a whisper, a hissing coming from the side alley. Bobby peaked into the alley and saw three boys beside a cluster of bikes. With spray paint cans in hand, they were tagging an abandoned row house with great bubble letters: "69 Squad."

"Hey, you kids!" Bobby hollered, fueled in equal parts by a rush of civic pride and the lingering frustration at Suzie. He expected an easy victory, anticipating that the boys would flee like cockroaches from sunlight. But the boys didn't flinch. They continued to ply their delinquent trade, indifferent to him.

Bobby hesitated, caught off guard by their lack of response. He was tempted to let the matter go and continue his afternoon wandering as if he saw nothing. But he could not go. He would not be ignored. "Hey! You there!" he exclaimed again and marched into the alley. He stood up straight and puffed out his chest as one might try to look bigger to scare a bear.

His initiative caused a visible, if subdued, reaction. A brown haired boy in the middle glanced over his shoulder and briefly assessed the threat posed by Bobby. Seeing little to worry about, he returned his attention to the graffiti.

Undeterred, Bobby stomped up behind the boys. "What do you think are you doing?" he growled in a voice intended to overwhelm and intimidate.

"We're doing calculus," the brown-haired boy replied, apparently immune to Bobby's inherent menace. He exchanged a spray can with a smaller blonde boy to his right and began to fill in an enormous "q."

Bobby was at a loss. His strategy had been based on the notion that even if they did not have respect for adult authority, they would at least defer to his relative size. But this was not the case. His broad brow blushing, Bobby continued.

"Who gave you permission to paint this house?"

"No one," a red-haired boy on the left answered. "We don't need it. Nobody lives here."

"Just because no one lives here doesn't mean you can paint it," Bobby said.

"Who says we can't?" the little blonde boy on the right asked.

"Well, for one, I do," he said, standing up to the pre-adolescent.

"You don't live here," the blonde boy said. "You can't tell me what to do."

"You're right. I can't tell you what to do," Bobby agreed. "But maybe the police can? What to do you think about that?"

"The police?" the brown-haired boy snickered. "Dude, this is Murderdelphia. There are like five people getting shot in Kensington right now. Do you think they're going to come out to Fishtown because some kids are tagging a wall? You're retarded."

The boys shook with laughter. On the side of Bobby's temple, a large blue vein began to pulse.

"Shouldn't you be in school?" Bobby muttered.

"Shouldn't you have a job, chum nuts?" the red-haired boy replied.

Bobby reached his limit and leapt at the spray paint can in the brown-haired boy's hand.

"Whoa-ho-ho, pops!" the boy cried. "Let go of me."

"Yeah, let go of him!" the blonde-boy yelled, cocked his arm back and thwacked a can of Krylon paint directly between Bobby's eyes.

Bobby fell to his knees and clutched his head, a string of curses dribbling from his lips. He looked up and saw the boys hop on their bikes, laughing and shouting as they pedaled away. Bobby threw an empty paint can after them. It fell to the ground in a flaccid arc far from where they disappeared around the corner.

Bobby still held his head when he staggered out of the alley. His face was bruised and so was his ego. But as he stumbled along, he noticed something that made him forget about that shame dealt to him by the feral street punks. At first he did not believe his eyes. He had to look twice. Up the road, where Belgrade intersected with his street, the door of St. Stephen's church was open.

It occurred to Bobby that he might have a concussion. The old church had been closed for more than a decade. For more than a decade its doors and windows had been shuttered behind iron grates and metal braces. Doubting what he saw, he walked closer. But there it was, plain as the sun in the sky, the door stood ajar, opening onto the musky black of the interior of the church.

Bobby stared at the open door and the blackness within. He filled with conflicting emotions. A part of him, an almost reflexive fear, urged him home. But some more vital core overcame this impulse. He gazed at the building as if mesmerized. He realized that his legs were moving, carrying him into the church, pulled by a force greater than himself.

He paused at the flat stone step before the open door. He had not stood on this spot for years. He could taste the air inside the church, drafting into the street. It was cold and stale as from a tomb. He peered into the dusty depths, but he could see nothing. He looked at his feet. They stepped inside.

It did not take long for Bobby's eyes to adjust to the blackness. Although they were covered with iron bars and grimed with years of debris,

78

the stained glass windows cast lattices of dull light across the sanctuary, illuminating the outlines of the pews and the nave. But the altar, located in a recess at the back of the sanctuary was, shrouded in gloom.

With the tentative steps of a penitent, Bobby shuffled up the aisle. He began to make out more details of the interior. He saw the mosaics, smeared by time and water damage on the walls and ceilings. The pipe organ, still in place, snaked up the far wall. He discerned the dim outline of the raised pulpit. But when he reached the foot of the chancel, he was shocked to discover that he was not alone. There was a groan of creaking wood. Footsteps echoed through the silent church. Something emerged from behind the altar. It descended down the steps, resolving into the contours of a man. It stopped several paces from Bobby, still in the shadows, just out of the light.

The silhouette stared at him from the darkness. Bobby gazed back, his heart shivering like a wet kitten.

The silhouette spoke. "Can I help you?" it asked, politely and rather anticlimactically.

"I'm Bobby. Bobby Bright. I, uh, live down the street."

"You live down the street?" the silhouette asked.

"That's right. I live just around the corner. Off Belgrade."

The silhouette nodded. A man emerged from the shadows. "My name is Jeff. I just bought this place. I'm your new neighbor."

Chapter Eight: Love Thy Neighbor, or At Least Try

"Don't we already have a coffee grinder?"

"Not like this one. Not an antique one," Suzie said, turning the creaky appliance in her hands, studying it from every angle.

Bobby regarded the contraption from a more objective distance. It was a hand-crank grinder, an old specimen with cast iron mechanics, but a hideous orange paint job had been applied to its wooden body by a previous, possibly colorblind, owner.

"Don't we have enough junk?" Bobby asked.

"You see junk. I see treasure. I saw one just like this on Antique Road Sow. It went for almost $100. And this one is only," Suzie upended the grinder and looked at the price tag on its bottom, "two dollars. It's a steal! It would go great next to that antique juicer I bought last month. Or maybe the Fiestaware!"

Bobby frowned at the pumpkin-colored dynamo. In his opinion it would go better in a dumpster. Or maybe on the train tracks. He cursed the Goodwill, the abomination of commerce where they had been rummaging for the last half hour.

Every Saturday Suzie dragged Bobby to the Goodwill. Unfortunately, it was on Frankford Avenue, less than a mile from his house. Although the inventory rarely changed and Suzie never bought anything they actually needed, Bobby had no excuse not to go.

"Put it wherever you want. You're the expert," he said in surrender. "Maybe it is nice. I don't know." Then, with a rancor that had nothing to do with the grinder, he grumbled, "That paint ruins it though. I hate it when people take a really nice old thing and, just, you know, ruin it. It's horrible."

"Oh heavens, Bobby. Please don't start this again."

"Start what?"

"You know what. Getting all worked up about it isn't going to make it better."

Bobby crossed his arms and pouted. "But how can I not get worked up about it? It's St. Stephen's. It's my church!"

"It isn't a church anymore. It's just a building."

"It is not just a building. You can't just make a church not a church."

"Will you keep your voice down," she shooshed. "You're making a scene."

"I grew up going to the church. I was an altar boy there. I spent every Sunday at that church for years. Suzie, that church belongs to the neighborhood."

"The church belongs to the guy that bought it," she said in well-rehearsed reply. "You need to get over it."

Bobby picked up a chintzy metal lamp and looked at it without really looking at it. "I need a drink. I want a coffee," he muttered and surveyed the store like he wasn't sure how he arrived there.

"Well, Sputnik is right around the corner," Suzie suggested, happy to have a break from him. "I can just meet you there."

He nodded absently and left her to hunt amid a shelf of tarnished pewter pots.

As Bobby stepped outside, the diesel-perfumed air had an immediate, settling effect on him. Looking south towards Center City, he gazed at the skyline as though it were some object of Buddhist meditation. Between the skyscrapers that dominated it, he contemplated the square and overly Baroque city hall with the statue of William Penn perched atop. The longer he gazed at its embellished terraces, the more it resembled a gaudy birthday cake of concrete and stone, a confection baked in plaster and sprinkled with rococo. Gradually his vision receded to the foreground and

81

he saw the rows of buildings that radiated from the center of the city, connecting it with the outskirts where he now stood. With the image of the city firmly before him, he once again felt grounded in person and place.

Bobby walked up the street and entered the Sputnik Café. Although it was a coffee house, the fact that it sold coffee seemed irrelevant to most of the clientele that lounged in its salvaged furniture, read its library of books, chatted endlessly, but rarely seemed to buy anything. Bucking the trend of consumer abstinence, Bobby purchased a coffee and scone. As he paid, a man at a nearby table with a broken pair of tortoise shell glasses and a copy of *Atlas Shrugged* glared at him contemptuously as though any medium of exchange more evolved than barter caused him personal offense.

Bobby maneuvered towards the back of the coffee shop to the only empty table, which stood by a window covered in shredded flyers that advertised, among other things, a soul dance night, several lost kittens, and a thugged-out Latina entertainer called "Fingerbang." Concluding that none of these flyers applied to him, Bobby picked up a *City Paper* off the table, prepared to fritter away however long it would take for Suzie to work her way through the Goodwill. But Bobby had barely read the front page headline when he was interrupted by a voice that made him cringe.

"How's it going, neighbor? Bobby, right?"

Bobby looked up from the paper with a reluctant fatality. Standing over him was a man he recognized instantly. "Jeff Kaye," the man said. "I just moved in on your street."

Jeff needed no introduction. Bobby knew precisely who he was.

"St. Stephen's…" he whispered.

"Yeah, that's right. I moved into the old church."

"It's called St. Stephen's," Bobby said.

"St. Stephen's. Right. Whatever," Jeff obliged with a smile.

Bobby smiled back, pinching out a thin, rat-like grin.

Jeff stood by the table, mug in hand, scanning the cafe for an empty seat. Bobby followed his eyes and realized that there was only one empty seat in the place and it was at his table.

"Do you come here often?" Jeff asked.

"Sometimes," Bobby mumbled, hoping in vain that one of the layabouts in the coffee shop would leave. "My girlfriend is up the street. In the Goodwill."

"The Goodwill? That's cool. On Frankford, right?"

"Yup. Just up the street," he said curtly, wishing that Jeff would just disappear.

Jeff did not disappear though. He said "awesome" and hovered above the table.

There was a moment of awkward silence. Biting his lower lip, Bobby confronted the reality of the situation. Jeff was not going anywhere. "Would you like to take a seat?" he asked grimly.

Jeff accepted.

If nothing else, this forced proximity to his neighbor afforded Bobby the opportunity to observe him more closely. Jeff was about Bobby's age, but he wore his thirty-plus years far better. He had a strong face lined with fine wrinkles, giving him the appearance of gravity and suggesting a life lived outdoors. Jeff had a lean, athletic body, accentuated by a well-fitted, collared shirt. Crowning his manly form was a fetlock of curly hair. Bobby gazed at his impressive mane and had a suspicion that the more he got to know this man, the less he would like him.

"Have you lived here long?" Jeff asked, disrupting Bobby's unneighborly ruminations.

"My whole life," he said, still distracted by Jeff's lush scalp.

"In Philadelphia?"

"In Fishtown. In the same house. My whole life."

"In the same house? Wow. I don't know anybody who has done that." He shook his head in disbelief. "Man, I can't even count how many places I've lived anymore. L.A. London. Miami. New York. You must really love it here."

"Yeah, I like it here," Bobby said. "If I like something, I don't see much point in changing it."

"If it's not broken, don't fix it?"

"Something like that."

Jeff smiled again. "You should like it here," he encouraged. "This is a great neighborhood. It has a lot of potential."

Bobby frowned. He was of the opinion that Fishtown had long ago realized its potential and was perfectly fine the way it was.

"What do you do around here?" Jeff asked.

"Like how?"

"Like a job."

After an unhappy pause, Bobby replied, somewhat incoherently, "I'm a writer. I work with computers. Programming. Internet stuff, you know. Sort of."

Jeff's optimism was indefatigable. "That's great. Computers are a great line of work."

"Yes, they are," Bobby agreed, although he didn't know the difference between Big Blue and Big Bird.

The conversation reached a natural ebb. Bobby could have easily picked up the paper and ignored his new neighbor. But despite his dislike for Jeff, his curiosity was piqued by the man who had appropriated his church.

"What are you doing in Philadelphia exactly?" he asked.

"Living, man. Just living," Jeff replied very seriously and sipped his coffee with an almost spiritual abstraction.

84

"I mean, what do you do for a living?"

The new neighbor looked very thoughtful and said, "I'm a photographer."

"A photographer? Like for newspapers or something?"

"No, no," Jeff laughed, tickled by the suggestion. "I'm a *commercial* photographer," he said in a tone that implied Bobby should know the difference. "I take pictures for advertising. Billboards. Magazines."

"What kind of pictures?"

"Pictures of everything. Liquor. Food. Fashion. But I specialize in cars. Actually, is that this week's *City Paper*? Let me see."

Bobby complied and handed him the paper.

"That's the one," Jeff said. "Check out page twelve."

Bobby turned to page twelve. There was a full-page ad featuring a sleek foreign sports car tearing across some baked stretch of desert.

Jeff scrutinized the picture. "It looks better in color," he said with measured self-criticism. "But you get the idea."

"Get the idea of what?"

"Of my work. I took that picture."

Bobby looked at the picture again and then looked back at Jeff. "You took this picture?"

"Yep."

"So you've come to Philadelphia to take pictures?"

"Not exactly. I work mostly out of New York. But I've been looking for a place there with sufficient studio space and I just couldn't find anything. You know how expensive New York can be."

Bobby nodded and plainly did not.

"Well, I've been looking for a decent studio for years," Jeff said. "But Manhattan is priced out. Brooklyn is no bargain anymore. Even

Hoboken went and got ridiculous. And there is no way I'm going to Queens, you know what I mean?"

Still no reaction.

"Well, this friend of mine tells me about Philadelphia. At first, I admit it, I was skeptical. But I started looking at places here and I liked it. I really liked it. So I'm meeting with a real estate agent one day and I see this beautiful, old abandoned church and it hits me. Bam! A church. Bam! This place has so many churches. More than it knows what to do with, you got me? So I talk to the real estate agent and it turns out there is one for sale. And it's going for a song. So I bought it."

As Jeff related his story, he became increasingly enthusiastic. The story had the opposite effect on Bobby.

"So you used to go to… What was it? St. Stephen's?" Jeff asked.

"I used to be an altar boy there," he said. "When I was a kid, I went there three times a week. Twice on Sundays. Once on Wednesdays."

"So you have history there?"

Bobby looked at Jeff with sudden severity. "You have no idea," he said.

Jeff's smile was inscrutable as Mona Lisa's. He tapped his fingers on the table and silently considered.

"Let me throw something out here," he said. "I would love to talk to you about the church. Really talk. I'm going to do some renovations on it, but before I do, I'd like to know more about the place. So I can make some informed decisions about maintaining the integrity of the space. Not only the architectural, but spiritual integrity, too, if you get me. It would be great to hear from someone who actually went there. Someone who has history with it. Would you be interested in getting together and talking about the church?"

86

"I don't think so," Bobby said and gave his head a little shake. "There's nothing that I could tell you that you'd be interested in," he lied.

"I'm sure you could," Jeff pressed. "Anything would be really helpful."

Bobby frowned and glanced towards the door as if to flee.

Jeff was undeterred by the cool response. He looked at Bobby slyly, as though he had a fifth ace in a stacked deck. Leaning back in his seat, he asked, "Would you feel differently if we talked about it at the Eagles game this Sunday."

Bobby's ears perked. "At the Eagles game?"

"At the Eagles game," Jeff confirmed.

"You mean in the stadium? Playing the Cowboys? You have tickets?"

Jeff shrugged nonchalantly. "I just did some work for a buddy of mine at the Hilton who handles the team's travel arrangements. He sent a couple of extra tickets my way."

"I haven't been to an Eagles game in years," Bobby said, more to himself than Jeff. In a city of diehard fans, Eagles tickets were always expensive, a precious item to be coveted. But the rivalry between Philadelphia and Dallas put a premium on what was already a luxury item.

"They're not the best tickets," Jeff said. "They're only in the end zone."

"Only in the end zone," Bobby chirped. "You'd really let me have one?"

"One? I'd let you have two. My friends are Giants fans. I can't give these things away. You can bring your girlfriend or whoever. It's up to you."

"You're serious?" Bobby asked, practically salivating.

"Why wouldn't I be?" Jeff checked his phone. "Listen, I need to run. Here's my card. Think about it. If you're free on Sunday and up for it, give me a call."

Bobby took the card, but he did not need to think about it. Unable to contain a toothy grin, he blurted out, "I'm free. I can go."

Jeff nodded with cool approval. "Awesome, man. I'm glad to hear it. Give me a call and we'll work everything out."

"I will. Thanks." He shoved the card deeply into his pocket as though hiding a golden ticket.

In what seemed like seconds after Jeff left Sputnik (although it could have been much longer, as Bobby was absorbed in happy football thoughts), Suzie sunk into the empty seat and propped up two bags overflowing with fabric on the table.

"What's all this?" Bobby asked, wincing at the rainbow of flannel, fleece, terrycloth, and corduroy exploding from the bags.

"Aren't they awful?" she asked with giddy irony.

"Yes, they are," he agreed, minus the irony.

"The Goodwill just got this enormous shipment of wonderful, tacky old pajamas in. I had to buy them."

"What are you going to do with them?" Bobby asked, lifting a tattered velvet sleeve covered in dust. "You're not going to wear that are you?"

"Of course not, silly. Some clothes are for wearing. Some clothes are for something more." Suzie beamed at the bag. "These rags are destined to be dolls."

"Rag dolls, huh?" Bobby said skeptically.

"All kinds of dolls. Boys, girls, cats, dogs, bears…"

Bobby thought about the prospect of Suzie littering his house with what would inevitably be half-finished, malformed stuffed animals. It

88

wouldn't be pretty. It would be the Muppets meet Charles Manson. But he only shrugged and chuckled "Why not?" He was feeling good today. Besides, anything was better than more knit hats.

Chapter Nine: Judas Probably Would Have Liked Football Too

Bobby knew it was a sin to wish away time. Thanks to his Catholic upbringing, he knew more personal prohibitions than even the guiltiest conscience could make us of. But Bobby couldn't wait for the Eagles game on Sunday. Damp October slogged by and the shortening November days stretched on forever. In the morning he would stuff himself on scrapple sandwiches. In the afternoon he would watch TV while Suzie hunched over the sewing machine, stitching delicate second-hand fabrics into rag dolls with her thick sausage fingers. At night there was no rest. Just waiting.

All week long Suzie worked on her dolls, churning out lumpy, irregularly-shaped pieces that resembled hearts and livers rather than the limbs and torsos she intended. The living room filled with these botched attempts, becoming an abattoir of paisley, plaid, and polka dot. But by week's end, Suzie had sewed together her first finished product. It was a cat with no analog in nature, a specimen that was like no other that ever came before it. It had a tiny corduroy head, outsized argyle ears, and a stubby body draped in gingham. When she showed Bobby her creation, he could only nod with the vaguest approval, perplexed by the doll's Frankenstein sensibilities.

Yet, while the week was generally one of eager anticipation, Bobby could not shake a nagging feeling. Although he would never complain about free Eagles tickets, he was bothered by accepting them from Jeff. This felt like an act of betrayal. After all, Bobby was fraternizing with a man who had bought St. Stephen's and was transforming a house of God into just a house, albeit with a studio. When Bobby thought about it, he felt like a traitor, a Benedict Arnold or, more appropriately, a Judas. Instead of thirty pieces of silver, he received two passes to an Eagle-Dallas game, Lower Sideline Section 135, Row 28, Seats 2 and 3 to be exact.

90

One evening Bobby stepped outside to go to the store. His Eastern European neighbor was on his stoop, smoking a cigarette, admiring a new handrail he had installed. Across the street, two silhouettes in a window waved their arms like Japanese shadow puppets, regaling the block with a fuck-you conversation. As he walked around the corner, Bobby saw a dumpster sitting outside the church. Loaded on top were tattered wall hangings, faded banners, ornamental lamps, and other sacred artifacts that Bobby remembered from his childhood. Like a slap in the face, a punch in the gut, and a wedgie, all performed in a simultaneous trifecta of pain and shame, it hit hard. Abandoning his errand to the shop, Bobby turned to the darker side of the street.

***

"You did the right thing inviting me," Ronnie said, shouldering through a huddle of dudes in football jerseys. "An Eagles game is no place for a girlfriend. Especially when we're playing Dallas. Hey, coming through here!"

"It wasn't my decision exactly," Bobby said, following in his wake. "Suzie didn't want to come."

"She didn't want to come to a Birds game? Where's her Philly spirit?"

"She's from New Jersey."

"Ah . . ." he said sighed as they finally reached the car. Ronnie, his arms akimbo, looked back with pride as if he'd just climbed a mountain or crossed the ocean, which in a sense he had. Before him, lolling between rows of RV's and vans, was a sea of Eagles fans, dressed in black, green, and white. Somewhere in the distance, a husky someone chanted, "E-A-G-L-E-S! EAGLES!" as if ecstatically participating in a spelling bee.

"Well, it's just good that you brought me," Ronnie said, beaming at the spectacle.

"I certainly hope so," Bobby said with a touch of uncertainty.

"And what does that mean?"

"For starters, that hat makes me a bit nervous." Bobby gestured to the bright orange Texas Longhorns hat on top of Ronnie's head.

"But it's my lucky hat. This hat got me out of a lot of tight spots when I was in the Navy. And besides I look good in orange."

"I wish you hadn't worn it. They're playing the Cowboys. You know, from Texas? People might get the wrong idea."

"Then I'll just have to straighten them out, won't I?" Ronnie declared and puffed up his chest. "But if you're such a fan, why aren't you wearing some Eagles gear?"

"I wore a green t-shirt," Bobby said defensively. He unzipped his black winter coat and pulled down his gray sweatshirt down, revealing a thin stripe of forest green around his collar.

"Oh, that's some team spirit. How about we get some beer and just change the subject?"

Bobby opened the back of his station wagon and cracked the cooler inside, revealing a trove of Kenzinger. As they drank their beers, a voice cried out "Dallas Sucks." Like a spark in a saw mill, this shout caught fire, igniting other exclamations of "Dallas Sucks," which flared out into the distance.

"So where is this photographer guy?" Ronnie asked, seating himself on the bumper.

"Jeff said that he had a few things to take care of. He's going to meet us here."

"He better get here with those tickets. I'm not freezing my ass off for nothing in the parking lot. Damn, this is sloppy. What a hot mess."

And what a hot mess it was. Philadelphia fans are, depending on one's perspective, either the best or worst fans in the country. When they lose, they take to the streets, breaking bottles, assaulting police, raping, fighting, climbing light posts, and flipping cars in an orgy of destruction that would make the Mongols blush. When they win, it's pretty much the same thing. And at that moment, tens of thousands of them were packed into the parking lot outside the stadium like some latter day Woodstock – albeit one fueled on aggression, cheap beer, and grilled meats.

Ronnie took a long drink and belched. "How well do you know this Jeff guy?" he asked.

"Not very well," Bobby said.

"And he gave you two tickets to the Eagles-Cowboys game? Possibly *the* game of the year? Does that seem strange to you?"

"A little, I guess. But he got them for free. He said he didn't have anyone else to go with. Why?"

"Maybe it means something. Maybe it doesn't." Ronnie shrugged with tantalizing indifference. "Oh, never mind…"

"What are you getting at?"

Ronnie assumed a philosophical repose. "I don't know the guy. And I don't know the circumstances of your acquaintanceship. But I've never heard of getting something for nothing. Are you sure there isn't some sort of *quid pro quo*?"

"A *quid pro* what?"

"A tit for tat?"

"I'm not following you."

"He scratches your back. You lay on yours?"

"Not really sure where you're going with this, Ronnie."

"Are you sure he's not gay?"

"I take it you don't mean happy."

"No, I don't. I mean *gay*. Like in "h" to the "o" to the "m" "o" sexual."

93

Bobby considered the suggestion with skeptical silence. "No way!" he exclaimed.

"Just think about it," Ronnie said. "It makes sense."

"I am thinking about it. And it doesn't make any sense. Jeff is not gay. Not that I care or anything. But this isn't like what your filthy mind is getting to at all."

"Really, huh? How many gay guys do you know?"

"Not many," Bobby admitted.

"I was in the Navy," Ronnie said. "And I met my fair share. When you're stuck on a lonely hunk of metal with boatload of frustrated seamen a thousand miles from shore, you learn to spot the type quickly. It can be a matter of survival."

"And what is the type then?"

"Think about it. He's an artist. He hangs around coffee shops. He gives men expensive gifts. He's gay for you, Bobby. Totally," Ronnie concluded with a swig of beer. "You shouldn't sell yourself short. You're kind of cute in this broken, balding sort of way. Gays are into fixing things up. It's that Queer-Eye-This-Old-House bullshit. They love your type. You're a hopeless fixer-upper."

"This is nonsense."

"Is it then? Hmm? Just don't be surprised when he wants something in return for those tickets."

Bobby declined to continue the conversation.

Across the lane a horde of tailgaters ate sausages and chugged beers, intent on getting even fatter and more belligerent. Bobby and Ronnie watched a girthy, shirtless man with more tattoos than teeth emerge from an RV with two poles constructed from Bud light cans, approximately six feet in length, duct-taped end to end. The crowd hurrahed. A man with dreadlocks took one of the poles and hopped onto the girthy man's back.

94

www.ingramcontent.com/pod-product-compliance
Lightning Source LLC
Chambersburg PA
CBHW051305120626
46547CB00015B/2096

Another man clothed in green and gray grabbed the second pole and ran some distance down the lane and mounted a fourth man, just as voluminous as the shirtless wonder but more seasonably dressed. The two teams pointed their poles at one another and erupted in a round of ornithological cries: "Birds!" one exclaimed; "Eagles!" was the reply. They charged.

Despite their size and lumbering, the noble steeds closed the distance with surprising speed. The jousters on their back scrambled to hold on, aiming their poles unsteadily. As they met, a beer can struck the shirtless man squarely in the shoulder, sending him and his rider to the ground. The other team, however, did not have a chance to celebrate. They tripped over their opponents and joined them on the pavement. A cheer erupted and echoed up and down the parking lot. The participants arose, dazed. The shirtless man's flabby torso was red and wet. His chest was skinned and blood flowed from his right nipple, cascading down his belly.

Ronnie shook his head. "Some people should not go topless."

"Truth," Bobby agreed. "Speaking of topless, how did things work out with that redhead from the bar?"

Ronnie grinned wolfishly. "Do you really need to ask?"

"Probably not. Did you have a good time?"

"I had a great time."

"So she wasn't completely passed out when she got back to your place? Not that it matters to you?"

"No, there was some mileage left in her. You should have heard her motor purr."

"So you're going to see her again?"

"Definitely. She's a good time. I appreciate that in a lady. I like it when they know how to enjoy themselves."

"I thought you liked it when they were easy."

"I do. I like that, too. All the better. And Beth, let me tell you, she was a real fun. And real easy. Everything that you could want in a lady."

A chant of "Dallas Sucks" began in the distance and spread across the parking lot. At first it was sporadic, but it grew in intensity, moving in their direction, accompanied by a wave of boos.

"Dallas fans?" Bobby asked.

"Definitely," Ronnie answered.

"What the hell are they doing out here?"

"Must be suicidal."

There was a commotion in the lane and the sea of green separated, revealing a figure in conspicuous blue and gray, the colors of the Dallas Cowboys.

"Bobby! Hey!" Jeff called out. Dressed in a Navy coat and light gray jeans, he was oblivious to the snipes and curses hurled at him.

Bobby reluctantly lifted his hand and waved weakly back.

"Oh, that's beautiful," Ronnie laughed. "You didn't tell me your boyfriend was a moron."

Jeff reached the station wagon and smiled. "Sorry, I'm late. It's a circus out here."

"It's the way we do in the Bird's Nest," Ronnie said cooly.

"The what?" Jeff asked.

"The stadium," Bobby said, trying to ignore the harassment of the Eagles fans around them. "You want a drink or something."

"We have Kenzinger and Kenzinger," Ronnie added helpfully.

Jeff opened his beer and a sordid set of females wearing pink Eagles jerseys and Mardi Gras beads staggered past. Seeing Jeff, they shouted in unison "Dallas Sucks" and made novel combinations of

96

derogatory gestures with their fore and middle fingers. The squattest and most demonstrative went so far as to bare her pale Irish ass in his direction.

"Some girls shouldn't take their pants off," Ronnie cringed.

"I never thought I'd hear that from you," Bobby said. "Never in my whole life."

"What was that about?" Jeff asked, more confused than insulted.

"Well, in case you hadn't noticed, buddy," Ronnie said, "you're dressed like a Cowboy's fan."

"Cowboy's fans wear Patagonia parkas and Diesel Jeans?"

"No, it's not what you're wearing," Bobby explained. "Blue and gray are the Cowboy's colors."

Jeff looked at his outfit and shrugged. "I guess you're right."

In Bobby's opinion, he was a bit too cavalier about being the object of the coincidental hatred of thousands of Eagles fans.

The three drank steadily. Jeff and Ronnie sat on the bumper of the car. Bobby, under the pretense of stretching his legs, stood in front of Jeff doing his best to hide him from the other Eagles fans.

"What took you so long, Jeff?" Ronnie asked as he pounded his fourth beer. "We thought you weren't going to show."

"I was touching up some photos from a shoot. The client wants them tomorrow. Getting over here from Chinatown was a nightmare."

"We have a Chinatown?"

"Yes, we do," Bobby said. "You never saw that big red Chinese arch near Center City?"

Ronnie shrugged. "So, what were you doing in Chinatown," he asked.

"I'm renting studio space in a loft."

From his beer hand, Ronnie stuck out one pinky, as though he were holding a champagne flute. "Clients? Lofts? Very fancy. What kind of pictures were you taking?"

Oblivious to his mockery, Jeff replied, "We did a shoot up in New York for the new Audi coup. Out on Chelsea piers."

"Chelsea, huh?"

"Yeah, Chelsea. You get a good view of the city from the piers. It's a nice backdrop."

Ronnie sipped his beer with a cunning expression. "That's very interesting. Working as a photographer must be a pretty great job."

"I can imagine worse."

"Lots of perks, I expect?"

"Sometimes."

"Must be very popular with the ladies? Meet a lot of ladies at work?"

"I'm sure he does," Bobby interjected. "Now will you give it a rest?"

Jeff looked between the two uncertainly. But before he could ask what they were talking about, a new chant swept across the parking lot.

"Boo B.O.! Boo B.O.!" the fans cried. Suddenly a book flew through the air and skidded along the lane, stopping in front of the station wagon.

"Who's B.O.?" Jeff asked.

"B.O. is Barry Omens," Bobby said, happy to divert Ronnie's line of inquiry. "He was the Eagles star wide receiver last year. But he had a meltdown with management and got traded."

"To none other than the Dallas Cowboys," Ronnie added.

98

More books were thrown after the first, coming from every direction. The crowd cheered as someone emptied a box of paperbacks into a pile.

"What are those?" Jeff asked.

Bobby peered at the cover of the books. "Those would be copies of Barry Omens biography."

"But what are they doing with them?"

No answer was necessary. Just then a burning book flew through the air, landing in the heap. The pile burst into flames. A cheer sounded from the crowd.

"You have got to be kidding me," Jeff muttered.

"You have no idea. Give it time," Bobby said ominously. The flames' reflections danced on his face.

"It can get worse than a book burning?"

"Give it time," Ronnie said. "Just give it time."

The smoke from the fire went up like a signal, drawing other Eagles fans to the flames. The crowd around the pyre grew thick and vicious, derogating B.O. and the Dallas Cowboys in the most unseemly terms. The fans brought more books to feed the flames. But the books weren't the only things committed to the fire. They burned Cowboy jerseys and fan flags. One crafty Eagles acolyte had a cardboard model of the Dallas cityscape, which he raised over his head and cast down into the flames. But the climax occurred when a procession of fans painted in ceremonial green arrived swinging baby dolls dressed in Cowboys uniforms from nooses around their plastic necks.

The procession chanted "Kill the Cowboys" like some unholy monastic order, lowered the dolls into the flames. The crowd whooped and hollered. Across the lane a motorcycle revved its engine along with the cheers. Gorging on the bloodlust, one of the men removed his doll from the flames and swung it in circles like a poi at a Hawaiian fire dance before dashing it in on the ground. The man with the motorcycle rode into the lane and positioned his back tire over the doll's head. He gunned the motor, burning asphalt and launching a spray of smoldering plastic behind him. The parking lot roared in ecstatic approval.

Even Bobby and Ronnie, well accustomed to the exuberant excess of their native city, were shocked. Jeff removed a digital phone from his coat and took a picture. "I wish I'd brought my good camera," he said.

It wasn't long before the fire died down, assisted by a circle of fans who decided to empty their bladders on it. As the flames hissed and sizzled, the crowd dispersed.

Bobby finished his beer and reached back for another. There were only ice cubes in the cooler.

"Where'd all the beer go?" he asked. His cheeks were a bright, blossomy red that could only partly be explained by the cold.

"We drank it," Ronnie burped.

"I think we've tailgated enough anyway," Bobby concluded with a hiccup. "I definitely feel the spirit. What time is it?"

"It's almost seven-thirty," Jeff announced after consulting his watch. "Kick off is 8."

"What are we waiting for then?" Ronnie jumped up from Bobby's bumper and slapped his hands together. "Are we ready for some football?"

They worked their way to the stadium. Although those without tickets continued to drink, the tailgating portion of the football experience was coming to a close. The grills were extinguished. The lawn furniture was folded and stowed. The last Italian sausages were eaten. The last beers were crushed. Fans were weaving through the cars and stalls, converging on the stadium.

While they were drinking, Bobby hadn't noticed that night had fallen. As he approached the stadium, Lincoln Financial Field was lit up before him, blazing brightly in the autumn sky. He trembled with excitement. His breathing quickened. His legs moved faster as he made his way through the parking lot. But as he progressed, the lane became more and more congested. One hundred feet from the gate, their progress came to a halt.

The crowd was held back by a column of burly gorillas dressed as security guards. Beyond security line, a television production crew armed with boom mikes and movie cameras dashed around the empty lane, filming seven twenty-somethings lounging in folding chairs, sipping beers in a damnable, leisurely fashion. Although each of these pretty young things was very well-dressed and telegenic, no two were attractive in quite the same way. They were a living, breathing Benetton ad, a virtual color wheel of diversity ranging from white to yellow to black and several hard-to-place mélanges in between. It seemed statistically impossible that such a perfectly proportioned swath of multi-culture could meet and become friends. It was even more difficult to believe that they would be at an Eagles game, where the overwhelming demographic was comprised of white and trash. But there they were: drinking and laughing, happily ignorant to the mob of Eagles fans growing around them.

"What's all this?" Ronnie asked. "Some sort of beer commercial?"

"No way," Jeff said. "They'd never shoot one out here. The lighting is way too harsh."

"Then what is it?" Bobby asked.

"It's that freakin' tv show, *Real Life.* That's what it is!" a brawny man behind them grumbled. "Move it, you freakin' metrosexuals!" he yelled, showering spit and fouling the air with his yeasty breath.

101

"Metrosexuals!" some echoed, while others selected different expressions from the rich Philly vocabulary of abuse.

Despite the anger around them that was growing to a riot pitch, the *Real Life* cast continued to take their sweet time, luxuriating in the spotlight, sprawling casually in their lawn chairs.

"Oh, this is ridiculous," Ronnie said. "We got to get to the game."

"But what are we going to do?" Bobby asked, pressed by the surging masses behind him.

"If they aren't going to let us through, we're going to have to push our way through," Ronnie agitated.

Although the idea didn't appeal to Bobby, it carried currency with those around him, who growled with approval.

"Whose city is this anyway?" Ronnie cried. "Who do they think they are? This is our town. This is the freakin' Bird's nest!"

This rallying call was no exemplar of eloquence, but it had a receptive audience. The crowd roared with drunken enthusiasm. The more hooligan elements rushed forward against the security cordon. The brawny man at their side shoved down a security guard, breaking the line. Ronnie, Bobby, and Jeff charged through the breach, dashed across the television set and joined the line at the gate.

"That was great," Jeff exclaimed, enjoying the vigorous turn the evening had taken. "Way to start a riot."

"I do what I can," Ronnie said. He looked back. The security guards struggled with the mob, but the mob had the upper hand. The *Real Life* cast had already abandoned their chairs and retreated from the mayhem. "What a bunch of jerks!" he chortled.

Bobby and Jeff joined in the laughter. Their good time attracted unwanted attention however. A doughy Eagles fan finishing an Italian sausage eyed them suspiciously. He glanced from Ronnie's Longhorns hat to Jeff's blue and gray color ensemble. He sucked the last slices of pepper and meat from the hoagie roll and glared.

"Who are you calling a jerk?" he barked with his mouth full.

The three stopped laughing and regarded the offended fan. This was a delicate situation. With the right words, it could have been defused. But Ronnie was not known for his delicacy. He never backed down and, given the least provocation, he would rise to any unnecessary occasion.

Ronnie's eyes gleamed with devilish intent. "Shut up, Fatty McFatterson," he said.

The man flushed with stupefied anger. "Fatty McWhat? Who do you think you are?"

"Hey, my friend here is sorry," Bobby attempted to mediate. "He had a little too much to drink and..."

"Blow it out your ass, fat man! You look like a Sunday ham!" his friend interrupted, scuttling any hope of rapprochement.

The Eagles fan was incensed and grabbed at Ronnie with his flabby, sausage-stained hands. Although the man had six inches and at least fifty pounds on him, Ronnie knocked his hand away. "You want to go? You want some of this!" he cried, sticking out his jaw in a way that just invited a haymaker.

"No, I don't think anyone wants anything," Bobby stammered helplessly.

A venomous smile spread across the fat man's fat face. He said, "Well, giddy up, cow . . ." Before he could Ronnie clocked him in the nose.

The line around them exploded into a scrum of shoves and punches. But this anarchy only lasted a few seconds. Security, long accustomed to such incidents, rushed over and separated the warring parties with brutal efficiency.

When the dust settled, Bobby was sitting on the pavement, not at all sure how he ended up there. Jeff stood some distance away, gawking while Ronnie struggled to free himself from a security guard twice his size that presently had him in a headlock.

"Let me go!" he demanded, bucking and kicking. The security guard obliged his request and tossed him down on the pavement like a rag doll.

"What's all this brutalizing?" Ronnie protested. "This is how you treat ticket holders? We spent good money to see this game!"

"You're not going to see any game today," the apish guard barked back. "You're going to get the hell out of here."

"But we have tickets!" Ronnie exclaimed.

"Who cares? You're gone," the guard said.

"You can't eject us! We're not even in the stadium yet!" Ronnie replied, adopting a very losing argument.

"If you don't get out of here, we're calling the cops."

Bobby, trying his hand at peacemaking, rushed to the security guard.

"This is all a big misunderstanding," Bobby began, appealing to better natures. "We didn't want any trouble. That guy started it. We just wanted to see the game. We have tickets!"

The guard regarded Bobby impatiently. "You've got a ticket, huh?"

"Yeah, I've got a ticket. It's right here." Bobby withdrew it from his pocket, hoping that accommodation and goodwill would win the day.

Bobby, however, was wrong. The security guard reached out his long monkey arms and snatched the ticket from his hand, tearing it in half. "Now you don't. Scram!"

104

Bobby watched the shredded ticket float to the ground with disbelief. "You can't do that!" he said with disbelief.

"Call the *po-lice* then," the guard mocked. "I'll have you and your no-good Dallas friends see Philadelphia from a jail cell." All around them, Eagles fans who had watched the scene unfold with great delight, jeered and hooted. But Bobby was crestfallen and deaf to their heckling. He stared at what had been his ticket, torn and already soiled on the pavement.

Ronnie, undiminished by his ejection, launched a stream of provocative epithets back at the crowd. But Bobby had no words for them. He looked into their faces and winced as if he'd looked into the sun. Beyond them he noticed the cast and crew of *Real Life*. They had escaped the mob and were now being ushered through a VIP gate into the stadium. Bobby let out a little whimper.

"What a bunch of gomers," Ronnie said as they walked back to the car.

"You didn't help matters," Bobby sulked.

"Whatever. I only said the truth. I call it like I see it. They can all go and choke on a hoagie."

"That's really helpful." Bobby said. "But what are we going to do now?"

"I thought we were going to watch some football," Jeff chimed in. "There has to be somewhere around here to watch the game."

"There most definitely is," Ronnie said, eager to prolong his campaign of mischief. "I know a place. Lots of beer. Big tvs. It's right up the road."

"Then what are we waiting for?" Jeff asked, drunk and happy to carry on the party.

Only Bobby seemed disheartened by not getting into the stadium. While Jeff and Ronnie hurried back to the car, he hesitated and looked back at the stadium. A great cheer roared and travelled across the parking lot like rolling thunder.

Ronnie directed Bobby to a sprawling sports bar down the road. The lot brimmed with cars. They took several loops around the lot with the Taurus screeching at every turn. But there were no spaces. Bobby was eventually forced to pull into the narrow gap between the dumpster and the fence at the back of the lot. With Ronnie leading the way, Jeff in the middle, and Bobby bringing up the rear, they approached the bar. As Ronnie reached for the door, it opened of its own accord. A large bouncer with a cropped military haircut emerged.

"We're full," said the humorless goon. "You can't come in."

"You've got to be kidding me," Ronnie guffawed, a sentiment echoed by Bobby and Jeff.

"Take it up with the fire marshal," the bouncer said. "Nowhere to sit. Nowhere to stand. We're out of glasses too. We couldn't serve you a drink even if we wanted to."

"That's okay. I can drink out of a bottle," Ronnie volunteered.

"What if we wait until someone leaves?" Bobby proposed more helpfully.

"Sure. When someone leaves after the fourth quarter, you can go right in."

"Come on," Jeff said. "There are only three of us."

"Which is three too many." He took a closer look at Jeff's coat and frowned. "Besides, I wouldn't let you in wearing that anyway. For your own sake. They'd eat you alive, cowboy. We'd still be scraping you off the floor next Sunday." Without another word, the bouncer closed the door to the packed bar.

"What do we do now?" Jeff asked as they walked back to the car. "Try a different bar?"

106

Bobby consulted his watch. It must be the second quarter. But he didn't care anymore. "Let's just go home," he said.

"Nonsense," Ronnie said. "Toss me the keys, Eeyore. I have an idea," he announced with an impish grin.

Trekking into the urban scrub brush of South Philly, Ronnie turned onto Passayunk, navigating past a schizophrenic mix of industry. There were fish markets still soiled from the blood, guts, and chum of the morning catch. Windowless warehouses with inscrutable Chinese signs. Latino businesses offering tax services and quinceañera assistance. Liquor stores were reinforced like fortresses for a zombie holocaust. On an isolated piece of filthy real estate sat a solitary crab shack. Bobby stared at the decrepit bungalow as they passed, wondering who could possibly hate themselves enough to eat a Philadelphia crab cake.

The car turned down a desolate alley and stopped.

"There it is,' Ronnie said, indicating a brick building down the street.

"There is what?" Bobby asked.

"Where we're going to watch the game."

"That's a bar?"

"Something like that," Ronnie said cryptically and parked the car. "Come on. I don't want to miss the half-time show."

Bobby and Jeff followed Ronnie to the entrance. Ronnie pounded on the metal door three times. A scraping sound, like the gears of a great rusted dynamo, came from inside. A moment later the door creaked open, flooding the stoop with a dingy, red light. They stepped inside. Bobby's jaw dropped with the weight of his misgivings.

"What is this?" he muttered.

"The best damn half-time show you've ever been to," Ronnie said and slapped him on the back.

"But this…this… is a strip club?"

Strip club was too kind a name for it. Ronnie, Bobby, and Jeff were in a bonified titty bar – the skankiest nudie bar in Philadelphia County. On a stage at the far end of the room, a melon-boobed woman in a thong danced apathetically to a Whitesnake song that had been popular before her first abortion. On the bar along the wall, a second woman with long, weeping bangs and translucent heels was trying with limited success to grab her ankles. There were maybe a dozen patrons in the place and they showed only a little more enthusiasm than the dancers themselves. As the rock ballad blared, a weary old reprobate hobbled up to the stage and deposited a dollar into the dancer's thong with all the fervor of one feeding a parking meter.

"So what if it's a strip club?" Ronnie asked. "There are plenty of seats. No one cares that Jeff is dressed like Yosemite Sam. And most importantly," he said, pointing through the legs of the inverted stripper to a television on the wall, "it has the game. This place has everything!"

"I needed a drink anyway," Jeff shrugged and took a seat at the bar.

"I like your priorities!" Ronnie encouraged and turned to Bobby. "You could learn something from Jeff. I like him. He has a winner's attitude."

"Tonight was a disaster," Bobby said. "Take that for a winner's attitude."

Ronnie shook his head with exaggerated disapproval. Taking Bobby by the shoulder, he guided him to a stool next to Jeff and ordered more beers.

"So tell me, do you like what you see?" Ronnie asked Jeff suggestively.

"You mean, uh, these, *dancers*?" Jeff tried, and failed, to find the right word to describe the specimen on the bar thrusting her genitals at his face.

"Yeah, what do you think of the ladies?" Ronnie prodded.

Jeff glanced at the sagging spectacle of past prime flesh and cringed. Although everyone was someone's type, a woman stitched with c-section scars and speckled with sun splotches would not zazzle anyone who hadn't spent their adult life in solitary confinement.

Bobby frowned at the conversation, but was beyond caring about Ronnie's exploration of the undercarriage of Jeff's sexuality. He sipped his beer and watched the television. Half-time was over and the third quarter was about to begin. The Eagles had a comfortable two touchdown lead over the Cowboys. Taking consolation in this fact, he lifted his bottle and watched as the screen cut from the announcers to pan across the stadium and show notables attendees. A former Eagles coach visiting the sideline. A mayor in his usual seat. A movie star sitting in a cozy club box.

Then the screen flashed on an attractive and ethnically-ambiguous young man that Bobby recognized. The camera pulled out, revealing seven young people, equally attractive and representing a clinically-proportioned diversity. They wore crisp new Eagles paraphernalia and made quite a scene of having a good time, playing it up for the camera. Bobby's stomach churned, which only had a little do with the stripper who had thrust her rear directly into his line of sight.

109

Chapter Ten: Bobby's Winter of Discontent

Despite a commanding lead going into the second half, the Eagles did not win the game. After making two touchdowns in the final minutes of the fourth quarter, the Cowboys rustled up a last second field goal out of a Philadelphia fumble. It was a heartbreaking loss for the fans and, in usual Philly fashion, this defeat created a momentum of failure that toppled their team's playoff aspirations like a row of mislaid dominos. During the rest of the season, the Eagles dropped, steadily and irredeemably, through the floor of their division and sank to the bottom of the league. It was a painful ending for the fans who had spent the coldest days of December at the stadium, waiting in vain for a win.

Luckily, Bobby was spared that particular torment. After his expulsion from the game, he remained in dedicated ignorance about all things football. When the holidays came and the playoffs commenced, Bobby was as oblivious to the Eagles' fate as he was to the ingredients of fruitcake, the origins of the Christmas tree and, as the final days on the calendar ticked by, what "Auld Lang Syne" means.

Football wasn't the only thing that disappeared from Bobby's life. He hadn't seen Jeff since the game either. Although his neighbor never complained about how the night turned out, he did not stop by for visits afterwards. Bobby couldn't blame him. He would have held a grudge too if he'd been offered a feast of football and given a potluck of pillow tits and caesarian stitches instead. In such circumstances, ill-will was the right and proper thing.

Through autumn and into the winter, Bobby watched from afar as St. Stephen's underwent a full-scale renovation. Each morning a general contractor barked orders to the assembled workers. Every day laborers carried out refuse and debris, hauling the old oak pews one day and shards of drywall the next, loading them into the dumpsters on the sidewalk. Every day craftsmen lugged in lumber, pipes, and power tools, working into the night and illuminating the dull stained-glass windows with their droplights. But through these weeks Bobby never saw Jeff, who had vanished from Fishtown as suddenly as he came.

Bobby pressed his face to the window in his parlor and gazed onto the street one frosty evening just before New Year's. He could feel the cold from the glass leach across his forehead as he watched St. Stephen's. The workers had constructed scaffolding over the face of the church, covering it with plastic sheets that billowed in the bitter winter wind like the sails of a ghost ship.

Suzie sat at the kitchen table in the back of the house, sipping coffee and reading the *City Paper*. She had taken a break from her sewing and bits of a stuffed octopus – purple corduroy tentacles, button suckers, and bright rhinestone eyes – were scattered across the table. Amidst these scraps of crafty calamari sat a box of Whitman's Samplers. Suzie removed a mocha-flavored chocolate shell out of the clutter of wrappers and looked down the hall to where Bobby stood by the bay window. Hidden, with only his feet visible below the skirt of the drapes, he was like some low-rent Polonious. She placed the candy in her mouth and chewed with concern.

"Bobby," she said.

His feet did not move.

Suzie coughed to clear the chocolate film coating her throat. In a tone meant to sound off-handed, she piped, "They're re-opening the Fishtown Pavilion!"

The drapes rustled. "What's that?" Bobby said.

"It says in the *City Paper* that they're re-opening that old movie theater you always talk about. The Fishtown Pavilion."

"The Fishtown Pavilion?" he replied. His bald round head emerged from the curtains.

111

Suzie nodded.

Bobby emerged from the drapes and marched to the kitchen. "I used to see movies in the Pavilion!"

"I know," Suzie said. "You talk about it. A lot."

"That old place has been closed for years. I can't believe they're going to start showing movies again. I wonder what will be on the bill?" His eyes twinkled with possibility.

"Well, it's not going to be showing movies. Not exactly," Suzie said.

"But it's a *movie* theater. Of course it will show movies. That's what it does."

"That's not what it does anymore. It's re-opening as an Urban Apparel."

"What's an Urban Apparel?" Bobby asked.

"It's a clothing company. The sell t-shirts and stuff. They're converting the Pavilion into a new store." She consulted the newspaper, moving her lips as she scanned the page. "It says it right here. It will be the flagship store for the whole Philadelphia region. Right here in Fishtown. That pretty cool!"

Bobby's face crinkled with disappointment. "No. That's not cool at all. The Pavilion was great. I saw every Indiana Jones movie in that theater. Every one! They can't turn it into some sort of Gap."

"Who said anything about a Gap? This is an Urban Apparel. They're from Los Angeles," she cooed at the associated glamour.

"*Bah!*" he cried, channeling the rage of a disconsolate sheep.

"Give it a rest, Bobby. You bah-humbugging isn't going to change a thing."

"Maybe not. But that doesn't mean I can't try. I repeat: *bah!*"

"Suit yourself. Be a grinch. But I'm not going to let you ruin my holiday cheer." Suzie lifted up the *City Paper*, creating a paper shield against her boyfriend's petulance.

Bobby stood in the kitchen for a moment, at a loss. He looked around distractedly, overcome with a sense of purposelessness. For want of something to do, he recalled the bay window. He inched across the linoleum towards the living room, compulsively, like a drunk reaching for a bottle.

"Don't you have something better to do than stare out that window?" Suzie asked from behind the broadsheet.

Bobby considered. "Honestly? No," he replied.

"Well, if you're not tired of spying on the street, you might be interested in this."

"Interested in what?"

"The neighbor is Jeff Kaye, right?"

"Yeah. Why?"

"He's a photographer."

"I knew that."

"Well, apparently he's some kind of big shot. There is an article about him."

"Let me see that." Bobby took the newspaper. On the open page there was an article entitled, "Resurrecting Real Estate," which featured a picture of Jeff standing in front of St. Stephen's, his arms crossed in a proprietorial pose. The article began:

> For more than two decades, St. Stephen's in Fishtown has been in a kind of limbo. (Bobby groaned at the secular appropriation of theological doctrine.) Closed in the early 1980's because of budget shortfalls, the arch-diocese retired the old stone church and combined its congregation with a neighboring parish in

Kensington. Since that time St. Stephen's has kept a lonely watch over a crumbling stretch of Belgrade Avenue, adding to the list of churches all over the city, representing every major sect and denomination, that has been closed in the last quarter of the century.

With persistently declining attendance, the Philadelphia's Catholic authorities had little prospect of reopening the church. With its size and remote location, they could not find a buyer. Nor could they simply tear it down. More than a century old, it was a historic building protected against demolition. As such, the property remained on the Vatican's books – vacant and crumbling. Unwanted and unsellable, church authorities could only pray for a miracle to get St. Stephens off their hands.

And a miracle came from an unlikely source.

This year the church found an unlikely savior in a commercial photographer from New York City named Jeff Kaye, one of the many New Yorkers migrating to Philadelphia for its affordable real estate. But unsatisfied with the usual offering of town homes and condominiums, he tried something different.

"When I saw St. Stephen's," Kaye explains, "it was like a flash of light. Like a message from God. It was, like – BAM! – this is the place! It's a beautiful building, filled with history.

And I even like Fishtown," Kaye is quick to add. "It's a little rough around the edges, but it has lots of character. A lot of potential. It's

114

up and coming. I wanted to be here on the ground floor. At the beginning."

Bobby could read no more. He turned to the second page of the article. There was another picture of the church, some copy about the real estate market. But Bobby was drawn to several images of Jeff, apparently taken during his photo shoots. One picture showed him in a blistering desert lying flat on the sand, angling an enormous camera at a bottle of vodka, which was sweating like a Russian tourist on holiday in Thailand. In a second photo Jeff directed impossibly long-limbed models, scantily clad in what, given their pointy nipples, must have been a very chilly studio. The third and final picture found Jeff on a spit of desolate mountaintop, crouched against the gray sky, forming a frame with his fingers in a myth-making pose of artistic endeavor. Before him, teetering on the edge of a precipice was a shiny BMW. Bobby stared at the image for a long time, wondering how they got the car up there.

"So that's the neighbor?" Suzie asked. She had gotten to her feet and peered over his shoulder at the paper.

Bobby nodded.

"It looks like he has a pretty cool job."

"I guess. If you're into that globe-trotting sort of thing."

"I think he's cute. He looks exciting."

Bobby crumpled the paper into a jagged ball of print and threw it at the garbage can. It waffled through the air and landed short, skittering across the linoleum floor.

"What did you do that for?" Suzie complained. "I was reading that!"

"It's a stupid paper. Hackery. Yellow journalism at its most jaundiced."

Suzie pouted at Bobby. Then her lips composed into a knowing smirk. "Oh, no. You're jealous!"

"I'm not jealous," Bobby scoffed. "What would I be jealous of?"

Suzie eyed him accusingly.

"What if I am jealous?" he said, fidgeting under her stare. "Can't a guy be jealous? It's a perfectly natural human emotion."

Suzie shook her head and began to fiddle with her corduroy octopus on the table. "I'm not going to argue with you," she said. "Do you know what is funny about all this? If this photographer showed up at your door and asked you to another football game, you'd forget all of your complaining and jump at the chance."

"No way."

"Oh, really?"

"Yeah. And what if I did? What's your point?"

"My point, oh man of mine, is only that you're not doing yourself any favors by being negative about things you can't control. He took you to a football game. That was nice of him. I don't know why you would resent him for having an article written about him. I'm sure he has his own problems, too."

"Judging by those pictures, I'd love to have some of his problems," Bobby said.

"Jealousy is not attractive," she sighed and manipulated a purple tentacle. "I'm going to ignore you now. You can talk to me when you've worked all of this out of your system. You're projecting very hostile vibes right now. I can't concentrate with all of this emotional violence."

Bobby pursed his lips and arched his substantial brow as he considered an appropriate response. His retort was thwarted by a knock at the door. "Who could that be?" he said.

"If it's Ronnie, he can't come in," Suzie said, her fingers picking blindly through the chocolate box as she worked. "I didn't like how he played with my dolls last time he was here. It was just indecent."

Bobby walked into the parlor, grumbling softly under his breath. He opened the door. To his surprise, he was face to face with Jeff Kaye.

"Afternoon, Bobby," Jeff greeted with characteristic chipperness. "Mind if I come in?"

Bobby nodded, stunned by his neighbor's abrupt reappearance into his life.

Jeff entered the house and ran his eyes over the living room. "Nice place. So you like dolls?" he asked, nodding towards a menagerie of stuffed animals strewn across the couch.

"Those are my girlfriend's," Bobby said. "It's her thing."

"Ahhh…" was Jeff's reply. He walked to the couch and picked up a pug-nosed lion with a mane of ruby sequins.

"I haven't seen you in a while," Bobby began tentatively.

"I've been really busy," Jeff said, preoccupied with articulating the lion's canvas paw. "I was on a shoot for Toyota in Las Vegas."

"All month?"

"Before that I was doing a thing for Red Lobster in a fishing village in Nova Scotia," he informed casually.

"How'd that go?"

"Cold. Wet. Canadian." Jeff tossed the lion back on the pile. He inspected the rest of the house.

Bobby had a rush of anxiety at having his living space surveyed by a man with such a discriminating photographer's eye.

"So how is it going over there at the church?" Bobby asked and stepped into Jeff's line of sight. "I've seen a lot of trucks out there."

117

"I had the contractor go all out while I was gone," he said, his attention successfully diverted. "I wanted to get the heavy lifting done while I was away. They had to gut the place. Rewire. Do plumbing. Put in new drywall. Today they were refinishing the floors. It has a long way to go, but it's at least livable." He shook his head in wonder. "It's really amazing how much a place can change in a month."

"I can't imagine." Bobby tried to visualize the renovated church. "I'd love to see it," he said almost to himself.

Jeff clapped his hands together and smiled like a champion. "Well, you're in luck then. I'm planning on having a party on New Year's Eve. You should come. It will be chill. A few of my friends will be coming down from the city."

"What city would that be?" Bobby asked uncertainly.

Jeff laughed as though Bobby had made a great joke. "*New York City*," he said. "Listen, I've got to run. Sorry I couldn't stay longer. But feel free to stop by."

"Thanks. I'll think it over."

"Great. Maybe I'll see you then." He started to leave, but stopped. "I almost forgot why I came over here. I have a power washer if you need it."

"Why would I need a power washer?"

"Haven't you seen it?"

"Seen what?"

Jeff winced sympathetically. "I hate to be the one to tell you this," he said. "But you should probably come outside."

Bobby followed Jeff to the sidewalk. He shivered as a cold wind rustled up the empty street. "What's this all about?" he asked, wiping a winter tear from his eye.

Jeff pointed at the house. Bobby looked back at his home. Smeared across the face of his row home was "69 Squad," scrawled in thick red streaks from a spray paint can.

Chapter Eleven: Suzie Can't Find a Thing to Wear

"You need to let it go," Suzie said as she flicked through a pile of electric blue hoodies. "You're getting all splotchy."

"How can I let it go?" Bobby huffed. "They graffitied my house. They intruded on my castle. They desecrated my domain."

"Don't be so dramatic. The paint washed off."

"That's supposed to make it okay? Suzie, there are some things that paint can't wash away."

"They're just kids, Bobby."

"Kids?" he protested and followed her as she perused a rack of cotton dresses. "They're vandals! They're hoodlums! They're a pack of little huns roaming the streets!" Across the store a female sales associate in a tight fuscia dress and blue neon leggings glanced irritably in their direction.

"Will you keep your voice down? You're making a scene," Suzie said.

"It riles me up. Those little criminals shouldn't be able to get away with writing all over someone's house."

"But they did. And you need to get over it. Now tell me, do you like this dress in raspberry or lime?"

"It depends. Do you plan to wear it or make a sorbet out of it?"

"Be serious. Which one looks more 'New-Yearsie'?" Suzie held each dress in front of her in turn and assumed the uncertain smile of a QVC model.

Bobby looked at both dresses impatiently. "I don't know. The green?"

"Really?" Suzie crinkled her nose as though sniffing sour milk. "I prefer raspberry."

120

Bobby and Suzie had been at the Urban Apparel store for an hour. Bobby had followed Suzie from tank tops to sweat shirts and skirts and blouses, all of which adhered to a flagrantly boring design principle that exhausted the aesthetic possibilities of monochromatics. It was the day before the New Year's Eve party. Except for two sales associates behind the register, they had the run of the place. This was a good thing. Bobby was in an indignant spirit. With Suzie refusing to further discuss the crimes against his property, he projected his animus outwards.

"This used to be the Fishtown Pavilion," Bobby said. "I used to watch movies here. Double features on Sundays." He thrust his finger at a squad of baby mannequins mounted on the wall, getting physical in pink, lemon, and powder blue onesies. "That used to be the concession stand. You could buy a soda and large popcorn for three bucks."

"Do you have any idea how old you sound? I mean really old. Like grumpy old man old? You've got to lighten up."

"I can't lighten up. I'm in a mood. The world is trying to suffocate me. I mean, seriously, what is with that crap?" He gestured to a display with t-shirts that respectively featured a monkey in a space helmet, a velociraptor doing math, and the African continent with two fingers jutting out of Algeria, making a peace sign.

"Who would pay – jeez! – $30 for one of these? I could design a better shirt with a cookie cutter and a magic marker."

"Then maybe you should," Suzie said, tugging at the stitching on a knit top. "At least it would give you something to do."

Bobby frowned mightily and returned his critical eye to the store. He noticed the two sales girls by the register. Their neon wayfarer sunglasses projected hostility. The volume of the poppy punk playing in the store suddenly shot to a piercing treble pitch.

"I don't think they like us," Bobby said over the music.

121

"Who's that?" Suzie shouted back, showing no sign that she'd noticed the change in volume.

"The girls at the counter. I don't think they like us."

"They like me fine. It's you they don't like. Frankly, I can't blame them," Suzie said, inspecting a pair of tights that she could never hope to fit into despite the miracles of spandex.

Bobby left Suzie to her stockings and drifted to the back of the store. To his right was where the concession stand once stood. The back wall of the store was where the entrances to the two theaters used to be. But the theater doors were gone. In their place was a lingerie display and a blow-up of a girl in her underwear, perilously close to adolescence, with childlike eyes and a puckered rear upraised towards the camera to better model her panties.

Bobby stared at the wall, looking for some sign of the theater. For some seam or fixture that was overlooked during the renovation. But while his inspection was entirely innocent, his attention, fixated in the direction of the bras and bottoms, suggested an unseemly preoccupation.

"Can I help you?" a girl's voice asked behind him.

"How's that?" Bobby mumbled, his face just inches from a thong.

"Do you need any assistance, sir?" the voice asked snootily.

Bobby turned. A thick-set girl clad in mannish flannel glowered at him. She carried a broom in her hands like she was toting a battle axe. "Do you need help?" she asked again. "Something for your wife, maybe?"

"My wife?" Bobby replied vaguely. "No, my, umm, girlfriend is right over. . ." He pointed to where Suzie had been, but no longer was.

The burly girl narrowed her eyes menacingly. She gripped the broom more tightly. "Just to let you know, the men's section is at the *front* of the store."

122

"The men's section…" he repeated. He did not understand her meaning. He glanced back at the wall and noticed for the first time the print of the girl's ass framed by bras. Finally understanding the shop girl's accusing eyes, Bobby flustered, "Oh, wow. No. You've got the wrong idea. I'm not looking at this stuff." He fingered a lace bra on the rack. "I'm looking for the theater doors."

"The theater doors? This isn't some kind of peep show, pal."

"No. This store used to be a movie theater. The snack bar used to be right there. And the doors were back on this wall. I was just looking for the doors."

Bobby grinned sheepishly. The shop girl did not return his smile.

"I don't know anything about any movie theater. I just came here to tell you the men's section is at the front of the store. If you need anything, I'll be at the register. By the *men's* section." She pointed to the men's section with the broom, leaving no confusion about where Bobby should be.

After the sales associate had returned to the register, Suzie emerged from the dressing room wearing a red cotton wrap dress and a light hooded scarf. "What do you think?" she asked.

"Isn't December kind of cold for that sort of thing?" Bobby noted her large, white thighs exposed below the dress.

"I'm not buying it for an arctic expedition. We're just walking around the corner. Besides, that's why I have the scarf. How does it look?"

Bobby thought the ensemble made her look like a Russian peasant freshly impressed into prostitution. "You know I don't know anything about clothes," he said.

"But do you like it?"

"If you like it, I like it," he offered diplomatically.

123

Suzie puffed out her butt and grimaced into the mirror. "I don't think it fits right." She indicated to where the stressed fabric strained to accommodate her womanly curves. "I think it's a bad design. Poor stitching too. You can already see where it's tearing at the hip."

"Definitely shoddy workmanship," Bobby agreed.

With her legs banded by the skirt, Suzie scissor-stepped to the dressing room.

Bobby looked back at where the theater doors used to be. A spring of nostalgia welled up inside of him. He remembered the movies that he had watched in the old theatre. Low-budget slasher films. Spaghetti westerns. Action movies. Washed out noir with their dark nights, haunted figures, and empty streets. These movies were part of his childhood. He remembered them as he saw them for the first time in the dirty seats at the back of the Fishtown Pavilion. If he closed his eyes, he could imagine the mangy lobby carpet beneath his feet and the hypnotic drone of the popcorn machine.

Transported into the past, away from the aisles of bright spandex and teenage sex, Bobby breathed deeply. But instead of the sweet flavor of stale popcorn and raisinettes, he tasted something caustic. Something bitter and metallic burned his throat. He began to retch. As he gasped he saw the burly sales girl in the flannel, under the pretense of housekeeping, dousing him with Lysol.

Unable to find anything to accommodate her generous figure, Suzie left Urban Apparel without a single bag. By New Year's Eve she had still not decided what to wear to the party and exiled herself to the bedroom, trying on various combinations from her existing wardrobe with little satisfaction. Bobby insisted that whatever she wore would be nice and that the party was no big deal. But Suzie objected on the grounds that they "never went out" and she wanted "to make the most of it." Especially since it was New Year's Eve, which, she pointed out, "only comes once a year."

124

While Suzie rifled through the bedroom, Bobby waited in the living room by the bay window. Unfestively dressed in a sweatshirt and jeans, his head hidden behind the curtain, he kept watch over St. Stephen's, the interior of which was lit up for the occasion. Upstairs the sounds of sliding hangers, slamming doors, and stomping continued.

When Suzie finally descended the stairs, Bobby peaked out from behind the curtain. He was astounded. After months of relationship drift he had forgotten how nicely she cleaned up. Her hair was washed and curled. Her body was draped in black, exclusively in black, from her ebony shoes and charcoal leggings to a forgotten velvet dress that performed a minor miracle of slimming her waist while enhancing her breasts. Manly need twitched across his face. She smiled from behind a mask of freshly shellacked foundation.

Drawn to her, like a moon to its super Earth, he walked towards her and pressed himself against Suzie's matronly form, giving her a little squeeze.

"Stop it," she giggled. "You'll wrinkle my dress!"

"Then let's get it off of you," he whispered, nuzzling against her bosom.

"Oh, you!" she trilled and pushed him away. "There is plenty of time for that."

"Why wait?" he asked with the restraint of an over-sexed adolescent. "Come on, Snooze. Can't we fit in a snuggle before the ball drops?"

Suzie pushed him away and pouted playfully. "You romantic. Always saying just what a girl wants to hear."

"What do you mean?" he asked, oblivious to his coarseness. "You look beautiful!"

"Too little, too late, buster," she said. "I want to go to the party."

"But what's the rush?"

"I didn't spend all night getting dressed just to get undressed in the living room. Now let's go before I get a run in these leggings."

Despite its thick granite walls, Bobby heard a hum from inside St. Stephen's as soon as he stepped out of his door. The party sounded like a barely contained roar. Bobby stopped in the street, hesitant to approach further. He looked up at the church. His gaze fell and lingered on the broad stone step before its entrance. If it wasn't for Suzie, who was shivering without a coat, who knows how long he would have stood there, braced against the cold wind whipping up the street.

Bobby followed Suzie to the church. He opened the door, crossed the threshold, and was promptly greeted by a flash of light. Bobby stumbled blindly inside and certain parallels to Paul and Damascian roads sprang from the more Catholic recesses of his mind.

As he rubbed his eyes, a silhouette with an enormous camera exclaimed "Happy New Year!"

Chapter Twelve: Auld Lang Syne, Bobby

"I thought you said you were only having a few friends over," Bobby said, still blinking from the flash.

"You know how these things go." Jeff shrugged helplessly. "You invite one person and they tell a friend. Then their friend tells two friends. Then two friends tell their brothers. It's all exponential growth."

"Like a virus?" Bobby said.

"That's not the example I would choose. But, sure, why not? Like a virus."

"This is an amazing place," Suzie declared, overwhelmed by the exuberance of the party and the square footage of the venue.

"I'm glad you like it," Jeff said hospitably.

"Oh, I do. It's beautiful," Suzie said. "And so big. And, oh, what is that? A pipe organ?"

"Why, yes, actually. It is original. You know…" Jeff began, but did not complete his sentence. Behind them the door opened again. Another wave of guests were borne in on a gust of cold air. Like a tipsy gunslinger, Jeff made a quick-draw with his camera, blasting the new arrivals with his flash and offering a slurred greeting. Bobby only then realized that their host was already tipsy. With a broad grin stretching across both hemispheres of his face, Jeff turned back to Bobby and Suzie.

"I'm very sorry, but you must excuse me. I have things to take care of. Make yourselves comfortable. There are drinks over there," he indicated with a vague gesture towards the rear of the church. "I'm so glad you came!" he said, before returning his flitting attention to the new arrivals.

The sanctuary was mobbed with revelers celebrating the New Year like a pack of well-heeled heathens. Bobby followed in Suzie's wide wake as she moved towards the alcohol. He rubbernecked like a tourist, gawking at the church's transformation. In just over a month, St. Stephen's had changed almost beyond recognition. The basic dimensions were the same. But the symbols of religiosity – the pews, altars, tapestries, and candelabra – were gone. The stone walls were sheathed with new drywall that brightly reflected the colorful party lighting. As Bobby looked around, he could only recognize the old church in the unmodified rafters and the old pipe organ at the back of the chancel, rising over the sanctuary like a fountainhead of brass.

Beset by a sudden vertigo as he followed the pipes to the ceiling, Bobby let Suzie take him by the hand and drag him to the bar. As Suzie plodded forward, she jiggled to the music that echoed through the church. They made a wide sweep on the outskirts of the sanctuary. At what used to be the altar, they found two long tables provisioned with a rainbow of liquor and a kiddie pool filled with bottles of beer. Bobby forewent the beer and poured gin into a cup. Suzie fell upon the rum and coke with a vengeance. With drinks in hand, they gazed upon the crowd.

"This is a great party!" Suzie proclaimed.

"Why is it so great?" Bobby asked.

"Everyone is dancing. Having a good time."

"How do you know that everyone is having a good time? It looks like a riot. It is very possible that someone is being stomped to death on the dance floor at this very moment."

"Don't be such a downer," Suzie censured happily, her wobbly parts gyrating to the beat. "This is fun!"

"I don't see what's so fun about it."

"It's a party!" she cried as though the declaration were sufficient explanation in itself.

"I never know what to do with myself at a party."

"It's simple. You drink. You dance. You do whatever you want."

"What if I want to go home?"

"Oh, just drink, baby. I promise if you drink the joy will come."

Bobby did as he was told and drank his gin. He finished his cup. Unfortunately, the joy did not come. All he experienced was a burning in his throat and the off-putting realization that he was drinking on the spot where he had taken his first communion.

As Bobby mulled these things, Suzie danced. Already merry from her cocktail, she soft-shoed around Bobby, playfully striking him with her breasts. "How about a kiss, lover?" she whispered huskily into his ear.

"But it's not midnight yet," Bobby said.

"Do we have to wait for a ball to drop? You realize that we can kiss more than once a year?"

"I suppose."

"Then pucker up."

In what used to be St. Stephen's, in the place where the altar once stood, Suzie grabbed Bobby by the shoulders and bore down upon him with unsolicited intimacy. He winced and closed his eyes, awaiting the kiss. But the kiss never came. A girl with transparent glasses and a newsboy cap, who had been dancing on the edge of the crowd like a coked-up dervish, performed a pirouette into Suzie. Her rum drenched his sweatshirt.

"I'm all wet!" Bobby cried.

"Ooh, baby," Suzie cooed as she transformed from a lover into a nurturing mother. "Your shirt is all wet. Are you okay?"

"I'm sticky and cold and smell like a sailor."

"You should go to the bathroom and dry off. You'll get sick if you run around like that."

Bobby pouted and held his shirt away from his body with his forefingers as though it were a dirty diaper. "You'll be okay by yourself?"

Suzie smiled a crooked smile. "Don't worry about me. I'm a big girl. I can take care of myself," she said. She took the rum bottle from the table and poured another cocktail with a heavy hand.

Bobby pushed towards the chapel in the east wing where the bathrooms used to be. He hoped that, despite the cosmetic changes to the interior, Jeff had not gone so far as to rejigger the plumbing. As he trudged across the dance floor, he noticed a crowd congregating around a side altar that had once held a statue of a lesser saint whose only noteworthy achievement was a particularly gruesome martyrdom. In the place of the saint's contorted and gory likeness was a Christmas tree. Bathed in bright professional lighting, the tree was thronged by a circle of revelers who took turns posing with an enormous stuffed polar bear in a bathing suit. Within the circle Jeff pranced with his camera, posing his subjects and snapping pictures in a parody of a fashion shoot.

Pressing on, Bobby arrived at the bathroom, which was exactly where he remembered it. What was new to him, however, was the long line of drunkards eager to use the facilities. Bobby took his place at the back of the line. Unfortunately, he did not have to wait alone.

While Bobby did his best to keep his wet shirt from touching his skin, a man stepped beside him. His gleaming eyes met Bobby's. He bared his unnaturally bright teeth in a smile and set upon Bobby with an aggressive, almost sociopathic, affability. "Hello. I can smell the alcohol from here. Getting the New Year started on the right foot, I see?"

"It's a real barn burner."

"Have you been here long?"

"Long enough to have a stranger spill a drink on me. Which is long enough in my opinion."

"Oh, don't let a little spill get you down," the man said, apparently getting a kick out of Bobby's discomfort. "It's New Year's Eve. It only comes once a year."

"So they say," Bobby said and shuffled forward in line.

The man shuffled right beside him.

"So how do you know, Jeff?"

"I'm his neighbor."

"You're from the neighborhood?"

Bobby nodded.

"So you saw what he did this place start to finish? He's done one hell of a job, right?"

Bobby shrugged. "There have been trucks out here all month. It must be costing him a fortune."

"Between you and me, it is. But you can't argue with the finished product." The man surveyed the high ceilings and ground his teeth ravenously. "Damn. This is a fine investment property."

"How is buying a church a smart investment?" Bobby asked. "Isn't the square footage a little excessive?"

"Well, for one thing, Jeff is walling off that wing over there and converting it into rental properties. He should be able to pay his mortgage just from those tenants."

"And how do you know that?"

"Because I helped draw up the plan. My name is Paul. I'm Jeff's realtor."

"You're a realtor?"

"Yup. I've been doing deals all over Fishtown. The market is really hot. I just sold two neighboring row homes on Gaul to a couple from New Jersey. They're converting them into a his-and-hers duplex."

131

"You don't say," Bobby muttered, losing patience with the turn the conversation had taken. A man and woman fondling each other at the front of the line slipped into the bathroom together, giggling as the door closed. The line groaned collectively.

"I'm doing a lot of deals in your neighborhood," Paul continued. "You know, if you're Jeff's neighbor, the properties on this block are going to get a lot more valuable once this church is finished. If you are ever in the market to sell, you should give me a call."

Before Bobby could express his utter disinterest in selling his house, the realtor had removed his card from his wallet and pressed it into Bobby's hand. Bobby looked at the card with a mix of surprise and disgust, as though the realtor had pressed a small piece of poo into his palm.

Wishing to avoid another sales pitch, Bobby fled the bathroom line. He crumpled the card and threw it to the floor. With his shirt still sticky with alcohol, he tried to get back to Suzie. But this was no easy feat. Moving across the dance floor was like swimming against the current. The party had become oppressively crowded. The air was hot and sour with alcohol, sweat, and sex. Bodies beat against Bobby from every side. But when he reached the alcohol table, she was gone. Gasping and dizzy, he looked across the heads on the dance floor that bobbed like buoys on a carnal sea. At last he saw Suzie. She was in the midst of the crowd, lapping at her drink and chatting while a man with a neck tattoo stared earnestly at her chest.

Bobby pushed through the dancers and grabbed her by the shoulder. Suzie spun around, sloshed her drink and roared, "Bobby! Where have you been?"

"I see that you've made a friend," he said, gesturing accusingly at the stranger with the word "Freegan" scrawled across his jugular.

132

"Friend? Who?" Him? Oh, yes. *Him*. This is Ben, Bobby. Ben loves animals. Ben, this is my boyfriend, Bobby."

Bobby narrowed his eyes at the would-be paramour. Ben glared back, surveying Bobby from the top of his wide forehead to the toes of his beat-up Nikes. Reaching a low estimation of the competition, he smiled smugly.

"So you're an animal lover?" Bobby asked disdainfully. "What does that mean?"

"I'm in animal services," Ben replied and took a long drink from a forty of Steel Reserve. "I walk dogs. Professionally."

"You walk dogs professionally? Did you have to go to school for that?"

"Laugh if you want," Ben said. "I have clients. I walk the dogs of some of the most famous people in the city. You know Dawn Stensland? I totally walk her dog."

"That is *sooo* neat!" Suzie slurred, dousing her face with vodka as she drank.

"It's not that neat," Bobby disagreed.

"Whatever, Cochise. I work outside. Make my own hours. Get exercise. It's awesome. What do you do that's so great?"

The question broadsided Bobby. He hated having to justify himself to a man that made his living by picking up the poop from other peoples' pets. Luckily, Suzie, in her boozy enthusiasm, responded. "Bobby is a writer!" she declared.

Bobby was relieved by Suzie's quick, if inaccurate, reply.

"Whatever," Ben shrugged. "I don't only walk dogs. I also make t-shirts."

"Really?" Suzie asked.

"I've been doing it for years," he boasted. "I studied printmaking in art school. I'm trying to start a company, but in the meantime, I do contract design for a couple of stores. Ever heard of Urban Apparel?"

"Urban Apparel?" Suzie turned to Bobby. "We were just in there, weren't we, babe?"

"I saw some of those shirts," Bobby said. "What did you make? A monkey in a pirate hat? A sasquatch crapping out a velociraptor?"

"No. That would be stupid," Ben sneered. He spoke to Suzie in a voice husky with eroticism. "I designed a shirt with Isis. She is the Egyptian goddess of love."

"No, you're right. That's much cooler," Bobby said. "Isis is totally cool."

"You think it's easy to design a t-shirt?"

"It's not walking a dog, but I think I could manage."

"Oh, come on, Bobby," Suzie said. "You don't have a crafty bone in your body. You couldn't make the bed if you tried."

"Sure I could," Bobby defended. "I could make the bed too if you weren't in it until noon everyday."

"Now there is no need to get nasty, sweetie."

"So you really don't think I could make a stupid t-shirt?" Bobby asked.

Suzie did not need a second to consider the question. "No, I don't."

Bobby shrank at her perceived betrayal. Suzie then exclaimed to Ben, "I love art! I make art, too. I knit all kinds of stuffed animals: cats, sea creatures, horses, puppies, too…"

"That's cool. I'd love to see your puppies sometime," Ben said.

The thought of Ben seeing Suzie's puppies roused Bobby from his self-pity. He took her by the hand and pulled her away. "Come on, Snooze. I need a drink. Ben, good luck with all the dog shit."

"Why were you talking to that guy?" Bobby asked as they retreated to the liquor table.

"He wasn't so bad," Suzie replied, tipping a bottle of rum into her cup.

"He was a creep. He had designs. And I'm not talking t-shirt designs. I mean sexual designs, Suzie."

Suzie objected with a wet raspberry. "*Ptwwwt!* Who cares? It's not like I was going to do anything. You were gone for such a long time. I got bored. What's a girl to do?"

"Well, I'm sorry I was held up. There is only one bathroom. And if you didn't notice from my soaked shirt, I didn't even get to use it."

Suzie had not noticed. She took another drink. Her eyes glazed like two jelly donuts.

Bobby took the cup from her hands and sniffed. The fumes made his eyes water. "How many of those have you had?"

"Two," Suzie warbled.

"I think two is enough."

"But we just got here!" Suzie cried. She shambled back and forth, shifting her weight from one foot to another. "I want to dance!"

"I don't," Bobby said. He filled a cup from a punchbowl with brown mystery liquor.

"Don't be such a heel." Suzie jerked him by the arm. The brown liquor splashed out of his cup and re-moistened his shirt.

"Okay, okay! We'll dance. Just let me finish this drink first, all right?"

Suzie pouted mightily. "You're no fun," she whined. "You only like me when you're drunk."

Bobby did not dignify the remark with a response. He drank his punch. It was gritty and bitter, having the consistency and appearance of pond water. But beneath its aesthetic deficiencies, there was a robust base of booze that promised to enliven even the staunchest curmudgeon. Bobby guzzled the cup, eager that the alcohol should numb him to the party clambering about him. He finished his drink and resolved to drink another. But before he did, he saw a familiar face. At the far end of the table, he saw Marco Dominico.

"I'll be right back, Snooze," he said.

"Where are you going?" she asked, gyrating like a spastic to a Latin beat on the sound system.

"I see someone I know."

"But you said we'd dance!"

"I'll just be a minute. Hold on!"

Suzie tried to give him with a withering glare, but she couldn't keep her eyes from crossing. "You better hurry up. I'm gonna be kissing someone at midnight!" she threatened, punctuating her ultimatum with a dramatic swig.

Marco held an empty tequila bottle, gazing at the label like he was trying to divine some riddle inscribed on it. Bobby hadn't seen him since he was laid off. He approached his former colleague warily.

"How's it going, Marco?"

Marco didn't respond. At least not in any way that Bobby understood. Marco whispered into the bottle as if making an incantation.

"Happy New Year," Bobby persisted.

Marco slowly pivoted towards Bobby, but his eyes remained fixed on the bottle. In a voice of discovery he announced, "I can read this!"

"You can read what?"

"I can read this bottle. It's in Spanish. I can *read* Spanish!" Marco looked up at Bobby. His pupils were enormous black disks, all but crowding out his irises. His face seemed desolate and emptied of

136

personality. Then, from the void between Marco's ears, a smile emerged. "What's up, Kafka?" he asked.

"So you still know my name?" Bobby asked, only half-jokingly.

"Oh, how could I forget you, Kafka?"

They both laughed. Bobby uncomfortably. Marco with a sharp cackle before falling disquietingly silent.

"I didn't know that you knew, Jeff," Bobby said.

"Who is Jeff?"

"This is Jeff's party."

Marco looked around as though he had only just noticed that he was at a party. Without warning he dropped the tequila bottle. It shattered on the floor.

"Opa," he said. "I'm just following the stream."

"The stream, huh?" Bobby nodded without comprehension. "Have you been here long?"

"Where?"

"At the party."

"I've been at the party my whole life, man." Marco stared into Bobby's eyes as if he'd forgotten where, when, and why he was. "Do you want a drink? I want a drink."

"Thanks. But I already have one."

"Have another."

Marco picked through what remained of the ravaged bar. He made two rum and cokes, which he then splashed with gin.

"What's this?" Bobby asked.

"It's a drink."

"Does it have a name?"

"Does it need one?" Marco replied philosophically. "Come on then, chin-chin."

Bobby answered Marco's call and drank. It was not awful. At least it was better than the pond water that he had been drinking before.

After they drank, an awkward silence ensued. It was awkward for Bobby at least. Marco seemed content from the perch of his stoned little world. Trivial conversation topics presented themselves to Bobby, but there was really only one thing that he wanted to know. "How are things at DataCon?" he asked.

"Fine," Marco replied with irritating nonchalance. "Same as always."

"Really?" Bobby frowned. He had been the best writer at DataCon and had hoped that that, even if things could go on without him, the business would at least feel his absence.

Sensing Bobby's disappointment, Marco half-heartedly moderated his response. "I mean it's the same, but not the *same*. It's not the same without you."

"You mean it?"

"Definitely. Pops talks about you, like, all the time. He says that none of those Indians can write a campaign like you can."

Bobby brightened. He stood a little straighter. Held his head higher. Drank more surely. "So those jerks you outsourced my work to aren't much of a replacement, huh?"

"They don't hold a candle to your flame," Marco yawned and was immediately distracted by a long-legged specimen passing in a provocatively short skirt.

Oblivious to Marco's waning attention, Bobby continued. "I miss DataCon, too. Between you and me, if the opportunity ever presented itself and all the stars aligned, I wouldn't mind coming back someday. I mean, I don't have any hard feelings."

"If something ever opens up, we'd love to have you back, buddy."

138

"Really?"

"Sure. Why not?" Marco caught the woman's attention. Leveling his swarthy Latin eyes at her, he said, "I've got to go, Bobby. But, uh, why don't you give me a call sometime."

"About work?"

"Whatever."

Bobby's heart was filled with an excitement that he could scarcely contain. "That'd be great. I'll give you a call next week."

"Fine, fine," Marco muttered. He smiled wolfishly and set out after the girl.

"Happy New Year!" Bobby called after him.

Throughout the church buzzers, honks, and whistles began to sound as the guests tried out their party favors in advance of the new year. Midnight fast approached. Draining his drink, Bobby returned to where he'd left Suzie. He had a pep in his step that wasn't there before.

Once again, Suzie had disappeared. Bobby waded across the dance floor, but he did not see her anywhere. Suzie, who was not unlike a landmark in that she was easily identifiable from a distance, was gone. After several minutes of being battered by the thrusting and strutting dancers, Bobby retreated to corner, feeling very much like a delicate piece of laundry in a heavy duty spin cycle.

The clock ticked closer to midnight. Bobby searched with grim determination, circumnavigating the church. He traced the east side of the sanctuary, looping past the entrance, trudged back up the other side, and closed the circuit by the liquor table where his search had begun. He could not find Suzie.

Many voices rose. The countdown began, starting at ten and clicking past the single digits towards nullity. At zero a great cheer went up and the party erupted in shouts, howls, and horns. The party puckered and engaged in a collective, orgiastic kiss.

Bobby was close to despair when, imagining Suzie locked in the passionate embrace of a freegan with a neck tattoo, he finally saw her. She sat beneath the bright lights in the photo station in the bye-altar. Wearing a plastic yellow crown and leaning against the stuffed polar bear for support, she looked like a calling card for debauchery.

"Where have you been, Snooze?"

"I could ask you the same question," she slurred.

"Suzie, you're drunk," he roared hypocritically.

"So what? It's New Year's. It only comes once a year…" Suzie swooned and began to nuzzle the bear with her cheek.

With no small effort, Bobby pulled Suzie to her feet. After midnight, the party quickly cleared out, dissipating into street towards other venues where the most diehard would drink until dawn. Carried out the exit by the crowd, Bobby dragged Suzie down the street, through his front door and up the stairs to the bedroom. Suzie fell into the bed with a crash, snoring as soon as she hit the comforter.

Bobby undressed and staggered to the bathroom. By the time he came back, Suzie had unfurled herself, spreading her limbs to the four corners of the mattress and occupying the center. He tried to move her, but in her sleep she put up a heroic defense of the bed, moaning and kicking at him. Too tired and drunk to struggle with her, he grabbed a blanket out of the closet.

Bobby staggered down the hall towards the stairs. But he paused when he passed his grandfather's old bedroom. He shuddered before the door that had remained closed for so many years. He felt dizzy and sick in a way that had nothing to do with the alcohol. Seized with panic, he turned and stumbled down the stairs.

140

Chapter Thirteen: South Street is Just Awful

The old year had gone. On Belgrade Street, the only evidence that it had ever been were a dozen trash cans filled with broken beer bottles, toy horns, soiled streamers, and empty magnums of champagne. The garbage from Jeff's New Year's Eve party sat on his corner, leaking and leaving the sidewalk tacky enough to catch passing rats. Thanks to an oversight at the sanitation department, no garbage truck came anywhere near Fishtown during the first week of January. Trash piled in front of every house and in spite of the cold it created a funk, the rankness of which had not been whiffed in the neighborhood since fishermen mongered their catches in the streets a century before.

Suzie's hangover lasted almost as long as the lull in garbage collection. She did not get off the couch for two days, which, admittedly, wasn't entirely out of the ordinary. She held a damp towel to her head, sipped ginger ale, and nibbled saltines joylessly. When she finally did emerge from her convalescence, she was not her usual sunny self. Sullen, dysphoric, and sensitive to light, she suffered the world and swore off alcohol at least ten times a day.

Even with the consequences of the last year lingering on into the new, it was a time for new beginnings. Although Bobby made no formal resolutions, he didn't waste time starting his new hobby: t-shirt design. Conceived from Suzie's doubt about his craftiness and driven by an arbitrary want of something to do with his time, he embarked on his first art project since the sixth grade.

Like any thoroughly modern man, Bobby's first step on his journey to self-expression was to consult the internet. After watching a tutorial on YouTube, he decided that making a t-shirt would not be particularly difficult. All the necessary supplies were available at any craft store. Bobby smirked, wondering why anyone would ever bother with school when they could learn everything from a computer.

But although the mechanics might have been manageable in theory, the creative process turned out to be somewhat trickier. Bobby knew nothing about design. He disliked logos and slogans. He had no eye for detail. He could not even draw a straight line. In short, he was fantastically ill-suited to the task and the last person one would expect to design anything. Days passed and the only ideas that came to him were so obviously inadequate that he discarded them outright. Seeking inspiration, he retreated to the medium that he knew best and settled in front of the television, watching the History Channel in marathon stretches.

During one of these epic viewing sessions, Suzie sat beside Bobby, sorting through mail piled on the coffee table. "You've got something here," she said.

"Anything good?" Bobby asked. He was watching a documentary about Cecil Rhodes aborted railway between Cairo and Cape Town.

"Do you like bills?"

"Not really."

"Then, no. Wait a minute. You got something from the Department of Labor."

Bobby opened the envelope.

"What is it?"

"It's from the unemployment office. They want me to verify my contact information and certify that I still don't have a job. Yet another bureaucratic hurdle to jump through. Why do they make you work so hard for unemployment?"

"I don't know, babe. It's a shame you can't get something for absolutely nothing."

Bobby wallowed for a moment in his government-subsidized pity before he started filling out the forms contained in the letter. When he finished, he asked Suzie where the stamps were.

"Who keeps stamps anymore?" she asked as she flipped through her copy of Glamour.

"People who need to send letters."

"Who sends letters? Can't you just email?"

"Not to the unemployment office." Bobby leaned back and caressed the bulge that had recently appeared around his waistline. "I guess I'll have to run to the post office," he groaned. "I had to go out anyway to buy some things at the art store."

Suzie rolled her eyes. Her pupils took an exasperated turn around her ocular cavities. "You're not still going on about that t-shirt nonsense are you? I told you I was sorry. I don't even remember having the conversation. It's all so… so fuzzy…" she recalled unhappily.

"What are you complaining for? You said I needed a hobby."

"Well, I was wrong. You don't need a hobby. You need a psychiatrist. Who cares if you can't make a stupid shirt? If it's that important, then I believe in you. Satisfied?"

"Not at all. You doubted me. I have to show you what I can do. It's a matter of principle."

"Good grief, Bobby. If you put as much energy into getting a job as you do into your principles, you wouldn't be home bored out of your mind right now and we wouldn't be having this conversation."

"So you have a problem with me not working?"

"No. It's every girl's dream to have a boyfriend on unemployment. You know those checks won't last forever, right? Eventually you'll have to get a job."

143

A lecture about work from his stay-at-home girlfriend struck Bobby as odd. But he kept the peculiarity to himself. "Don't worry about me," he said. "I've got some irons in the fire."

"I hope these irons don't include getting your old job at DataCon back."

"And what if they did? I have it from a credible source that there might be an opening soon."

"Marco is not a credible source. And why would they have fired you just to hire you back?"

"They didn't *fire* me. I was downsized. My job was outsourced. It's a very important distinction. And don't worry about my job search. I know what I'm doing."

Suzie crossed her arms and leaned back on the couch with a huff. The couch creaked in response.

"Fine," she said. "I won't worry about it. Just do what you're going to do. I'll do what I'm going to do. When you run out of money, we can live on the street." Suzie concluded the conversation and buried her nose in an article about Kim Kardashian's new nail polish line.

Although he had an errand to run, Bobby procrastinated on the couch. Unemployment was a morass of the will, a psychic quicksand, a spiritual black hole that sucked at his motivation and undermined his best intentions. Noon came and went. Delay begat dawdling, which gave way to idleness and culminated in fuck all. By the time he took a shower, brushed his teeth, ate lunch, brushed his teeth again, and watched a cultural documentary about the history of the European schtetl, it was close to four. He only had an hour before the post office closed.

Bobby drove out of Fishtown and puttered down Columbus Boulevard. Heading south, he snaked along the river, looping around the comparatively clogged arteries of Center City. Taking a hard right on

144

Christian Street, the transmission groaned. He turned onto Seventh and arrived at South Street with time to spare. But getting to South Street was only part of the journey. Parking was something else altogether.

South Street had once been like any other neighborhood in Philadelphia. It had the same cramped streets and blocks of row homes that were as much Philadelphia's architectural signature as the stately Victorians in San Francisco or the slinking shotgun houses of New Orleans. Like Fishtown – or any other American city for that matter – it had its beginnings in immigrant communities, but it diverged in the mid-century from its working class roots, evolving alternately into a mob stronghold, a garment district, a doo-wop capital, and hippy Mecca. As the last decades of the millennia ticked away, South Street became a haven where suburban trash came to have their sensitive bits pierced, buy leather accessories, squat in the streets, smoke American Spirits, and alternately glare at/ask for change from anyone who passed.

Bobby loathed South Street and avoided it whenever possible. Unfortunately, avoidance was currently impossible because he needed to go to the art store. He braced for the packed intersections and pedestrians. He drove slowly, stopping at every light. As he crawled towards the post office on Fourth, Bobby searched for a parking spot. But both sides of the street were filled without space for as much as a Vespa, let alone a full-size American family car. As he approached 8th Street, all hopes of parking were dashed when stretches of broken asphalt and scaffolding replaced the road.

Bobby pulled onto a side street, but the situation was no better. The cars displaced from South Street had migrated to the neighboring blocks, occupying their narrow avenues completely. As the dashboard clock ticked towards five, Bobby grew more desperate. He was about to give up and go home when he found a 30-minute spot in front of a bar off Bainbridge. He

145

stomped on the accelerator and swerved into the space. His nose kissed the bumper of a dull green Tercel teetering off the sidewalk and his rear ever so slightly peeked into the loading zone behind him.

Bobby looked at the clock. It was 4:40. The post office closed in twenty minutes. With his unemployment forms in hand, he exited his Taurus and buttoned up his coat. On a nearby stoop, a homeless man shivered in a wad of blankets, mumbling something that almost certainly dealt with spare change. Bobby had no time for charity. As he belonged to the unemployed ranks, he had no change to spare. Bobby set out at a trot.

He ran down Bainbridge, nearly getting hit by a Suburban as he darted across Passayunk. The SUV blared its horn, which drew the spirited jeers of a group of rubberneckers loitering on the corner. Ignoring their catcalls and unkindly references to his head, which was flushed and bristled like a ripe strawberry, Bobby cut down 4th towards the blue awning marking the post office.

Throwing open the door, Bobby steeled himself for the long lines that always seem to be associated with government services. But to his happy surprise, there was no line. The office was empty and for the first time in his life he enjoyed the undivided attention of the postmaster. He headed directly to the counter, handed over his letter along with thirty-seven cents for the stamp. Their transaction complete, the postmaster tossed his letter with a practiced flick of her wrist, causing it to helicopter like a maple seed as it landed in the mail bag. With his letter in the mail, Bobby experienced the simple satisfaction of a mission completed.

Or half-complete anyway.

Stepping back out onto South Street, Bobby emerged into a strange universe. A bizarre sort of Disney Land imagineered for high school hookies, junkies, drunks, thugs, their plugs, and all the other trash that

146

washed up from the Jersey shore. More trailer park than Hershey Park, more Five Points than Six Flags, it was a lot like Dorney Park.

Bobby marched through the dismal street show and was swallowed by the wretched humanity. Carried on by the masses, he saw a visibly intoxicated street musician pining for attention. A crew of hack breakdancers flailed and flopped on flattened cardboard boxes before an apathetic crowd. A tourist bus passed and a tinny voice on the loudspeaker pointed out the birthplace of Larry from "The Three Stooges" with little enthusiasm.

As Bobby travelled down South Street, he was treated to a parade of such half-assed spectacles. But he was most struck by the crowds on such a chill winter evening. There were crowds in record stores and crowds huddled around heat lamps on outdoor patios. There were crowds in front of the pizza places and crowds, despite the cold, at iced custard stands. But of all the crowds on South Street, none was greater than the mobs laying siege to the cheese steak shops.

History is a funny beast. There is no clear answer for anything and there are an infinite number of explanations for why South Street turned out the way it did. But when Bobby saw the lines outside the cheese steak shops snaking around the block, he was certain that whatever was wrong with South Street had to do with cheese steaks.

The simple combination of chopped steak, cheese whiz, and a hoagie roll belonged to all of Philadelphia, but no neighborhood had seized upon it like South Street, clinging to it like a monkey grasping a big, soft banana. Every bar served them. A shop on every corner claimed to have invented them. Sometimes they got no fancier than fried onions and sometimes they were gussied up with truffle cream. But despite their variations, the cheese steak was a beacon to everyone in the tri-state area to come to South Street to get fat, drunk, and tattooed.

Looking past the lines of bundled tourists, twitching for their greasy fix, Bobby saw the art store and pushed his way inside. At once the bewilderment of the street was replaced by the labyrinth of cluttered aisles of the arts emporium. Overwhelmed by the volume of the place, Bobby took a few steps, paused and wavered, wandering with senile distraction among the brushes, easels, glue knives, paints, specialty papers, and fine-tipped pens.

When Bobby emerged from the store after what seemed like an eternity, it was already dark. In both arms he carried bags brimming with the tools needed to make a t-shirt. With his awkward load, he walked back up South Street. Pushing against the street traffic, he had only a slightly less difficult time than a salmon swimming upstream to spawn. By the time he returned to Bainbridge, Bobby was panting. His arms felt like lead. Between the cold and the heavy bags, his fingers were pink, lifeless sausages.

He continued up Bainbridge and reached the block where he parked. The homeless man still dozed on the stoop, nestled in his rags. The dull green Tercel was angled onto the sidewalk as before. But the Taurus was gone. Bobby forgot to breathe. His heart dropped into his stomach like a penny falling into the bottom of a deep black well. He had to set down his bags as he was overcome with dizziness. Trying to stay upright as the asphalt seemed to tilt and crumble, Bobby walked gingerly to the homeless man.

Bobby spoke haltingly like a little boy having an asthma attack: "Did you see? What happened? To the Taurus?

The homeless man muttered under his foul breath as he slept.

Bobby persisted. "Did you see? What happened? To my car? You were here. When I parked."

148

The homeless man opened his eyes. His pupils were cloudy and gray like oysters rotting in a half shell. "I ain't seen nothing in years," he said.

Chapter Fourteen: Rhodesia Was Super!

After Bobby's car was stolen, he didn't leave the house much. Frankly, he couldn't have left if wanted to without transportation. He might have taken the bus of course, but that really wasn't a choice for reasons known to anyone that has had the misfortune of riding a SEPTA bus, a thing that gives true meaning to the phrase "hell on wheels." No, Bobby spent his time at home, working on his t-shirts, and maintaining an uneasy peace with Suzie, who had concluded that his latch-key existence wasn't doing either of them any good. To get him out of the house, she even suggested that he see Ronnie, which, given her distaste for Ronnie, was an act of extreme desperation, the last of last resorts. But Bobby wouldn't see his contemptible friend or budge from his isolation. His sphere was reduced to Fishtown. His primary contact with the outside world consisted of his solitary vigils by the parlor window watching the old church and his morning expeditions for scrapple sandwiches.

But even this breakfast link was soon severed. One morning when he went for his scrapple infusion, the gas station on Aramingo was closed. The windows were black and a sign on the door announced new management. Bobby peered into the windows. No one was inside. There were only empty shelves peeking out of the darkness. Bobby turned to go. As he passed the idled gas pumps, he stepped on the Miller bell, which dinged a melancholy ding.

Deprived of his daily dose of pork by-product, Bobby went home. His bald brow angled against the bitter wind, he walked as though he was trying to butt heads with something in the distance, some looming belligerent thing on the horizon. Because he looked down, he didn't notice the "For Sale" signs that had sprouted in front of the many row homes in his neighborhood. If he'd glanced at St. Stephens, he would have seen that the scaffolding had been removed as well as the metal grates on the stained-glass windows. The windows were cleaner and brighter than they had been since he was a child.

As Bobby fumbled with his keys at the door, he noticed people coming out of the house across the street. The cranky Eastern European was nowhere to be seen, but a young couple was on the sidewalk, surveying the finished product of his renovation. Their attention was directed by a woman whose vulture eyes and prom queen smile could only belong to a real estate agent. Bobby loitered, watching the exchange until the real estate agent turned her all-appraising eye on Bobby. She glared and willed him away, deeming him a blemish on the property's curb appeal. Bobby went inside, making a point to slam the door behind him.

Suzie was at the kitchen table. Surrounded by her patchwork menagerie of stitched animals, she worked on her newest creation. Suzie's doll-making skills improved remarkably over the months. She improvised animals from every phylum with commanding proficiency. Now, as if her handiwork paralleled the course of evolution, she moved beyond simple beasts and started producing nature's most complex creation: man. Skinned in canvas and coifed with long strands of ruby beads, the doll was dressed in a cowgirl number of pastel gingham and pleather that was vaguely reminiscent of a tranny Annie Oakley. While Suzie worked, her original creations – the cat, the octopus, the Zebra, and an owl outfitted in more tweed than a country squire – looked on unhappily, slouching on the table, their button eyes filled with the envy of the first born.

Suzie held a pair of bloomers against the doll's bare bottom, checking the size. "So I was reading in the paper. A company in Cherry Hill is looking for people to do consumer response surveys."

"Are you looking for a job?" he asked as he rummaged a bowl and a packet of Quaker Instant Oatmeal out of the cabinet.

"I wasn't thinking about me. I'm starting classes next semester."
She paused and threaded a needle. "I was thinking about you."

"Me?"

"Yeah, you. It kind of sounded like what you used to do. I thought
you might be interested."

"But it's in New Jersey. Suzie, you know that I hate New Jersey.
And besides, I don't have a car to get there. Do you expect me to walk
across the Ben Franklin?

"There's always the train."

"But I hate the train. And besides, I don't ask consumers about
their opinions. I *make* consumer opinion.

Suzie heaved a heavy sigh. "I just thought you might be
interested."

"Thank you, Snooze. But I'm not. Besides, I've got something
better to do with my time right now."

"The t-shirt?" she asked wearily.

"Yes, the t-shirt. Today I should finish my first *spec,*" he related
with exaggerated expertise. "You can't wait, can you?"

Suzie did not answer. She pinched her nose and sutured the
bloomers to the transgender cowgirl's thighs with unnecessary violence.

After an unsatisfying, fat-free oatmeal breakfast, Bobby went
upstairs to start his work. Once he had bought the necessary supplies and
decided on a design, he realized that he needed a proper studio. Parts of
printing require total darkness, which excluded the parlor or the kitchen.
The standing water in the basement made it a non-starter. His grandfather's
bedroom would have been perfect, but the thought did not even cross
Bobby's mind. With his other options eliminated, he settled on the one
room left: the half-bath on the second floor.

A half-bath is not an ideal work space. After all, it is only designed for one very inartistic act. But Bobby adapted to its confined dimensions like a mole in its burrow. Keeping his elbows tight at his sides, he inched backwards onto the toilet. Upon the sink, which pressed uncomfortably against his knees, he had fashioned a stand where he baked an emulsion coating on a silk screen with a high wattage bulb inserted into the vanity. Bobby looked at his watch and muttered to himself. It wasn't quite time yet. He crossed his arms and waited, increasingly woozy, as the ceiling fan whinnied and imperfectly ventilated the chemical fumes in the room.

After several minutes, dizzy as much from anticipation as the toxic vapors, Bobby washed the excess emulsion off the screen and blotted it with a towel. When it was dry, he held it against the light. His eyes twinkled. With an excitement he could hardly contain, he took a plain t-shirt from a stack beside the toilet bowl and laid it on a rack between his legs. Fastening the silk screen over the racked shirt, he poured purple paint across the screen and proceeded to squeegee.

Bobby emerged from the bathroom wearing his new shirt. He marched down the stairs with no small pomp. He strode into the kitchen like the cock of the walk, his potbelly cinched, his sloped shoulders squared, and a shit-eating grin like a boy who had made his first poo. Suzie was still at the table, fitting a felt Stetson to Tranny Annie's head. Despite his dramatic entrance, she paid him no attention.

Undeterred by her blatant ignoration, Bobby cleared his throat and pronounced, "So, what do you think?"

Suzie looked up slowly from her work. She examined his shirt, blinking with incomprehension and a little annoyance. "I don't get it," she said.

"What's not to get?" he asked and pulled at the shoulders of his shirt to better display its design. Against the white fabric stood a cartoon

153

elephant with its foreleg held high. In its trunk it carried a furling banner with the phrase: *Rhodesia Was Super.*

"Eh?" Bobby arched his eyebrows hopefully.

"What's Rhodesia and why was it super?"

"Are you serious, Suzie?" he scoffed, forgetting that not everyone was such a diligent student of the History Channel. "Rhodesia was the south African colony named after Cecil Rhodes? There was a war there in the 70's when its white government refused to recognize the rights of its black majority?"

Suzie digested the information. "What's so "super" about a racist country in Africa that no longer exists?" She frowned as if the concept caused her indigestion. "Why would you make that?"

"Because it's funny. It's ironic!"

"It's definitely something. But ironic is not the first thing that comes to mind. You'd better not wear that out. You'll probably get shot."

"Oh, Snooze. Anyone who gets it would love it. It's hilarious."

Suzie was skeptical. "Don't quit your day job," she said. "Better yet, get a day job." She returned to her work.

"Don't start that again now. Today is a day of celebration. It's my first shirt day!"

Suzie set her doll aside and breathed carefully and deliberately. "You made your shirt. I was wrong. You're brilliant. You're crafty. Now, please, try to find a job. Call Marco about your old job. Try something. Try anything."

"I'll call Marco when I'm ready. I just haven't felt like it yet," Bobby said. "Besides, why are you bugging me about working? I haven't seen you bring home a paycheck lately."

"Bobby, don't change the subject. This is about you. Not me. Besides, I'm comfortable with unemployment. I'm very good at doing

154

nothing. But you're not handling it very well." She grimaced at the apartheid elephant striding across his shirt. "I'm worried about you."

"Worried about me? Snooze, you're being ridiculous. You should listen to yourself."

"I'm not trying to fight with you. Please just try to get a job. If not for me, do it for yourself. You weren't made for so much free time. Leisure time isn't something everyone can handle."

Bobby muttered under his breath. He abruptly announced that he was going to work in his studio. Suzie shook her head, more disappointed than angry, and returned to her sewing. As he went up the stairs, he thought he heard her whisper, ever so softly, to the doll.

Bobby cleaned the upstairs bathroom, making all the noise that he could without actually breaking anything. After several raucous minutes of slamming cabinets, banging the toilet seat, and copious flushing, he emerged with a garbage bag packed with scraps of stencils, paper towels, paper, paint, and sinews of emulsion that had clogged the sink. He stomped down the stairs and looked into the kitchen. Suzie was still at the table, ignoring him.

He glared backwards over his shoulder at Suzie as he walked through the living room and out the front door. Suzie never batted an eye. Bobby cursed and closed the door behind him. Then, with his first careless step onto the stoop, his right leg slingshot from beneath him. His body rose and then plummeted onto the steps. Something cracked as his coccyx hit the cold concrete. The garbage bag flew through the air and spilled across the sidewalk.

Pain surged up Bobby's spine. His first panicked thought was that his back was broken. He craned his neck towards the house, instinctively looking to Suzie for help. But the door had closed and Suzie could have no idea that Bobby was on his back, writhing like a capsized turtle on the cement.

Out of lingering spite, Bobby swallowed his pain and fought back the urge to call out to her. After several long moments on the frozen step, the throbbing in his back began to subside. He could eventually wiggle his toes and fingers. Fairly certain that the fall hadn't crippled him, he got to his feet. Unable to stand up straight, Bobby examined his stoop. The steps were littered with soda cans and cigarette butts. A waxy wrapper from an Entenmann's Apple Pie was caught against the iron railing, crinkling in the wind. Bobby's eyes traveled to a broken glass bottle, which he deduced was the cracking sound that he heard when he fell. As he hobbled up the steps, he noticed three cans of empty Krylon spray paint that had been discarded over the railing. He glared down at the paint and his temple pulsed with rage.

When Bobby finally entered the house, Suzie was no longer in the kitchen. Presumably she had gone to the bedroom to nap after a long day of handicrafts. Bobby grabbed Suzie's purple corduroy octopus off the table and returned to the living room. Placing the doll behind his back, he sank gingerly onto the couch.

Bobby ruminated silently. He glanced at the stairs and listened for Suzie, uncertain about whether he wanted her to come down or to remain tucked away in the bedroom. He was still undecided when he picked his cell phone up off the coffee table. Making sure that Suzie was not coming down, he made the call. The phone rang and rang and went to voicemail. It was just like every other call that Bobby had made to Marco over the last two weeks.

He didn't leave another message. He tossed his phone on the couch and limped up the stairs. He walked to the bedroom door and stopped. He could hear Suzie breathing inside, snoring like a well-fed house cat. He lifted his hand to knock, but hesitated. He lowered his hand and went back down the stairs. He grabbed his coat and left the house.

Bobby searched for a reason to be outside on a cold winter night. He had not seen Jeff since New Year's and concluded that a neighborly visit was as good an excuse as any. But as he walked to the corner, Bobby saw that there were no lights on inside the church. Its stained-glass windows reflected the street lights in dim purples and lifeless browns. Despite Jeff's obvious absence, Bobby knocked on the heavy wooden door anyway. When there was no answer, he knocked again. He tried a doorbell that he'd never seen before. A dull clang in a minor key echoed inside, but there was no reply. As he shivered on the broad concrete step, Bobby searched for something else to do. It was not long before his thoughts turned to alcohol, which was always a good reason in a pinch.

Bobby hobbled down the street in the direction of the nearest bar. The Silhouette was only five blocks away, but with his back aching the short distance seemed as far as a continent. Each step on the broken sidewalk made him wince. But he continued on towards the promise of undiscriminating company and cheap liquor.

On a Wednesday night, Bobby did not expect much of a crowd. He never expected any sort of a crowd at the Silhouette. So it was curious that half a dozen bicycles were locked to road signs in front of the bar. As Bobby stepped inside, he was shocked to see that almost every seat was taken, which was an unprecedented first. A group of grizzled regulars still defended the far end of the bar like a phalanx of dissipated Spartans. But the rest of the clientele were young, energetic, and, uncharacteristically, not depressing. In a radical departure from the norm, the Silhouette seemed like a place where people went to enjoy themselves, rather than to grow old and die.

157

Speaking of growing old and dying, Bobby looked for Mitch as he took an empty seat at the bar. But the ancient proprietor was nowhere to be seen. Bobby ordered a beer from a bear of a bartender that he did not recognize. He drank his beer and tried to ignore a man to his right in Buddy Holly glasses and a neck tattoo of a butterfly. The man cackled manically to anyone who would listen, his enthusiasms commensurate with the empty shot glasses and crushed tallboy cans strewn before him. When the man ordered another City Wide, Bobby looked in vain for another seat.

It is no secret that that life is orchestrated by unseen forces of chance. In European theater, Oscar-caliber cinema, and second-rate fiction, this point is hammered home with existential verve. Sons murder fathers and marry their mothers. Strangers meet on trains. Etc. And here, as Bobby surveyed the bar, he had his own encounter with fate. Sitting at a table by the jukebox was Marco Dominico.

Bobby had to look twice. He doubted his eyes. Naturally, he was surprised to see Marco, the man he had been trying to contact for a month. But even more startling was that next to Marco and three of his friends was a chimpanzee, which had its hairy knuckles wrapped around a pint glass.

Bobby stared at the beer-drinking chimp. A number of jokes came to mind. But the reality of the situation was anything but funny. Even from a distance, Bobby could see that the chimp wasn't happy. It had the red eyes and unmistakable slouch of a problem drinker. With its shoulders pitched and its head hung low, it monkey-lipped its pint and snarled at the occasional passerby.

One by one Marco's companions hopped off their stools and went to the bathroom, walking like ducks in a stumbly row. When Marco was alone, Bobby forced a brave smile and approached. But once he reached Marco he stopped and hovered. With his face pinched in an achingly

158

artificial grin, Bobby had suddenly lost the power of speech, struck by a crippling self-consciousness.

The monkey was the first to sense Bobby's brooding presence and looked up at him. Marco followed the monkey's fuzzy gaze. The monkey rolled its eyes with tippled indifference and continued to drink. Marco, however, was more welcoming.

"Kafka!" he roared. "What are you doing here?"

"I live in the neighborhood. I came in for a drink," he said stiffly, his words were short and starched.

"I thought you might know Jason," Marco replied, oblivious to Bobby's unease. "We're having a little party for him. It's his birthday." He leaned forward, as though he were taking Bobby in the strictest confidence, and tapped the side of his nose with his forefinger. "He's in the bathroom."

Bobby nodded ignorantly and gestured to the monkey.

"Him? He's the entertainment," Marco said. "Kafka, meet drunk monkey."

"Drunk monkey?"

"His real name is George. Like 'Curious George'?" Hearing his name, the monkey bared its teeth and swatted in Marco's general direction. The monkey missed and fell off its stool. Marco shook head. "We felt that drunk monkey was more appropriate."

"Where did he come from?" Bobby asked, looking on the simian with pity.

"He's a rental."

"A rental?"

"This guy rents him out by the hour for parties. You know, party with a monkey? How awesome does that sound?"

"Pretty awesome, I guess."

"We thought so too. But it isn't." Marco regarded the monkey disapprovingly as it crawled back onto the stool. "Judge for yourself. He's a mess. He only wants beer. He won't even touch the bananas." Bobby noticed a dozen untouched bananas on the table. "Who wants a monkey that won't eat bananas? We should have gotten a stripper."

"You don't have to be so mean about it," Bobby advocated on the chimp's behalf.

"Why not? He can't understand you. After as much as he drank, he can't even sit on his stool."

"It still doesn't seem right to make fun. He can't help being a lush any more than he can help being a monkey. It's all genetic."

"Okay, Bobby. I'm sorry. You hear that? I'm sorry, drunk monkey," Marco mocked and patted its hairy back. The chimp rolled its shoulder aside and bared its enormous white teeth. "All better. See? Now, Mrs. Goodal, how about you pull up a stool and wash down that sympathy with a beer?"

Bobby took a seat at the table and examined the monkey more closely. George was in a pitiful state. His breathing was labored. His belly was as round as a beer keg. The hair on his head was thinning. Bobby didn't even know that monkeys could have alopecia. George's hands trembled as he lifted its pint. Between sips he muttered, an inarticulate chimp. When the monkey finished its beer, it grunted and slapped the table for another.

"See what I mean," Marco said. "Take, take, take, and no give. If George wasn't a monkey, he'd be an asshole."

Bobby decided not to respond. He changed the subject.

"So how are things?" he asked.

"Great, man. Really great," Marco said distractedly.

"How's your Dad?

"Like he always is."

160

"And DataCon?

"Same as ever."

"And the new office in India?"

"Little by little. Day by day."

Bobby could get nothing out of him. Marco was like some master of conversational judo. He parried and deflected Bobby's every attempt at conversation. Bobby, however, would not be dissuaded. He leaned forward, determined to discuss employment possibilities. But before he could put things bluntly, one of Marco's friends returned from the bathroom and whispered in Marco's ear. Marco jumped out of his stool and disappeared into the bathroom.

Bobby was left alone. Technically he had George, but the monkey was dreadful company. Marco was in the bathroom for a long time. For want of something to do, Bobby got a beer. But the beer caused more problems than it solved. While Bobby drank, the monkey grabbed at his bottle. Bobby moved to the far corner of the table. The monkey lunged at him, spilling bananas and bottles onto the floor. It was not until Bobby bought the chimp a Guinness that it left him in peace.

Marco and his friends returned from the bathroom. During his absence, Marco had developed a certain pep in his step. His friends seemed more engaged and their eyes flicked after anything in the room that moved, beeped, or otherwise twinkled. Clearly, his time in the bathroom had concentrated their minds. Bobby was hopeful that they could now get down to brass tacks.

"Geez, Marco. I thought you fell in." Bobby said as Marco ordered a whiskey.

"Fell into what?" Marco barked back excitedly.

"Into the toilet."

Marco roared with unwarranted laughter and abruptly fell silent. He leveled his gaze at Bobby and strained a crooked smile. "That's funny, Kafka. But I'm fine. I couldn't be drier. I'm Death Valley dry. I'm parched. I need a drink. God, I love whiskey. Do you like whiskey?"

Bobby said that he did, but Marco's attention had already returned to his friends with whom he shared whispers and agitated laughter. Bobby repeated that he liked whiskey. Marco did not respond.

Marco's friends left the table and went to the bar. Bobby took advantage of their absence.

"So about DataCon." he said.

"What about it?" Marco replied.

"I was just wondering…" Bobby started to say but was interrupted when Marco suddenly bounced out of his chair to go to the jukebox.

"What were you saying?" Marco asked when he returned some minutes later without actually having selected any music.

"I was just saying that, well . . . ahem . . . I was wondering how things were looking at DataCon."

"In what sense, Kafka? I'm not following."

Bobby proceeded. "It's just that last time we spoke – at the New Year's Party – you mentioned that if a position opened up, I might, well, be considered for it."

"Of course, of course," Marco crooned like choir of crooked politicians. "If we have an opening again, you would definitely be a candidate. A major one. Top of the pile."

"That's good to hear. I really appreciate it," Bobby paused. "But I was wondering not so much *if* you'd have an opening, but *when.*"

Marco erupted, using many words to say nothing at all. "It's tough to say. 'When' is a very difficult question. An unknowable unknown. We're still in the middle of this whole reorganization. I'm sure you understand.

162

We have this operation spanning continents. Continents, man! I mean, have you ever considered how insane it is that we can communicate across oceans? Instantaneously? It makes my brain tingle." Marco ground his teeth in appreciation of the wonders of the globalized world.

"Yes, that is definitely something, Marco," Bobby said. "But when you get that all sorted out, do you think you might start hiring again here in Philly."

Marco threw his hands up in the air and roared. "Who the hell knows! We're all at the mercy of the market. Slaves to the global system!"

"Come on. You must have some sort of idea," Bobby persisted, growing frustrated with Marco's emphatic hyperbole.

"Seriously, Bobby. I don't have a clue. Those Indians are clever. I don't know when we'll have to hire anyone here again. Hell, my dad might fire me and replace me with some Indian. Wouldn't that be crazy? But really, all this work talk will make you morbid. All work and no play makes Marco a dull boy." Marco finished his whiskey and looked to his friends at the bar. "Tell you what. I have to get back to the party. If you just want to talk about a job, why don't you call me next week about it?"

"I have been calling you," Bobby said. "For a month. You never picked up."

"Didn't I?"

"No."

"And you called the right number?"

"Yes."

"That is a mystery, isn't it? Tell you what, I'll be sure to pick up next time. But now I have to go. My people need me."

After Marco joined his friends at the bar, Bobby sat and felt his heart pound. He finished his beer, but the alcohol did not have the usual settling effect. He watched Marco at the bar, swilling whiskey and rousing himself to sloppy excess. When Marco began throwing bar nuts at strangers, Bobby decided it was time to leave the Silhouette. He abandoned the monkey at the table. It was passed out, gurgling as it snored, its hand gripping the empty Guinness glass.

Chapter Fifteen: An Artist's Birth is Messy

Bobby did not call Marco again. There was no point. Despite his gleaming past with DataCon, there was no future there. The false hope of getting his old position back was a rickety bridge to nowhere. It was time to move on.

Bowing to Suzie's persuasion, Bobby broadened his job search. As he perused newspaper classifieds and scoured the Internet, his girlfriend looked up from her ragdolls with relief, delighted that he was using his time more constructively. Bobby complained less. He moped less. With no more scrapple, his stomach grew less. And, best of all, he was out of the house more often. It was like a great weight had been lifted off her soft shoulders. Suzie flipped the channel to HGTV and pulled a blanket over her legs, gladdened that things were getting back to normal.

Unfortunately, Bobby was not as sanguine about the order of things. The first day of the job search, he realized that he faced a steep and treacherous slope. Although he had years of experience, DataCon occupied an obscure and ethically-compromised field with little relation to other industries. He accepted that no job would be a perfect match. But he wasn't prepared for the fact that so many jobs did not draw on his particular skill set in the slightest. He was unqualified to be a medical assistant and he did not have the solicitude for sales. He lacked the natural graces to barista and the human touch needed for retail.

Eschewing the service sector and focusing on office jobs, most of the positions Bobby found were menial exercises in administrative servitude with little pay and fewer benefits. On the infrequent occasion he came across a writing job, he would bite his lower lip and spiderwalk his fingers across his scalp anxiously as he read the advertisement. Sadly, they almost always turned out to be conventional marketing positions involving churning out press releases. After reading them, his jaw would sink and he

165

would moan to the ceiling. Bobby had never written such routine commercial correspondence. It wasn't so much that he thought these jobs were beneath him. As a communications mercenary for hire, he had shaped consumer opinion, influencing the market, nudging it, in his own humble way, in his clients' favor. To waste these talents on drafting something as clunky and obvious as a press release would be a sin. And, in any case, his cover letters never got a response.

Despite the dearth of opportunities, Bobby was able to find two postings that seemed for a short while like real possibilities. The first was a reporter position at *The Fishtown Star*, a hyper-local weekly available exclusively at grocery stores and discriminating street corners in the neighborhood. He had no journalistic experience per se. But as a life-long Fishtown resident, Bobby was sure that he would have no problem cranking out the folksy fluff and scuttlebutt that the paper's readership demanded.

In an encouraging turn, Bobby quickly secured an interview. The morning of the meeting he got up early and slipped into his "good" suit: a dated, black, two-button number with pleats that he had bought from Sears the previous decade. Ignorant of his lapsed fashion, he left the house in high spirits, resembling, with his giddy smile and stark black suit, a Mennonite off to the county fair. But once he arrived at the newspaper's offices, Bobby's optimism collided with the brick wall of reality. It was immediately apparent that the editor, a newly-minted graduate from an out-of-state liberal arts college, failed to see any advantage in his long residence in the neighborhood. After an abbreviated interview, the editor pushed Bobby's resume aside and informed him that without solid journalism experience, he couldn't hire him at *The Star*. But before Bobby left, in a fillip of charity, he suggested that if he were to go to a smaller paper for a year or so and then reapply, he might have a shot. The editor did not answer the more daunting question of where someone could find a smaller paper than *The Fishtown Star.*

Not long afterwards, Bobby got another interview at a company called CapitalPoint, which sought a "Market Intelligence Procurement Officer." The exact nature of the position was unclear. The posting was riddled with unnecessarily technical gibberish about "probabilistic perception research," "bimodal shareholder analysis," and "competitive assessment infomatics." Bobby didn't understand any of it, but he applied anyway. He certainly had "superlative written communication skills." He prided himself on his ability to work independently, thriving in the most monastic isolation. While he was not particularly organized or "detail-oriented" in practice, Suzie frequently called him anal, which was probably close enough.

But what really attracted him to the position was the sound of one of its job duties calling for "corporate intelligence gathering." This appealed to the childish exuberance in the heart of all grown men for the cloak and the dagger. But, like the job at the newspaper, this too ended in disappointment. In its windowless office in an unmarked building in Center City, Bobby learned that the position's primary responsibility entailed cold-calling overworked secretaries at private companies in the hopes that they might divulge proprietary information. As it is in political espionage, so it was in its business cousin: regardless of the titillating fiction, the reality of intelligence gathering was more underwhelming and much more depressing.

Still not all was grim for Bobby. Although he struggled on the employment front, he thrived and underwent a renaissance in terms of creativity. Undissuaded by Suzie's lukewarm response to his designs (or her growing complaints about the converted upstairs bathroom), he continued making t-shirts.

167

Initially, he was content to repeat his original black and white shirt "Rhodesia Was Super" ad nauseum infinitum. But as he gained experience, his horizons expanded. He evolved beyond white shirts to adopt more vibrant palettes. He began to buy different paint colors. Soon these experiments in color lost their novelty and he considered new designs. Having exhausted the abilities of his first Rhodesia print, he lifted the silk screen over the sink and washed away the emulsion with the solemnity of one saying goodbye to a lover.

As his methods improved, Bobby's main influence remained the cultural medium closest to his heart: television in general and the History Channel in particular. Considering his next shirt, Bobby spent a quiet night at home with a six-pack of Pabst. Long after Suzie went to bed, he sat on the couch, dozing through commercials as he watched a heavily-edited presentation of "Full Metal Jacket." It was in those yawning hours after midnight that inspiration came to him like a bolt of lightning, or more aptly, a burst of suppressing fire from an M60. Grabbing a scrap of a sudoku and a pen from the coffee table, he frantically traced out his ideas, his eyes wide and glowing with the flames of the reflected explosions on the television.

The next day Bobby emerged from the bathroom and went to the kitchen to show Suzie his new shirt. Looking up from a copy of *Bon Appetit*, she saw her boyfriend holding a shirt exhibiting a dangling shape that simultaneously suggested the political borders of Vietnam as well as a limp penis drooping from the crotch of Southeast Asia. Beneath the image was printed: *Me Love You Long Time.*

From that time forward a cataract of imagination gushed forth. Bobby simply oozed with the concentrated pulp of his creative juices. Even on the most tedious, soul-crushing days of his unemployment, he couldn't go an hour without some new idea for a design asserting itself in his teeming brain. Anything could be a source of inspiration. He had become a thirsty sponge for external media and utilized in his designs everything from forgotten propaganda, dusty cultural footnotes, and dimly-remembered jingles from his youth.

Bobby showed each new design to Suzie, who constituted his one-woman audience. Together with Ronnie, she was the person he knew best in the world. (And knowing Ronnie's casual cruelty so well, Bobby would never expose his work to his friend's blistering criticisms.) At first Suzie played the part kindly. But, as time passed, her charity faded. Bobby's imagination was a roaming one, wandering through murky steppes for obscure nuggets of historical memory. He designed strange-seeming slogans like "Scando!" (an exercise in pan-Scandinavian pride) and expressed a recurring fixation on Anne Frank. Sometimes his designs, through the recklessness of his unbridled process and his own peculiar sense of humor, ventured into more controversial territory. When he exhibited his "Hitler on the Roof," a baffling stencil showing the Fuehrer dressed in the garb of a schtetl-dwelling Zero Mostel, Suzie's response was unequivocal. Under her supervision, Bobby washed the design off his silk screen. Then she personally collected all the copies of the Hitler tees, which she disposed of in an undisclosed location.

Bobby had truly found his calling. Although it wasn't putting any bread on the table, it was satisfying a spiritual hunger. He became consumed with his designs and delegated almost all of his free time to his t-shirts.

One afternoon, after squandering his day at a job fair in Center City, Bobby stopped by an art supply store. He wanted to pick up a second screen in order to create multi-color designs by layering his prints. His head filled with two-tone potential, he hurried home, anxious to throw off his workday wear and lock himself in the bathroom.

Bobby got off the bus with his arms filled with his purchases. There was an unseasonable warmth in the late winter air. With his unbuttoned coat flapping open, he raced home. As he navigated the crooked avenues, he hardly noticed the new condos that had sprouted across from the old park, which had recently been groomed and liberated from its homeless population. But when he turned onto Belgrade, he came across something that he could not fail to notice. Upon his front steps sat three uninvited guests: one with tawny hair, one towhead, and another with tight, titian curls.

The three boys munched candy bars with soda cans at their feet and cigarettes between their underage lips. Bobby squinted severely and saw that their hands and clothes were flecked with a rainbow of paint. His brow pulsed and he surged with a giddy fury. The delinquents were there. He had caught them red-handed. And blue-handed. And yellow-handed. And green-handed . . .

Bobby crept closer and took the opportunity to observe them, as prey might watch from beneath a shrub as its predator licked its paws between kills. He was anxious to learn more about his pubescent persecutors, but he gained nothing from his observation. The boys sat silently, inscrutably, their blank faces betraying no emotion. They weren't laughing. They weren't having fun. He could see no reason that they existed except to torment him. As they yawned and chewed, it occurred to Bobby that they were like the pixilated monsters in old video games that would lurk in pre-programmed places behind walls, their bodies imping in place as they waited for the hero to turn the corner.

Just then the large brown-haired boy stuffed a baked apple pie in his mouth and threw the wrapper over his shoulder, bouncing it off Bobby's front door. No longer able to stand by and watch, Bobby stormed into the open, his arms still filled with his packages, hollering "Get off my steps!"

170

Taken by surprise, their little heads snapped in his direction. Crumbs and dribbles of cola flew from their open mouths.

Seizing the initiative, Bobby strode forward, continuing to shout with the crotchedy crank of a man twice his age. The boys retreated from the steps and exchanged telepathic glances about how to respond. Before they could agree on a course, a very stout and square SUV – a diesel-powered Mercedes from the eighties – roared up behind them. Its growling engine, which was amplified by the echo on the street, sent them into flight down an alley.

Bobby watched them scurry out of sight and beamed with triumph. The SUV cut off its engine. Bobby tore his eyes away from the alley and looked at the unfamiliar vehicle just in time to see its driver-side door open. Jeff emerged, dressed in a thick parka. Although it was only late February, his face was sunburned. "What's going on, Bobby? Are you okay? Why are you screaming in the street?"

"Those kids," Bobby aspirated, exhilarating with victory. "Those kids have been messing with my house for months. But I . . . (he wheezed) . . . I finally caught them. I got them. I got you!" he cried down the alley, his chin quivering with victory. "I got you!"

Jeff furled his brow. "It's been a while, stranger," he said, likely wondering how far someone's sanity could slip in two short months.

"Yeah, it has been," Bobby said, his face still twisted in a grin. "I was starting to think you'd given up on Fishtown." Although this was meant as a joke, there was some hint of wishful thinking lurking beneath the statement.

"Given up on Fishtown? Not a chance," Jeff clucked with amusement. "I'm just busy this month. Traveling for work."

Bobby tried to hide his disappointment that Jeff would be staying on the block. Noticing his neighbor's peeling nose, he said. "It looks like you got some sun."

"I was down in Rio de Janeiro last week doing a shoot for Pepsi," Jeff said casually. "I was at Carnival."

"At Carnival?"

"It's like Mardi Gras but bigger. Better," Jeff explained.

"I know what Carnival is," Bobby said defensively. "It's like the biggest party in the world. Everyone knows that."

"Well, let me tell you something that not everyone knows. It's not all sun and beautiful women. Although there is lots of that. I nearly got myself killed."

"Do tell," Bobby replied, perhaps a bit too eagerly.

"I was in a helicopter getting some aerial shots of the parade. We wanted to photoshop Pepsi cans in place of the floats. Anyway, we're up in this helicopter and a big gale comes out of nowhere and nearly blows us into a high rise. It could have been a very bad day," he said with remarkable composure, shrugging as if near death were no more troubling than missing the bus. "But what's this, neighbor? What do you have in the bags?"

Bobby had forgotten about his bags. Suddenly, he became very bashful. "They're just some things I got at the store," he said.

"Things you picked up at the *art* store," Jeff clarified, observing the logo on the bags. "What were you doing at an art store?"

"I was just, umm, well, picking up a few things for a hobby of mine," Bobby choked out with difficulty.

"And what kind of hobby is that?

"I've been making t-shirts."

"T-shirts? Why you crafty devil! I had no idea you made t-shirts," Jeff said.

Bobby squirmed as if being interrogated beneath bright lights. "It's kind of a new thing," he confessed to his shoes.

"What kind of stuff do you make?" Jeff asked with genuine interest.

"Oh, I don't know. Just things."

"Have you shown these *things* to anyone?"

"I've shown them to Suzie," Bobby said with a sigh. "I'm not sure that she appreciates them though."

"You can't let one person's opinion get you down," Jeff encouraged. "If you ever want a second opinion, I'd be happy to take a look at them."

Bobby quit fidgeting. He looked at Jeff in a new way. His neighbor's affability was no longer so damnable. Jeff shone in a new forgiving light. The possibility of a more sympathetic observer than Suzie for his t-shirts was tantalizing. After all, Suzie was a woman. Maybe his shirts needed a more masculine audience to appreciate them, rooted as they were in the boyish preoccupations of B-movies and the History Channel.

"Really? You'd take a look at them?" Bobby asked hopefully.

"I'd be happy to. Whenever you're up for it."

"How about now?"

"Right now?" Jeff asked.

"Yes, now. Right now."

Jeff considered the proposal reluctantly. He was still covered in dirt from Brazil and inclined to go home after a long flight. But there was a hunger and desperation in Bobby's eyes, like something one might see in the eyes of an undersexed adolescent on prom night, that convinced Jeff that "no" would not be an option. "Sure. Why not?" he said with some reluctance.

Borne on a gust of manic enthusiasm, Bobby led Jeff into his house and told him to wait on the couch while he got the shirts from upstairs.

Jeff watched his host's legs disappear beyond the landing. Heavy footsteps shuffled above his head and the muffled sound of drawers and closet doors banging. Jeff settled back and crossed his left leg over his right. He crossed his right leg over his left. Bobby was upstairs for a long time. When he lifted his wrist to check his watch, Jeff finally heard the bedroom door open. Footsteps proceeded slowly to the landing and paused apprehensively. Bobby descended the stairs and stood before Jeff in profile. He breathed deeply and then turned to face the photographer, exposing himself like a virgin on her wedding night. He wore his "Rhodesia was Super," featuring a crisp white elephant on a green shirt.

"So? What do you think?" Bobby asked after a lengthy silence.

Jeff scratched his cheek and stared. "I don't get it," he said.

Bobby tried to explain the symbolism of the shirt, but was hopelessly flustered and ended up mumbling about the irony of Zimbabwe, Robert Mugabe, and some menacing thing called a "street sweeper."

"Now, tell me. Be honest. What do you think?"

Jeff did not know what to think. "I like the elephant," he said.

This was not the response that Bobby had hoped for and he started to deflate like a week-old birthday balloon.

Seeing that Bobby had taken his measured praise on the chin, Jeff mustered up a more positive spin, focusing on Bobby's skill rather than the beguiling subject matter.

"It's a good print," Jeff said. "It's really even and clear. How long have you been doing this?"

"A month. Maybe two," Bobby sulked.

"You did a good job. It looks great."

174

"You're just saying that."

"No, I'm not. It's good work. Especially after just two months."

"You think so? You like the shirt?"

"I admire your technique," Jeff replied diplomatically. "I tried screen printing when I was in school. You're better at it after a month than I was after a whole semester."

Bobby brightened. In gratitude, he offered Jeff a beer.

With Pabsts in hand, they sat on the couch. Jeff asked the very reasonable question, "So, why did you start making t-shirts?"

"I had to do something between unemployment checks."

"I didn't know you were out of work."

"Really? I was sure I must have told you. Suzie says that I talk about it to everybody."

"You never mentioned it to me."

"Well, I am," Bobby confessed and swirled the beer in his can meditatively.

"That's rough. I'm sorry to hear it."

They shared a sympathetic swig. Jeff glanced at the elephant on Bobby's shirt. An idea flashed across his rugged features. "I just had a thought," Jeff announced. "I think I know how to get you a job."

"Oh, really. And how would that be?" Bobby asked.

"If you like making t-shirts, I know this guy who runs t-shirt production at this store in the city. I met him during a photo shoot last year. I did a campaign for the company."

Bobby arched his eyebrow as if to say "go on."

"Urban Apparel. They actually just opened a store around here. I think it's in some old movie theater."

Bobby did not answer straight away. Ponderous and unresponsive, he seemed to gaze at something far beyond the boundaries of his cramped

175

living room. As Jeff regarded his stone-faced stare, he thought he heard a faint grinding sound coming from Bobby's jaw.

"I know the place," Bobby said. Then in a lower octave, as if swallowing back a bit of vomit, or possibly his pride, Bobby asked, "You really think you might be able to get me a job there? Making shirts?"

"I'm not promising anything, but I could at least ask this guy if they can use any help in the design department."

Bobby nodded severely.

"It doesn't hurt to ask," Jeff said and sipped his beer.

Bobby watched Jeff finish his Pabst. He stared at Jeff's can and his eyes started to cross as though he were focusing on something very small and very close, like a fish peering at a worm on a hook.

That night in bed, Bobby had a vision. Inspired like never before, he rushed to his computer and started to work. Utilizing all the design skills he possessed, Bobby gave painstaking life to his idea. He consulted encyclopedias. He perused fonts. He violated copyrights. But he finally had his design.

With stencil in hand, Bobby locked himself in his bathroom studio. He worked until the wee small hours of the morning, putting his design to ink. At some time around dawn he had his prototype.

Slipping the yellow shirt over his head, Bobby stood before the mirror. Printed in black ink was City Hall as seen from the wide expanse of north Broad Street. City Hall was positively baroque in its pomposity, with William Penn's statue lording over the city like some despot groom striding atop a wedding cake. Along the boulevard, the buildings that formed the skyline were replaced by ranks of thin fish – carbon copies of pikes, bass, perch, and salmon – standing tail to top, receding from the foreground all the way to the horizon. Beneath this piscine print, in a crisp, bold, and unapologetic font read the word "Fishtown."

Chapter Sixteen: And the Best Man for the Job is . . .

"I don't know why you had to bring that thing," Bobby said as he followed Suzie down the aisle.

"How am I supposed to buy the right buttons without her?" she replied, projecting her butt at Bobby as she bent before a carousel of buttons for sale. With her left hand Suzie fingered the various sizes and colors. In her right hand she carried a corduroy cat named Henrietta.

"Couldn't you have just guessed?" Bobby asked.

"Why make a guesstimate when I can compare the buttons against the genuine article?"

Bobby bristled at the portmanteau "guesstimate." He hated portmanteaus. "What difference would it really make if you were a little off? It's doll-making. Not rocket science. You don't have to be perfect. And, besides, I don't see what difference there is between one pair of buttons and the next."

Suzie snatched a pair of gray marbled buttons from the stand. "It makes a lot of difference," she said and held them to Henrietta's empty eye sockets. "See? These are too small for her head. How would I know that if I didn't have her right here?"

Bobby shrugged. "I was just saying."

"Just saying what? Hmm?" Suzie spun the carousel and searched through a new row of buttons.

"It's just…" he continued, his words hissing through his teeth, "Don't you feel a little silly walking around with that doll?"

"Why should I?"

"Because you're a grown woman and you're carrying a doll?"

"Bobby, no one cares if I have Henrietta. And even if they did, why should I mind? You can't live your life by what other people think."

177

"I know that. I totally agree. Generally speaking. But I don't see why you had to change the eyes at all. Its eyes looked fine."

"*Its* name is Henrietta," she said. "And, yes, her eyes do look 'fine.' But they could look better. Surely you can understand that, Mr. Perfectionist." Suzie selected a pair of ruby red buttons and dangled them between her thick fingers. "What do you think of these?"

"I don't know, Snooze. They're red."

"Could you be any less helpful?"

"I don't know. Maybe. If I tried."

Suzie frowned and regarded Bobby solemnly. "I know that you're nervous. But it's no reason to take it out on Henrietta and myself."

"Henrietta and *me*."

"What's that?"

"Henrietta and me," he said. "It's more grammatically correct."

"Please don't correct my grammar. It's obnoxious," she said and returned her attention to the button carousel.

As Suzie perused the buttons, Bobby began to fidget and look up and down the aisle like a child in search of a bathroom. "What am I even doing here?" he muttered. "I have an interview in an hour."

"We've already been over this," Suzie said without looking up. "I'm trying to keep you occupied. You know how you get when you're nervous. Just look at yourself now. You're getting all sweaty and flushed. You don't want to walk into your interview frothing at the mouth, do you?"

Bobby declined to answer.

"Of course you don't," she said. "So take it easy. You've done what you can to prepare. You're dressed up nice. You have your shirts. Now all you have to do is take a deep breath and help me pick out a new set of eyes for my kitty. Now tell me. What do you think of these?" she asked again, thrusting the ruby buttons into his face.

178

Suzie was right, of course. Bobby prepared as much as he could for the interview. Jeff had made no promises when he said he might be able to get Bobby an interview at Urban Apparel. But his neighbor's professional connections were potent. Per their conversation, Jeff gave Bobby the contact information of a manager at Urban Apparel named Kyril. Bobby called and left a voice message mentioning that he knew Jeff. Conditioned by his long unemployment to waiting for days for an employer to reply (if they ever did), Bobby didn't anticipate a speedy response. But just after he set the phone down, it buzzed and shuddered in his palm.

Bobby brought the phone to his ear and was greeted with a bubbly female voice that belonged to Kyril's assistant. After a brief dialogue with the assistant spewing out a chipper stream of information and Bobby responding in hiccupped replies, it was decided that he would come in for an interview the following Friday.

Although he had gleaned little more than a time and a place from the conversation, Bobby locked himself into the bathroom for days on end, perfecting his shirts for the interview.

Aside from the artisanal aspects of his preparation, Bobby also attended to a recently overlooked aspect of his person: his grooming. One day while sitting on the toilet, pulling the final version of his "Fishtown" t-shirt (his masterpiece, his "*tee de resistance*" as he repeatedly quipped to a consistently unamused Suzie) Bobby saw himself in the mirror. To his alarm, the image looking back at him resembled a yeti with a hangover. His eyes were sandbagged by dark circles. To say that he was unshaven would be incorrect. Mishaven was more appropriate, with patches of stubble traced by paths he had cleared with careless flicks of his razor. The hair on his head had grown thinner and what remained radiated out in cottony tufts, which, despite Bobby's attempts to pat down, sprung back to scruffy attention. In a matter of weeks, he had come to resemble the isolated, unemployed thirty-something that he was.

Spurred by these signs of neglect, Bobby rushed to the barber, who both tamed his hair and touched up his shave. He used Suzie's eye makeup on his dark circles and changed his clothes, slipping into an Oxford shirt and a gray pair of pants, which were tighter than he remembered and required much sucking-in. Notwithstanding his thicker waist, as he stood before the bedroom mirror, neatly dressed, with his receding hair revealing a noble island of pink scalp, Bobby looked much improved, exuding the aura and quiet competence of an office clerk.

It was in this outfit that Bobby now followed in the wide wake of Suzie, who swayed gently through the craft store, buying the needles, thread, and other paraphernalia of her hardcore sewing habit. It was not the most productive way of spending the precious time before his interview, but, as Suzie correctly noted, it had a mellowing effect on him. Shadowing her through the store, his eyes glazed over and his thoughts congealed into a thick, gray pudding, which was an infertile soil for anxiety to take root. In a commercially-induced coma, Bobby wandered the aisles. Time compressed into an inane singularity and without noticing it, he had completed a circuit in the store, passed out of the check-out line, and walked through the exit. It was not until they turned off Broad Street that Bobby realized he was on his way to the interview. There was an indistinct, nagging buzz in his ears. He noticed Suzie's moon face turned towards his, her lips pursed in a question.

"Well?" she asked.

"Well, what?"

"How do you feel? Are you nervous?"

"I don't feel much of anything," he admitted.

Suzie considered this answer for a moment. "At least you're not sweating anymore."

180

They walked on.

"You'll do fine, babe. Don't worry," she encouraged and bounced Henrietta on her shoulder as though she carried a small child. .

"I'm not worried," he said, still spacey from the store.

Suzie regarded him dubiously. Forcing a smile, she said, apropos of nothing, "Well, this is convenient anyway."

"What's convenient?"

"Going to Urban Apparel. I wanted to come here anyway. Henrietta's jumper is tired. Who wears denim anymore? I need an outfit to go with her new eyes. Oh, look. There it is now!"

The store was up the street, just beyond Rittenhouse Square, its lawn brown and muddy at the sloppy start of spring. Bobby then looked at Suzie with worry. "You weren't planning on coming in, were you?" he asked.

"Of course I was. What else would I do while you were in there?"

"I kind of thought you'd wait outside."

"In March?"

"What about a coffee shop?"

"But I don't want to wait in a coffee shop. I want to go into Urban Apparel. Is there some reason that you have problem with that?" Suzie asked.

"No. Not exactly," he said. "But won't it be a little weird if you show up to an interview with me?"

"I'm not going to the interview with you. I'm just going to the store."

"But you're my girlfriend."

"They're not going to know that, Bobby."

Bobby nodded and dropped the subject. Suzie let it go as well, charitably ascribing his being an asshole to his high-strung nature.

181

They walked up the street without saying a word. Suzie thought about Henrietta's new costume. Bobby was fantastically distracted, his thoughts inundated by unspoken concerns. Only Henrietta showed any enthusiasm, her corduroy limbs flopping in Suzie's arms. As they approached the door to Urban Apparel, Bobby slowed and stopped. Noticing that she was walking alone, Suzie turned back to him. Bobby urged her onwards, gesturing with his chin to the door. Suzie shook her head and went inside. Waiting until she disappeared amid the reflections in the window, Bobby followed.

Urban Apparel did not just sell clothes. The bulk of their receipts did come from shirts, pants, dresses, and other passing fancies of each fashion season. But they also sold books about politics and music, reproductions of vintage furniture, record frames, and kitsch in all its plastic forms. In short, the place peddled more than goods. It pushed a way of being, a worldview, a lifestyle.

As Bobby entered the store, he felt the overwhelming presence of the place bear down on him, as though it was imposing its personality, by sheer force of its corporate will, onto his own. With his head wobbling to and fro on his neck like an uneasy jack in the box, he crossed the sales floor. Trying not to lose himself in the store's vaulted post-industrial architecture, he looked at his shoes and relied on his peripheral vision to negotiate the customers and displays of frilly notebooks, gaudy décors, and irreverent plastic toys lampooning Einsteins, American presidents, and saints from every Semitic religion. His eyes flicking involuntarily, he caught sight of Suzie. Her back was to him and she was holding a high-waisted skirt with a bright floral print against Henrietta. He proceeded to the counter. A wire thin sales girl with long black bangs sat behind the sales desk. She looked up from her copy of *Ad Busters* and flinched, startled by

182

Bobby's polished brow barrowing down on her like the ramming end of a trireme.

"Can I help you?" she asked and reflexively lifted the magazine like a shield.

"I'm here to see Kyril," Bobby said with a smile that tried much too hard.

"Kyril?" she repeated skeptically.

"I have an interview." His voice dropped to a husky whisper. "I'm supposed to show him some of my work. Some of my t-shirts." By way of visual aide, he tilted his brown shopping bag towards her so that she could see inside.

The sales girl looked inside reluctantly, as though she would not have been surprised to find a bomb or a severed head inside. "So you want to see Kyril?"

"Yes. Kyril," he said. "I have an interview."

The sales girl thought for a moment, rubbing her studded tongue against an unusually long left incisor. "I don't know where he is right now. Give me a minute."

The girl made a phone call. While she spoke, Bobby continued to stare at her. Shifting beneath his gaze, she wanted to end the exchange with Bobby as soon as possible and send him along.

Fortunately for the sales associate, it was not long before an egg-shaped woman waddled across the store, calling out Bobby's name. The woman was a curious specimen. Her long, ovoid curves were accented by a pair of bright tights and what appeared to be a ballerina skirt cinched around her low waist. Her shirt was all sheer and ruffles. The totality of her frumpy ensemble suggested an egg that someone decorated as Cindy Lauper. As Bobby was led away by this funky humpty-dumpty, the sales girl exhaled with relief and returned to her magazine.

"Very pleased to meet you, Bobby," the egg-shaped woman chirped. Moving as fast as her stubby legs could carry her, they headed towards the back of the store. "My name is Molly. I'm Kyril's assistant."

"It's nice to meet you," he said. Despite his desire to project confidence and collegiality (which he read were prized in the workplace), Bobby was stiff and awkward. He doddered with each step as he followed the surprisingly swift assistant.

"Thank you for coming in today," she said, skirting past a stand of conspicuously pink paraphernalia. "I'd like to apologize in advance. It's been a madhouse here. I'm sure you've read that we're re-locating our headquarters."

"I haven't."

"Really? You haven't? That's odd. It's been in all the papers. Well, since you didn't know, the company has grown a lot over the last few years and we made a deal with the city to move into a site at the old Navy Yard."

"That should be neat," he said.

"It will be once they finish. There is so much to do, though. Mold. Asbestos. I haven't seen it myself, but they say there is grime six inches thick in some places. Can you believe it?" Before he could reply that he could not, she motioned for him to follow her through a large steel door. "Right this way!"

The heavy door groaned shut behind Bobby, blocking out the bright sales floor, and encapsulating him in a low, dim hallway. This space was stifling, almost tomb-like. His sense of confinement was aggravated by the boxes lining the floor and bulletin sheets tacked to the walls, which brushed him when he passed like grasping paper cilia. Whereas Molly's squat proportions seemed evolved for these bowels of commerce, Bobby had to stoop down to follow her.

184

"As you can see, we're a little crowded at the moment," she said. "Back here is where we house our administrative staff. Sales. Marketing. Distribution. In that dark little room is finance. Poor souls." She pointed to a box of products that had spilled out onto the floor. "Watch out for the fruit-powered alarm clocks!"

"Fruit-powered alarm clock? Do they work?" Bobby asked.

"Who knows? Just follow me."

They turned down a short hallway that ended at a door wedged between a janitorial closet and a restroom. Molly entered the door. "Please come in," she said.

Bobby hesitated. Peering through the doorway, he was not sure that he could follow. Molly stood in an office stacked floor to ceiling with boxes, folders, records and product displays. He guessed that there was a desk in the corner where the papers were stacked like castle ramparts, but he couldn't see how he was supposed to get to it.

"I know it's cramped, but there is a seat right there," Molly said. As she pointed towards the corner, she knocked over a pile of stapled reports with her broad, elliptical ass.

Following the path of her finger, Bobby saw a narrow path cut into the stacks that led to a chair. Lifting his bag above the mess, he shuffled towards it.

"Can I get you something to drink? Coffee? Water?" she asked once he reached the desk.

"No. I'm fine," Bobby said as he searched for a place to set his bag. Unable to find one, he steadied it on his knees, which pressed uncomfortably against the desk.

Molly paused for a moment and then nodded in silent confirmation that her role in the interview was complete. "I'm sure Kyril won't be too long," she said. "Good luck!" she chirped as an afterthought.

Bobby mumbled something in the way of thanks and proceeded to wait, bent-kneed, his arms wrapped around his bag as if he was a child scrunched at the back of the school bus.

Despite Molly's assurance that her boss's arrival was imminent, this was not the case. Once she was gone he heard someone in the bathroom. Assuming that the person in the bathroom was Kyril, he listened to the ambient noises of the commode – the creaking stall, the soft grunts, the expulsions, the crumpling paper, and the final flush – with anticipation. Literally on the edge of his seat, he heard steps and running water. The faucet stopped and in the subsequent silence Bobby imagined that the person was examining himself in the mirror, perhaps inspecting a new pimple or noting how harsh a fluorescent light was when compared to an incandescent bulb. The bathroom door finally opened and Bobby flexed his face in a professional grimace. But the anonymous steps went down the hall, echoing into obscurity.

So began Bobby's wait, every moment expecting Kyril's arrival and every moment disappointed by his absence. While he sat, he peeked at the papers lying around the office, first guiltily, then with brazen interest, and ultimately apathetically as he tossed aside a sheaf of paper filled with lists of indecipherable acronyms and meaningless sales figures. Bobby's knees began to hurt, buckled up against the desk as they were. He stood up to stretch them, but almost immediately sat back down when he heard footsteps in the hallway. Sitting up straight, Bobby adopted the posture of the motivated employee, only to slouch into dismay as the steps passed the office for the bathroom. Bobby was so bored that when Kyril did appear, he almost missed it.

From down the hall came a tinkling, like bells on a winter sleigh. Footsteps clicked closer and the tinkling built to sharp clanks. Shaken from his torpor, Bobby turned towards the door just in time to see a man appear.

186

Tall and fashionably scruffy, he wore a black t-shirt and tight black pants. He had rings on every finger and a silver crucifix dangling from his neck. When he saw Bobby, he smirked in a way that resembled Eric Bana if Eric Bana were a practicing satanist. From the top of his benighted head to the soles of his leather boots, he was Gothic in the most Teutonic sense, an image that was completed by a pair of steel spurs, spinning slowly on the back of his heels.

"Bobby Bright? I'm Kyril. I apologize for the mess. Things are very busy here. Lots of important things. I'm quite sure you understand," he said, slipping his way through the room's clutter. Although he spoke matter-of-factly, there was an intonation of mockery, a congenital sarcasm that left Bobby unsure whether he was being poked fun at.

"Thank you for taking the time to talk with me," Bobby began, attempting to lay the groundwork for a more amicable dialogue.

"A pleasure I'm sure," Kyril replied, sliding into the chair behind the desk and peering at Bobby down his long Norman nose.

Bobby paused uncertainly. "Jeff told me a lot about you…" he began again.

"Unfortunately, Jeff told me next to nothing about you," Kyril interjected, reclining, but losing none of his cynical intensity. "Last week Jeff gives me a call and says that I should meet with someone named Bobby Bright. I don't know Bobby Bright. But I know Jeff. He's a good photographer. So I say all right. I'll meet with Bobby Bright. And now here you are. So tell me, what can I do for you, Bobby Bright?"

"Ahem," Bobby coughed. He clutched the bag on his lap more tightly. "I was interested, I guess, in getting a job here."

"So why do you want a job at Urban Apparel?" Kyril asked, resting his finger on his cheek in a pantomime of inquisition.

"Well, it's my understanding that you make t-shirts."

187

"We do a lot more than t-shirts," Kyril said. "I make dresses, pants, skirts, sweatshirts, pillows, wall paper, posters, and notebooks."

"But you also make t-shirts?"

"Yes, we also make t-shirts," he confirmed, visibly irked by having his output narrowly characterized.

"Well, I'm really interested in t-shirts," Bobby said. "I've been doing a lot of screen printing." He lifted his grocery bag as a way of introducing his work. Kyril, however, was preoccupied with picking his thumbnail and failed to notice the bag.

"It's great that you do screen printing," he yawned, intently observing the cuticles on his right hand. "But if you're looking for a job in that, I'm afraid I have to tell you that we have machines that handle merchandise production. At Urban Apparel we like to take advantage of the Industrial Revolution at every opportunity."

"Excuse me," Bobby stuttered, confused.

"Don't get me wrong," Kyril continued. "It's nice if our employees are interested in their work. I like screen printing. If you like it too, kudos!"

Bobby twisted out a smile. "Actually, if you're interested, I brought some of my work." Once again, he raised his bag above the wall of stationary on the desk.

"I'm sure it's very nice," Kyril said. "But I don't need printers. What I need is simpler. Urban Apparel is ramping up to be a more national company. This spring we'll be moving out of our current offices and into a new site at the Navy Yard. In anticipation of that move, I'm going to need people moving boxes, writing invoices, talking to vendors. It will be a lot of logistical and administrative grunt work. I'll be honest with you. It isn't glamorous. But if you're interested in the position, we could possibly use you."

As Kyril described the job, Bobby's forced smile sagged in clearly defined stages: first into a diminished grin, then incomprehension, next a hopeful smirk, then back to incomprehension, which was followed by a jowly disappointment. It was this gloomy mug that he wore when Kyril asked him what he thought.

Bobby prefaced his reply with a sigh that sounded like a balloon deflating. "So would this position have anything, at all, to do with designing t-shirts?" he aspirated in long, breathy vowels.

Kyril leaned forward and rubbed his whiskered chin. "You want to know if this position would in any way involve designing t-shirts for Urban Apparel?"

Bobby looked into his probing eyes. "Yes," he said.

"Absolutely not," Kyril replied, punctuating his answer with a chuckle. "This job would have next to nothing to do with design. If you're worried about this job involving design, don't be. Absolutely no experience is required. Frankly, a chimp could do it. You're perfectly qualified."

Just then a rumbling came from somewhere on the desk. Kyril fished out a Blackberry from the papers, snickered at a message, and typed out a reply. After he pressed send, he stood up and said, "I've got to go. I'll see you out. Walk with me. Talk with me." With that Kyril scooted out of the office, the spurs on his boots jingling with each step. Bobby skulked out behind him, holding his bag to his chest like a life preserver.

"The way I see it," Kyril said, "we'll be trying to get people in as soon as possible. They'll work part-time for a few months so they can get used to the position. Currently, I've got a few..." He droned on about the job, but Bobby did not listen. Instead he focused on the spurs, which spun like pinwheels, clanging with each step. In this way he followed Kyril through the dim back halls and back out onto the sales floor.

"I don't need an answer now," Kyril concluded hurriedly. If you're interested, we can use you. A reference from Jeff is good enough for me. When you make up your mind, give Molly a call and we can move forward on this."

Bobby nodded vaguely. Overwhelmed with the weight of lowered expectations, he couldn't quite lift his head to look Kyril in the eye. He just wanted the interview to end so that he could go home, crawl into bed, and pull a blanket over his head. For that reason alone, he experienced a very qualified happiness when he realized from Kyril's speech (his words slowing, growing farther apart, and losing momentum) that the disappointing interview was coming to an end. But, unfortunately for Bobby, he couldn't count on anything ending quickly or cleanly, which were simple virtues enjoyed even by the condemned.

Out of corner of his eye, Bobby saw a large shape coming towards him. It was Suzie, visibly uncomfortable and carrying her Henrietta doll whose eyeless sockets seemed to share her ire. Bobby's first impulse was to shoo her away, but he resigned himself to her approach, reasoning that things couldn't get worse.

Apparently, she didn't see Kyril because she interrupted the conversation, speaking directly to Bobby.

"Let's get out of here. I've been waiting an hour. People are starting to talk about that lady with the corduroy cat!"

As could be expected, Kyril jerked around, annoyed by Suzie's interruption. But the moment he set his eyes on her, his expression softened. His lips puckered. His eyes moistened. His whiskered cheeks seemed to blossom.

Bobby was stupefied by the thaw in Kyril's demeanor and the only conclusion he reached was that Kyril had fallen in love with his girlfriend at first sight. As unlikely as it seemed, he could think of nothing else. This

190

thought seemed to be confirmed when Kyril's eyes angled downwards, staring in the direction of Suzie's breasts.

A strained hush settled between them. "Who is that?" Kyril asked, almost in a whisper.

"That's *my* girlfriend," Bobby said defensively.

Kyril flicked his eyes askance. "Ptwwwwt," he raspberried. "Not the girl. Who is that wonderful cat?"

"Her name is Henrietta," Suzie said, confused by the interest that the oddly Byronic figure was taking in her doll.

Kyril bent down with his hands on his knees, eye-level with the rag doll. "Her name is Henrietta," he said softly.

191

Chapter Seventeen: Bobby Puts His Foot in It

"What was I supposed to do?" Suzie said. "It's not my fault he liked Henrietta."

Bobby did not want to respond. He hated fighting. In his opinion, the only thing that could make fighting worse was fighting in public. And a fight did not get more public than doing it on a SEPTA bus crawling up Frankford Avenue at 5pm on a Friday afternoon. The bus was filled with riders occupying every seat and clogging the aisles. Of course no one actually made eye contact with Bobby. That is except for the bum in a purple tracksuit and a 76er's beanie who had no qualms about watching Suzie and Bobby with his bleary, bug eyes. But regardless of the other commuters' thousand-yard stares, Bobby knew they were hanging on every word, paying silent witness to their bickering.

"What should I have said?" Suzie continued. "Don't you dare look at Henrietta? Keep your hands off of her? No, I have no interest in your store licensing her? Is that what you wanted?" She crossed her arms and leaned back against the seat, which creaked beneath the heft of her discontent. "I thought you'd be happy. You always wanted me to get a job."

The bag with Bobby's shirts lay discarded at his feet. A shirt had spilled out of the top. Bobby stared down at the Elephant stencil on the front. He looked up at Suzie. In her arms, Henrietta's buttonless eye sockets guiltily avoided his gaze.

"I never told you to get a job," he said.

"Come on. You hate that I spent so much time in the house."

"I did not. I loved that you sat around the house."

"Don't start, Bobby. You're a terrible liar. You are telling me that you never, ever wanted me to get a job?"

Bobby chewed on his lower lip. He glanced between Suzie, the other riders' prying ears, and the homeless man smirking toothlessly at them.

"Maybe a little. Sometimes," he confessed.

"So then why are you angry? I got a job. You should be happy."

"But you weren't supposed to get my job!"

"Oh, Bobby. Get real. You were never going to get that job. You should just be happy that one of us got something."

"Maybe you're right, Suzie," he muttered, growing angry despite himself. "Somehow I'm not happy though." He grimaced at the stuffed cat on her lap. "You weren't even supposed to be there! I didn't even want you there!" he cried suddenly. It was not clear if he was speaking to Suzie or to the doll.

The other riders stopped pretending that they weren't paying attention. A few polite commuters peeked over their shoulders, stealing glances. Most just gawked.

Suzie's cheeks burned with fiery indignation and then went deathly pale. She raised her fist in the air. Bobby cringed, afraid of a hit that he recognized he probably deserved. But instead of a wallop, Suzie pulled the signal cord above the window. The bus came to a stop. She got up from her seat with Henrietta.

"This isn't our street, Suzie," Bobby called after her.

Suzie did not reply. She shoved riders aside as she marched to the exit. Bobby stumbled after her, forgetting his bag of shirts on the floor.

The bus pulled away. Suzie marched up Frankford with Henrietta under her arm. She walked quickly, and Bobby struggled to keep up.

"Hey, Snooze. I'm sorry. I didn't mean what I said back there."

Suzie did not respond. Her wide hips swayed ferociously as she walked.

193

"Come on, baby. Slow down. I said I'm sorry. I'm serious. I'm happy for you. I'm glad that you got the job. It doesn't bother me."

"I, I, I. Me, me, me," Suzie parroted bitterly without losing a step. "That's the problem with you. Everything is about you!"

"What are you talking about? I don't make everything about me," he pled to the back of her head.

"Of course you do. Your job. Your life. Your t-shirts. When do you ever think of me, Bobby?"

Bobby could not keep up with the expanding scope of her grievances. "But I do everything for you, Suzie. Rent? Food? I don't even know what you're talking about."

Suzie finally stopped. "Of course you don't. You only think about yourself. You completely take me for granted." Suzie threw up her arms, whipping Henrietta in a wild arc through the air. "You can't even remember a stupid date on the calendar!"

Bobby bridled at the accusation. "What are you getting at now? I can remember lots of dates. Halloween is October 31st. Christmas is December 25th. Thanksgiving is the third Thursday of November, I think."

"Don't even bother," Suzie said, disdainful of his recall of major holidays.

"No, really. What do you mean?

"What is today's date?" she asked, barely containing some secret fury.

Bobby furled his brow. He actually had no idea what the date was. Dates rarely came up during unemployment. "Friday," he said.

"Do you have any idea what the date is?"

From his vacant expression, he plainly did not.

"It's our anniversary, Bobby. It's our anniversary and you did not give me so much as an M&M."

Bobby was floored by the revelation. As he processed the information, his heart beat with a sickening, heavy haste. He mentally calculated the date. Ticking off the days from the last date he knew, he cycled through the week, slowing gravely as he reached the wrenching conclusion that Suzie was right. Today was their anniversary.

Bobby forgot about Urban Apparel and the job and even Henrietta, who hung limp like a pelt from Suzie's arm. All of this was pushed from his mind, replaced with a singular, Catholic impulse: contrition.

"Oh, Suzie," Bobby blathered in apology. "I'm so, so sorry. I just forgot. It completely slipped my mind. . ." He continued in this groveling vein for some time. All in all, it was a good start. On the occasion of grievous relationship missteps, spineless was the appropriate posture to assume. Unfortunately, Bobby's clumsy apology inadvertently veered from the shame into self-justification. "But, Snooze, why didn't you say some something?" he said. "If only you had told me."

"Why didn't I say something?" Suzie's spurned ears pricked.

"Yeah, I mean, it's my fault. Absolutely. I'm a jackass. I should not have forgotten. But you didn't remind me either."

Suzie's face seized as though Bobby was watching her on videotape and someone pressed pause. She began to tremble like a volcano about to explode. Then she became still. Ominously still. "I didn't remind you? What does that even mean? It's our anniversary. You shouldn't have to be reminded. It's the same day every year."

"I know, Snooze. You're right. I didn't do anything. But you didn't say anything. If you think about it, it's kind of like we both forgot. Right?"

Bobby smiled at her with a crooked hope that went well beyond delusion.

Suzie returned a stare more frigid than the chilly March evening.

195

"It's our anniversary," Suzie said with icy deliberation. "You did not give me candy. You did not give me chocolate. You did not give me roses . . ."

A spark went off in Bobby's brain. He recalled a Hispanic man on Girard who routinely thrust roses at passing cars. "If this is about roses, I'll get you roses right now," he interrupted.

She did not respond to the kind offer.

"I mean it. I don't mind. I'll do it."

"It's not about roses. I don't care about the roses!" she cried, shaking with womanly fury. "It's not even about our stupid anniversary."

"Then what are we talking about exactly?" Bobby was flabbergasted and well out of his emotional depth.

"We are talking about your total disregard for me. Don't you even care about me? Don't you think I'm worth your time?"

"Of course you're worth it," Bobby replied feebly. "The anniversary just slipped my mind. That's all. I just didn't think about it."

"Exactly. You didn't think." Suzie's eyes were wet with emotion. She tilted her head back as though she were trying to balance on her cheek a tear that had just formed. "You don't think about me at all. It's all about you. Your job search. You locking yourself in the bathroom all day and doing who knows what. Your weird fixation on that crummy old church. It's about everything in your life. Everything but me."

"That's not true."

"Yes, it is," she said, choking back a sob.

"No, it's not. You're wrong. It's just not true."

"If you care about me, why don't you show it?"

"I don't know, Snooze," he muttered in his throat. "I just don't know."

196

"I don't know? Is that all you can say to me?" She looked imploringly into Bobby's eyes.

Bobby hated to fight. Ever since he had followed Suzie off the bus, he felt woozy. His head swam and the sidewalk seemed to tilt and crumble beneath his feet. Bobby tried to still the teeming in his brain. Sensing the importance of the moment, he returned her gaze and fought back the nausea bubbling in his stomach. They had reached a crossroads. Their future together depended on what happened next.

Bobby knew that he had to say something. He wanted to say something. He wanted to let her know what she meant to him. Despite the way he acted. Despite the things he did and did not say. He cared for her deeply. But, despite all of this, he could not find the words.

They did not speak. A pregnant silence clouded the sidewalk between them. Suzie waited, hanging on some ill-defined hope. But whatever she hoped for did not occur. Bobby was silent.

"You have nothing to say? You don't have one thing to say to me?" she asked.

Bobby's hands began to tremble, but his tongue would not move.

"Jesus, Bobby. After all these years, you have nothing to say? I have . . . I've just been wasting my. . ." Suzie choked. She did not finish her sentence. She turned to go.

Bobby finally became unstuck. He reached out after her, grasping desperately. Suzie was too quick though. His hand missed her entirely. It swept behind her shoulder and clasped Henrietta's corduroy head, which was poking out from under Suzie's arm. Bobby heard tearing fabric.

Suzie stared with disbelief at the headless torso beneath her arm. She looked at Bobby with horror. In his fist was Henrietta's severed head.

"Bobby! How could you?" she cried. She picked at the cotton gore spilling from the kitty's neck. "How could you do this to Henrietta?"

197

"You don't think I meant to do that, do you?" Bobby said frantically. "It was an accident!"

"What am I supposed to think? You've always been jealous of her."

"Jealous? That's ridiculous, Suzie. I didn't mean to. It was a mistake."

"Bobby, please."

"Snooze, it was an accident," he begged.

Suzie shook her head as though she were being swarmed by flies. "Just don't say anything else. Please. Don't talk. I. . ." She did not finish. She ran up Frankford.

Bobby chased after her. But within a few steps his ankle twisted in a gaping crack in the sidewalk and he fell to the concrete. Trying to outrun her tears, Suzie made excellent time. She reached the intersection at Palmer and disappeared into the narrow streets of Fishtown. Bobby yelled after her, "It was a mistake, Suzie. I made a mistake!"

But she was already gone.

Bobby got to his feet, but he could only stumble as far as a bench by a small square of urban park. He looked up at the sky. The evening clouds seemed to swirl above his head. His brain pounded. As a car approached, its headlights caught his attention. Bobby watched, frozen in disbelief, as a Ford Taurus wagon with a squealing transmission passed him. He stared stupidly at the driver, a stubbled Hispanic man, who paid Bobby no mind. Somewhere in the distance, beyond the northern borders of Fishtown, a siren sounded.

Bobby did not go directly home. He went to a ratty bar on the corner that he had never been to before. He ordered a beer, but did not bother to drink it. No one noticed him. No one bothered him.

He limped home from the bar at closing time. On his stoop, he fumbled with his keys before he discovered that the door was already open. He stepped inside and saw that Suzie's sewing crafts – the stuffed animals on the couch, hats still piled on the chair – were gone. He went upstairs. Suzie was not in the bedroom. Nor were her clothes in the closet. He went downstairs to the kitchen. On the table sat her empty coffee cup and a set of keys. Suzie was gone. All that she had left Bobby was the riddle of how someone could disappear so quickly, so completely, after so many years.

Chapter Eighteen: Ronnie is a Riot

"Forget about her," Ronnie proclaimed from his bar stool. "Suzie sucked in all the wrong ways. You're better off, dude. It's for the best."

"How do you know that? How can you possibly know that this is for the best?" Bobby asked, sloppy with melancholy. Slouched against the bar, his face was rouged with pain, regret, and alcohol.

"You're looking at this the wrong way. This is a good thing," Ronnie explained with the tone of a therapist –a demented, misogynistic therapist. "You should be glad that she's gone. Now you can make a fresh start. This is the best thing that could have happened, buddy." He lifted his beer to Bobby and punctuated his salute with a belch. "Honestly, you should have dumped her a long time ago. I'm not trying to bad mouth her or anything. I mean she was a total bitch. I'm not trying to say anything negative though. But if you have to know, I really didn't like her."

"I guess you two were even then," Bobby said and picked at the label on his bottle. "She didn't like you very much either."

"No skin off my back, bucko," Ronnie laughed. "I don't care if she thought I was Satan's second coming. It doesn't matter. And do you know why? Because she's gone and there's nothing you can do about it. So you might as well look on the bright side. Don't think of it as one girl lost. Think of it as a city of available women gained."

"Thanks for the advice."

"I do what I can."

Bobby sneered without gratitude and looked away. He had never seen the Silhouette so crowded. Every table was full. Every stool at the bar was taken. There was even a line at the door. Only two or three of the old regulars from the neighborhood were present among an overwhelmingly brighter, younger demographic. Bobby hardly recognized the place.

Evidently, neither did its owner, Mitch. He slouched at the end of the bar, champing his gums and glaring at the crowd. Although Mitch had been there all night, he was not working. A man resembling a younger, more erect version of him – likely a son or nephew – attended to the bar. Without his bartending duties, Mitch seemed lost. Bobby could empathize. He wanted the quiet and the comfortable dilapidation of how the Silhouette used to be. The new Silhouette was, stated simply, not to his bitter taste.

It agreed with Ronnie though. He even said so.

"I like this place. Why don't we come here more often?" Ronnie asked, eyeing a group of girls that ponied up to the bar.

"Because every time I brought you here, you said you hated it," Bobby said.

"Did I really?"

"Yes. You did."

"Well, apparently things have changed."

"Yes. I suppose they have."

Ronnie assumed a wolfish grin as the girls retreated across the room, their drinks swishing and swashing out of their low balls. He stared with such amorous intensity that it was unclear whether he wanted to kiss them or punch them in the face. As Bobby recalled his friend's record of emotionally abusive relationships, there probably wasn't a meaningful difference between the alternatives.

"I see that you've gotten over Beth," Bobby said.

"Beth who?" Ronnie replied.

"Feisty redhead? We met her at the bar? You had a threesome on the dance floor? This isn't ringing a bell?"

Ronnie cackled and clapped Bobby's shoulder with such force that he nearly knocked him off his stool. "Come on, you chuck. I remember who Beth is. But to answer your question, yes, I've gotten over her. I was over her at goodbye." Ronnie looked back at the girls. His face darkened as a frown paved over his smile. "Oh, crap. Will you look at that? Just look at those busted-up assholes they're here with!"

The girls sat down a table occupied by four generically preppy jocks who resembled extras from the set of a John Hughes film. From their blocky shoulders to their negligible necks and the angular regimentation of their crew cuts, they were square in a very literal sense. They fell perfectly into Ronnie's big-tent definition of assholery.

Bobby shrugged. "A girl has a right to choose," he said.

"Not if she chooses like a retard," Ronnie replied. "Did those goombahs get lost and wander across the Ben Franklin? They're kind of far from New Jersey, aren't they?"

"It's a free country," Bobby hiccuped and slugged his beer. "They can go wherever they want."

"Since when have you become so democratic?"

"I guess I'm feeling patriotic."

"Well, so am I. I care about my fellow man. And *woman*," Ronnie declared. "I just can't stand seeing them waste their lives with those chucks. My grandfather didn't fight in World War II to see this abortion of civilization."

"Your grandfather didn't fight in World War II. My grandfather fought in World War II."

"Yours? Mine? What's the difference? It doesn't change the fact that those girls are wasting their youth on a pack of closeted gorillas. I mean, look at those pastel polos! Is that jerk wearing 'mint'?" Ronnie gestured belligerently at the offending shade of green.

"Don't point at them," Bobby said and batted at his finger. "They'll come over here."

"That's the idea," Ronnie said with great braggadocio.

202

"I've had a bad enough day. I don't need to get into a fight too."

Ronnie chewed the inside of his cheek and regarded Bobby unkindly. "You've got no heart," he said with disappointment. He ordered whiskey shots.

Bobby surveyed the brown shots that the bartender set before him with unease. "I don't want this," he said.

"You're talking crazy. Of course you do," Ronnie said. "You're in shock. You don't know what you want. Bottoms up!"

Reluctantly, but with little resolve, Bobby folded. He drank and immediately gagged.

"Now was that so bad?" Ronnie soothed with a jackal's grin, offering a morbid impersonation of his professional bedside manner as a nurse.

"Much better," Bobby rasped. He prayed that he would never be admitted to a hospital where Ronnie was on duty.

"I'm glad. It would have to be. Anything would have to be better than seeing those ladies with those chucks!" he cried suddenly, spinning around on his stool in a complete revolution and projecting his words for all to hear.

"Stop it!" Bobby barked. "Can't you forget about getting laid for just one night?"

Ronnie slapped both hands on the bar to arrest his rotation. He sat there for a moment, leaning forward, seriously considering Bobby's question. "No, I can't," he said at last and uttered the most honest phrase he ever would in his life. "When it comes to the women, I just can't control myself."

"I know you're hurting," Ronnie continued as he beckoned for more beers. "Although I don't agree with your choice to moan about 'Suze, the Snooze,' I respect your decision to be a bitch. But there is no reason

203

why your personal pain should be incompatible with my pursuit of pleasure."

Bobby glared at Ronnie. His friend luxuriated on his beer, blatantly proud of his little speech. Sipping his own beer with a less felicitous spirit, Bobby's head had started to spin. His longing for Suzie combined with his irritation at Ronnie. His thoughts became frothy and mean.

"You know? I've been listening to your mysognistic megalomania shtick for twenty years," Bobby said, chewing through his portentous word choice. "And I have to tell you that it's getting old."

"You don't say?" Ronnie said with a yawn.

"Yeah, I do say. It was really cute when you were fourteen. But you're in your thirties now. You've got to grow up."

"Says who?"

"Me."

"You, huh? I should get right on it then," he said with a smirk.

"Yeah, you should. And what's so funny about my opinion then?"

"Do you really want me to answer that question? Do you want me to tell you what is so damn hilarious about you doling out advice? I don't think you do."

"Oh, yes I do," Bobby said. The whiskey shot had lit a fire in his belly. He propped himself up on the bar, leaned forward, and glared at Ronnie. "I've never been so sure of anything in my whole life."

Ronnie regarded his old friend seriously, almost solemnly. Then, with almost inhuman speed, his lips twisted and his face flushed a deep crimson. His eyes burned like a furnace. He slammed his beer down on the bar and let out a bitter laugh. "If you really have to know, Bobby, I guess I'm gonna have to tell you. So here it is. I don't know why I should take life lessons from a thirty-something sad sack with no job, no talent, no car, and a dead-beat girlfriend who just left him."

Stung by the specificity of Ronnie's casual cruelty, Bobby's brief flirtation with a backbone ended. He expressed his betrayal in a single, shocked syllable. "Dude," he muttered.

"I didn't enjoy saying that," Ronnie said, although a smile tugging at the corner of his mouth raised doubts about that claim. "Bobby, you see the world in these tragic terms that are total crap. If you want to shackle yourself to one woman and die bitching about it, fine. But don't take your frustration out on me because I see a world of possibilities populated by many, *many* available women. And don't you dare try to push your wisdom on me. If you want to see the world your way, that's peachy. But I like things the way I see them. And right now I see a possibility passing me by." With that, Ronnie stopped speaking. His eyes stalked a woman wending through the crowd on her way to the bathroom. Ronnie jumped up from his stool and set out after her.

Bobby was left alone at the bar, defeated. Patrons jostled him from behind as they clamored for drinks. The Silhouette was filled with people, but Bobby was isolated, a man apart. He watched the crowed as though from behind a one-way mirror. He looked from side to side at the faces around him, but no one looked back. Bobby drank his beer and reflected on his solitary dimension, a space he alone inhabited. Almost alone anyway. At the far end of the room, Mitch gummed ice cubes from a glass of gin. He watched the crowd with estrangement, an alien in his own bar. By chance, their gazes met. Bobby looked at Mitch yearningly, eager for recognition. But Mitch looked away, lowering his milky eyes towards his gin.

It was at that moment – or maybe the next moment – it would be hard to say when exactly as Bobby's perception of time blurred and acquired that timeless quality characteristic of periods of both deep insight and heavy intoxication – that he had an epiphany. Maybe there was something to what Ronnie said, he thought. Maybe his outlook was flawed.

Was he really such a damn depressive? A gloomy Gus? An existentialist Eeyore? Was it possible that he had more in common with Mitch, the ancient bartender, than the happy crowd around him? He considered the question for a long time and finally shook his head.

"*No, I can't be!*" he concluded emphatically.

Bobby wasn't prepared to adopt Ronnie's philosophy of maximum sleaze. But maybe, just maybe, if he looked on the bright side of things, sought out the silver lining, and wrung his meager lemons, luck and lemonade would flow and fill his cup.

Bobby drank, and the more he drank, the more convinced he became of this belief. He sat up a little straighter. He held his head up higher. Fortified by his new resolve, he looked back at Mitch with pity rather than solidarity. No, Mitch was not his destiny. Isolation was not his fate. Bobby smiled a crooked, cavalier smile like some sop in a Franz Halls portrait and ordered another beer to inaugurate the new chapter in his life.

As he reached for the fresh pint, Bobby sensed a presence occupy Ronnie's seat. With his new optimism raging, Bobby turned to tell Ronnie about the personal breakthrough he had just achieved. But when he looked over, he did not see Ronnie. Perched on the stool was a girl. A pretty girl with a boy's haircut, a loose tank top, and the precocious curves of an African fertility goddess. And she was smiling at him.

Bobby rubbed his eyes as if he'd seen a mirage. The girl, still wearing a smile, leaned towards him as though she was offering her breasts like a tray of Christmas cookies. Bobby had no idea where she had come from or why she was there. But he couldn't discount the possibility power of positive thinking.

"Do I know you?" he asked, finally finding his tongue.

"I don't know," the girl replied. "But I know you."

"What do you know about me?"

"I know you like screen printing," she hinted with a wink.

"And how do you know that!" he asked, much more sharply than he intended.

"Well, for one thing, I watched you buy your silk screen."

Bobby's face flushed with surprise. His head resembled an enormous beet in contour as well as in color.

The girl took pity on him. "It's alright, pal. Don't freak out," she giggled tipsily. "My name is Zoe. I work at Pearl. I was working at the register when you came in."

"And you remembered me?" He was unaccustomed to anyone, much less a stranger, taking any interest in him.

"What can I say? I have a thing for faces. And, anyway, you were hard to forget. You looked really lost. You kind of stuck out."

Bobby vaguely recalled a girl working at the register in the art store the day that his car was stolen. Seeing her now, he cursed himself for being in such a rush. "Oh, yeah. The store. How's it, umm, going? What are you doing all the way up here?" he asked, groping for a sustainable topic of conversation. "It's kind of far from Pearl."

"I only work at Pearl. I don't live there."

"Of course you don't. Ha! Right! I mean what are you doing way up in Fishtown? It's kind of out of the way, isn't it?"

"My friend is having a birthday party here," Zoe said and nodded to somewhere across the room. Bobby didn't look. He couldn't care less about her friend. Zoe's splendid physique was quite sufficient to hold his attention. "I could ask you the same question," she continued. "That is if you told me your name."

"My name?" Bobby muttered. He was still unable to process why this girl was speaking with him. "My name is Bobby. Bobby Bright. It's very nice to meet you." Unaccustomed to courtship after his long

207

relationship with Suzie – not that he was ever particularly gifted in that regard – he thrust his hand forward in a very business-like fashion.

Zoe hesitated for a moment and then took his hand, indulging the formality. Their palms embraced a beat longer than necessary before she pulled her hand away.

"So tell me, Bobby Bright. What are you doing at this obscure little bar?"

"The Silhouette? I've been coming here for years. I live just up the street," he said distractedly. He fingered his palm. He could still feel the warmth of her touch.

"So you live in Fishtown?" she asked with a hiccup of excitement.

"Yes. Just off Belgrade. Only a few blocks away," he replied warily. "Is that some sort of problem?"

"It's not a problem at all. It's cool."

"Is it?"

"Yes. It is. It's very cool, Bobby Bright. Fishtown is the place to be." Zoe's lips blossomed into a smile that suggested a wonderland of tantalizing, if undefined, intimacies. She leaned closer towards Bobby and knocked over one of Ronnie's empty shot glass with her breasts. "Fishtown is so hot right now," she purred.

The shot glass rolled off the bar and pinged on the floor.

Bobby didn't know if Fishtown was hot or not. Frankly, he couldn't care less. But he nodded at Zoe's every word and encouraged each of her enthusiasms.

"You bet it's hot. And I've lived here my whole life!" he declared.

"And have you been printing your whole life too?"

"No. That's more recent," he said. "I just started screen printing t-shirts."

"You make t-shirts?" she chirped, teetering on the end of the stool as she scooted closer still. "I love screen printing!"

"You do?" he asked. His Adam's apple was aquiver with possibilities. He did not know how this – whatever *this* was – could be going any better. If he had been able to think about anything but the top-heavy nymph beside him, he would have been amazed to recall that only minutes ago he had been pining over . . . what? What was he pining over again?

"Yes. I do," Zoe said, drawing him back into the conversation. "I'm a big fan of art. I think more people should make art. Everyone should do it. All the time. Don't you think people should do it?"

"Yes. Sure. Absolutely. People should do it," Bobby agreed, not at all sure if Zoe was still talking about art.

"That's why you interested me. One look and I knew you weren't an 'artist.' (*"Whatever that means!"* she giggled to herself.) But I thought it was really cool that you were buying art supplies. You know, I wanted to talk to you then. To get acquainted. Figure you out. You seemed so mysterious. But you ran off!"

"I guess I was in a hurry," Bobby muttered, viciously kicking his inner-self for always being in such a damnable hurry.

"You're not in a hurry now, are you?" Zoe asked. "Maybe we can get to know each other a little better?"

Bobby nodded his head with the sincerest approval.

Zoe and Bobby shared a charged silence in the noisy bar. Bobby had no idea what he had done to deserve this girl's attention. But he was certain of one thing. He had become a devout believer in the powers of positive thinking.

Buoyed by this new faith, Bobby threw back his beer, choked down the frog in his throat, and parted his lips to speak. But before he could

209

utter a syllable, he heard words – alarming, angry words –and clamped his mouth shut, afraid that he had suffered a sudden onset of Tourette's. His lips were sealed. But the words continued, doing much to undermine the mood.

"What a waste of tits!" a voice roared above the crowd. "So what if she had a boyfriend? What's her man got to do with me?" Ronnie pushed past two modest-looking fellows waiting to order and inserted himself at the bar. "But excuse me! What do you have here?" he asked as he took a tactless inventory of Zoe's womanly charms.

With dread bubbling up in his belly, Bobby tried to gauge Zoe's reaction to Ronnie. Her face went pale, her head tilted to the side, and her mouth opened ever so slightly – a combination of gestures that conveyed shock, confusion, and disgust.

"Bobby, do you know this person?" she asked.

"Yeah, I guess I do. We're kind of old friends," Bobbie confessed reluctantly. "Zoe, this is Ronnie."

Zoe raised a skeptical eyebrow at them both. The existence of a friend like Ronnie demanded that she reevaluate her opinion of Bobby.

"Very nice to meet you," Ronnie slurred to Zoe's breasts and addressed Bobby. "Does she know that she is sitting in my seat?"

A tense moment ensued. Ronnie squeezed a cock-eyed grin. Zoe glowered back. Bobby frowned as though a beloved pet had just died.

"I'm just joking!" Ronnie barked. "My name isn't on the seat." He torpedoed his empty his beer glass down the bar and signaled for another. "You can sit wherever you want. I need to stretch my legs anyway."

"What a gentleman you are," Zoe said.

"That's just the kind of guy I am. I'm always looking out for the ladies."

"I've known Ronnie since I was kid," Bobby said, more as an apology than anything else.

"We've known each other our whole lives," Ronnie declared and wrapped his arm around his old friend. "I know everything about this guy. He's one talented son of a bitch. I mean it. He's a regular Calvin Klein. Did he tell you about his t-shirts?"

"Yes, he did," Zoe said flatly.

"How about Suzie?" Ronnie asked. "He must have told you about Suzie. He has been talking about her all night."

"Dammit, Ronnie. Come on," Bobby flustered, nearly spitting out the beer he had been drinking.

"My buddy here just lost his girlfriend," Ronnie continued roughshod.

Zoe's discomfort spiked. "Lost? Like she died?" she asked.

"Not literally. But she's dead to him. He's in mourning."

"I don't think she wants to hear about Suzie, Ronnie."

"Of course she doesn't, Bobby. No one *wants* to hear about Suzie. The woman was a bitch of a bore. But it's important that she knows." He turned to Zoe. "I just want you to know that he's a little delicate right now. You should be gentle with him."

"Why are you saying this?" Bobby hissed at Ronnie. His pitifully strained smile couldn't camouflage the sinister turn the night had taken.

"Why? I'm doing it for you! She should know about your situation. I wouldn't want her to take advantage of you in your fragile state."

Bobby frowned apologetically at Zoe. She regarded them both with contempt.

"Thanks," he muttered through clenched teeth.

"I do what I can," Ronnie said with great humility. "But what's this? What do we have here?"

There was a bustle by the front door. A ratty pack of dudes in flannels smoking by the entrance were violently parted. All eyes turned towards the commotion. A hush settled on the bar. Then the quiet was replaced by a collective gasp. A man with a video camera backed into the bar. He was followed by a septet of multiracial twenty-somethings who stumbled in his wake.

"You've got to be kidding me," Bobby groaned. But no one paid him any mind. The entire bar was captivated by the new arrivals.

Zoe, forgetting her hate for Ronnie, declared, "It's the cast of *Real Life*. I can't believe they're actually here!"

"Neither can I," Bobby agreed unhappily.

"Who cares about *Real Life*?" Ronnie grumbled. "They can choke on it. Beth is here! That little . . ."

"Beth? As in your ex-girlfriend Beth?" Bobby asked.

"Do we know any other Beth? And looksy. She is here with a fella!"

Beth, the diminutive redhead in question, had entered behind the camera crew. She pumped her short legs to keep pace with a lanky man wearing tortoiseshell glasses. Arm in arm, the couple weaved through the crowd.

"Look at that bozo she's with," Ronnie guffawed. "What a bitch!"

Ronnie's outburst reminded Zoe of her loathing for him. Her face puckered with disgust. "Who crapped in your shoes? What the hell is wrong with you?"

"Beth and Ronnie had a complicated relationship," Bobby explained hopelessly.

"I'm a complicated guy," Ronnie said.

212

Zoe opened her mouth as if she wanted to speak, but she could summon no words that adequately described her feelings about Ronnie. She could only shake her head. "I need to get back to my table," she said at last. She turned to Bobby. "It was…" she hesitated, considering her words carefully. "I can't say it's been nice. Good luck with the t-shirts. A word of advice: your friend is an ass. You're better off without him."

Zoe hopped off the stool and stomped away. As she and her extraordinary curves, bulging with such sensual promise, disappeared into the crowd, Ronnie yelled after her. "Nice meeting you!"

Bobby crumpled against the bar. Zoe was gone. She had taken with her his faith in happy turns and rosy outcomes. His depression returned viciously, worse than before. Adding to his grief, the *Real Life* cast pressed into the space Zoe vacated at the bar.

"Why did you have to be that way?" Bobby asked. He shifted uncomfortably as the camera man backed into him.

"I'm a complicated guy," Ronnie repeated and slugged his beer.

"I'm serious. Why are you such fantastic asshole? You say, go out and meet someone. So I do. And then you do everything you can to scare her away!"

"Give me some credit, buddy," he smirked. "I didn't do *everything* I could think of to frighten her. I could have been much more persuasive."

"You did enough."

"If she can't handle a simple conversation, a little tête-à-tête, she isn't worth your time. Besides," he paused to belch. "She had a dyke haircut anyway."

"I liked her hair," Bobby said.

Ronnie laughed and punched Bobby in the shoulder "See? It's a good thing that you have me around to keep you from making these mistakes."

213

Bobby rubbed his shoulder and glared at his old friend. But Ronnie didn't notice. His attention had drifted to where Beth and her new man had occupied a nearby table. Beth did not notice Ronnie. But Ronnie was powerfully aware of her. His eyes twinkled with a conniving glint. Bobby had seen Ronnie's eyes shine like this before. Bobby knew him well enough to be worried.

Inhaling and inflating his diaphragm like an opera singer preparing to belt out the first note of an aria, Ronnie began to heckle: "Bethy! Bethy-Beth-Beth!"

"Stop it. Leave Beth alone," Bobby said, trying to squelch whatever Ronnie was up to.

Ronnie ignored his friend and crooned Beth's name again. This time she paused mid-conversation. Her ears perked.

"What are you trying to do?" Bobby muttered.

"I'm just saying hello," Ronnie replied. Abandoning musicality, he barked out her name, exclaiming "Beth!" above the roar in the bar.

Beth heard her name clearly and looked in Ronnie's direction. She recognized Ronnie at once. Her smile promptly inverted into a frown.

Ronnie lifted his hand, waived, and blew her a kiss.

Beth clenched her jaw and tried to ignore him.

"I don't think she wants to say hello," Bobby said.

"You don't think so?" Ronnie smirked. "Well, that ungrateful…" He pressed back against the bar as though he were a tightly-coiled spring.

"Just leave her alone."

"What kind of man would I be if I left her alone with that jerk? I'm a gentleman."

"Give her a break. She isn't bothering anyone."

"Sure she is. She is bothering me by just being here." Ronnie began his "Bethy" chant again. From across the room, Bobby saw Beth flex her fists angrily.

When his heckles didn't produce a reaction, Ronnie concluded aloud, "I don't think she can hear me." Reaching into a bowl of nuts, he picked out a peanut and plucked it in Beth's direction. It flew in a wobbly arc and fell to the ground well short of its target.

"I needed a little more on that one," Ronnie said.

Bobby was deeply troubled by Ronnie's escalation to nut missiles. He wished that the bartender would see the unsanctioned use of bar snacks and throw Ronnie out. But the bartender, like everyone else at the bar, was distracted by the television cast, which seemed impossibly bored as they drank a round of City Wides.

Some distinguished, dead white guy once said that all that evil needs to prevail is for good men to do nothing. Bobby Bright was not the best man. He was so-so at best. In a word: "meh." But Bobby was the only man who knew what Ronnie was capable of. He had to do something. He cleared his throat and choked out, "Ronnie…"

Ronnie promptly cut him off. "Don't worry, little buddy. I'll get her this time. I just need to put some English on it." He spat in his palm and rubbed his hands together. He rummaged his moist fingers through the bowl, selected, and flicked another nut, which again fell short.

After the second barrage, Bobby tried to get the attention of the bartender. But he was wrist-deep in manhattans, vodka tonics, and a round of red-headed sluts.

"I need something with more weight," Ronnie said. He picked up the snack bowl to judge its mass. He tossed it down, scattering nuts across the bar.

215

Bobby watched with great concern as Ronnie lifted an empty beer bottle up and down in his hand. Fortunately, Ronnie decided against the glass projectile and let it fall and shatter on the floor.

Finally, Ronnie reached into his pocket and withdrew a quarter. His eyes gleamed and the quarter, reflecting the red "Exit" sign, twinkled demonically. Ronnie cocked his arm back, as if to skip a stone, and winged the coin. It shot across the room, sailing through the air like a tiny metal Frisbee, whizzing between bystanders until it found its mark on the soft side of Beth's temple.

Bobby watched the quarter's trajectory and impact with awful fascination. Beth clutched the side of her head and shrieked. Although the little metal blow came as a surprise, its source was no mystery. She immediately turned towards Ronnie, who confessed everything with his hysterical laughter.

Retribution came quickly. In a second Beth was on her feet, raising a chair nearly as large as herself over her head, and charging Ronnie with the berserker fury of a bull moose. The crowd before her fell away, but Ronnie didn't bat a lash. He leaned casually against the bar. His smile widened as if he welcomed the chair intended for his skull.

When Beth was within striking distance, she let the chair fall. At the last moment Ronnie leapt into action, stepping forward and deflecting the chair with his hand. Bobby watched dumbly, shocked by the sudden escalation, as the misdirected furniture missed him by inches and struck the cameraman beside him. The chair broke on the cameraman's back and he was propelled into the *Real Life* cast. Their glasses and bottles shattered as they fell to the floor.

Panic spread through the bar. The room erupted in a scrum of shouts and shoving. Amidst this chaos, Bobby remained still. A strange tranquility overcame him. Time slowed and seemed endless. The shouting was muffled like he had cotton in his ears. Bobby looked beyond the immediate violence towards the end of the bar where the owner Mitch sat. The old bartender, as inscrutable and weathered as a Bedouin goatherd, lifted his glass and drank. He was unmoved by the orgy of alcohol-fueled carnage. There was some secret wisdom that Bobby could have gleaned from his expression and white, milky eyes. But Bobby was interrupted before he could divine its meaning. On the periphery of his vision, he became aware of a fist-shaped blur hurtling in his direction. This was the last thing he saw before his head concussed against the floor and everything went black.

Chapter Nineteen: The War at Home

"Shoot him!" Bobby's grandfather yelled.

Trembling like a frightened hamster, Bobby jumped at the command. The shotgun bucked in his arms, sending him flying back onto the bed and the gun crashing to the floor. Bobby's eyes had been closed when he fired and his eyes were clenched shut as he massaged where the gun butt bruised his shoulder.

Showing little regard for his grandson's present well-being, Pop-pop peeped out of the window. "You missed!" he growled. "How could you miss?"

Bobby did not have a good answer to the question. But before he could even give a bad answer, a gunshot shattered the window. A shower of glass blew into the room and Pop-pop fell to the floor. Bobby screamed and rolled off the bed. His grandfather lay on the floor, bloodied by the debris, glaring at him. "He was right there!" he barked, angrier about Bobby missing his shot than being peppered by broken glass.

There was another blast. Chunks of plaster and dust rained down from the ceiling.

"If you aren't dead, I'd recommend you stay out of it, you son of a bitch!" Grauwickel called up from the street. "This is none of your business!"

"None of my business?" Bobby's grandfather muttered, his cataracts filling with milky indignation. "None of my business!" he hollered at the shattered window. "You shoot up my house and it's none of my business?"

"That's what you get when you poke your nose into someone else's goings on," Grauwickel hollered. "This is a family affair. Between me and Ed Flood."

"Dammit, Grauwickel," Pop-pop yelled back, "if this is was a family affair, you should have kept to Susquehanna Avenue. When you came over here raising hell and spreading your trash on my street, you made it my business." While he spoke, Pop-pop got to his hands and knees, retrieved the shotgun, and started picking up shotgun shells off the floor.

"Just sit tight, old man. I'll be finished here in a minute," Grauwickel declared.

"Sit tight, old man," his grandfather parroted under his breath. He broke the action on the shotgun and slid in two shells.

Bobby shook his head with dread as he watched his grandfather prepare a counter-attack. "Pop-pop," he whispered. "No!"

His grandfather closed the stock and cocked the gun. "You wouldn't understand, Bobby," he grumbled. "You always were delicate."

Using the gun as a crutch, the old man lifted himself up and poked the barrel out the window. "Grauwickel, you know what your problem is," he shouted. "You got no civic pride!" He punctuated his sentence with two shotgun blasts in quick succession.

A crackle of small arms fire answered from the street. Bobby screamed and fled from the room. His mind was wild and his body was sick and mad with terror. He ran down the stairs and dashed through the living room, crunching broken glass underfoot from the broken bay window, and burst through the front door.

Bobby's frantic thoughts could not keep pace with his hysterical flight. He operated on instinct and his only impulse was to escape. With his home descending into a war zone, Bobby turned to the only other refuge he knew: the church.

Bobby ran up the street to St. Stephen's. He fixated on the church and the rest of the world receded, relegated to the dimmest corners of his tunnel vision. Oblivious to the gunfire that burst around him and the large

219

lump of man unmoving in the middle of the street, Bobby sprinted towards Belgrade. He did not hear the police sirens speeding to the scene. He did not see Ed Flood's would-be escape car pressed against the telephone pole, still steaming and sputtering. He did not feel his dress socks, always too large for his feet, slip around his ankles and tangle with the undone laces on his second-hand dress shoes. Stumbling, he flailed to the ground and skidded across the pavement. He scowled and grabbed his knee. When he opened his eyes, he saw a revolver lying in the road.

Without thinking, Bobby picked up the gun and limped to the church. He went to the heavy wooden door and tried to open it, but it was locked. He pushed and it would not budge. He knocked and beat against it, but there was no answer.

Exhaustion overwhelmed Bobby. He turned from the door and crouched on the sidewalk, looking over the intersection with vacant eyes. The street was empty and still. There was no trace of Father Landy. Ronnie was gone too. The houses were shuttered and silent on the street. Deaf to the ambient violence up the block, he embraced his knees, dangling the gun between his legs. The sun was high overhead, burning the back of his already pink neck. Bobby stared at the long shadow the pistol made.

Then Bobby jerked to life. He heard footsteps behind him. He spun around and thrust the gun in the direction of the noise. When Ed Flood turned the corner, in his final flight towards freedom, Bobby didn't remember pulling the trigger.

Chapter Twenty: The Perfect Picture of a Maniac

Bobby opened his eyes and blinked at the pressed-tin ceiling. His head throbbed with a raw, thick aching that was worsened by the noise around him. From every direction he heard shoes scuffing and stomping. It was as though he'd awoken in the middle of a pack of Irish step dancers clomping out a heavy-footed slip jig. With each tremor on the floor, the square patterns on the ceiling shivered and quaked in his vision, threatening to break from their fixed geometry and shatter down upon him.

Fighting the tumult in his head, Bobby pulled himself up and leaned against the base of the bar. His memory was hazy and fractured. His confusion only settled slowly, like sediment in muddied water. He remembered faces and events, but they were jumbled and incoherent. He touched his chin and a sharp throbbing heat burned from his jaw to his ear.

The Silhouette was empty. Bobby lolled his head from side to side, looking for Ronnie. But Ronnie was gone. Bobby placed his hands on the ground to get up and something sharp stabbed into his palm. The remnants of a video camera lay beside him, broken into a million little pieces, a number of which now made a gory mosaic in his hand. Bobby pulled a long shard of glass from the center of his palm, which uncorked a thin stream of blood.

Bobby staggered to the exit, negotiating overturned tables and shattered glass. There were many muffled voices on the street. Alternating blue and red lights reflected in the Silhouette's windows. He opened the door and was greeted by chaos.

It was like witnessing the aftermath of a natural disaster. The street was congested with cop cars, ambulances, dazed civilians, and uniformed men. Medical personnel attended to the injured. Police restrained the disorderly. Bobby saw a pretty girl sitting on the sidewalk at his feet. She wore a tawny number, the color of cocoa, which was stained with something thick and red like homemade marinara. She blubbered to a camera man, who held his movie camera inches from her mascara-streaked face. Beside her a pretty white boy held a bloody compress to his head. His naturally vacant good looks were made even more modelesque by a witless expression brought on by a concussion.

Bobby skirted by the traumatized lovers and trudged past the remnants of the riot. As he was ambulatory and comparatively free from blood spatter, the paramedics paid him no mind. The police, who had their hands full with bona fide belligerents, were equally indifferent. But when he passed a police car at the intersection, a banging caught his attention. Pressed against the back seat window was the flushed face of a highly irate redhead. Beth, her arms shackled behind her, stared sabers at him through the window. He stared at her for a moment, but beat a hasty retreat when she started to scream. Bobby lurched away, fleeing around the corner, leaving the Silhouette behind him.

He ran as fast as his bandy legs could carry him and soon the sound of the sirens and shouting receded, replaced by the dense silence of the deserted city. Bobby did not know what time it was. He did not even know where he was. Although he spent his whole life walking these streets, Fishtown had become strange and foreign. He tried to read a street sign, but the letters crumpled in his vision, distorting and bleeding into meaningless calligraphy. The sidewalk also gave him highly unusual problems. It seemed to float and bob as he walked. Abandoning all concern about location, Bobby applied himself entirely to verticality, holding out his hands with palms to the ground in a desperate attempt at balance.

With each step his legs felt heavier. His feet sank into the sidewalk as if the concrete were reverting back into the clay, fly ash, and broken limestone of which it was comprised. Bobby panted with each exertion. The

222

air tasted hot and foul. It seemed impossibly muggy for the time of year. He wiped his brow and his hand came away wet and sticky.

Bobby stumbled down a street with no lights. The buildings around him were grim and decrepit like undertakers dressed in black rags. Even the sky chose that inconvenient time to cloud over, winking out whatever stars could be seen. Staggering blindly, he tripped on a crag of asphalt poking up from the sidewalk. He yelped in pain, but his cry received no answer. The night was dark and thick like a tumor.

Everything was silent and still. Not a soul stirred. But as he walked along, Bobby had the sense that he was not alone. He saw forms in the night, shadows flitting through the darkness. The air was pungent and sour and the breeze felt like something was breathing into his mouth, forcing air into his lungs. Gagging on the vile taste, Bobby started to run and fell down again. As he lay on the ground, he heard a whisper coming from the street, which looked like a river of pitch and stone. He strained to listen. The murmuring came from the storm drain.

Bobby crawled towards the gutter. He stared into the blackness beneath the storm drain, the void beneath the city.

The void stared back. The void seemed to whisper.

Bobby jerked to his feet and ran. He fled without direction, lost in the schizophrenic streets that adhered to no grid or plan. He ran blindly, crashing through trashcans and flinching at every noise. He ran until he emerged on a large wooded square the size of several city blocks. He stuttered to a stop, his heart pounding and his brain thumping to the rhythm of some excruciating, internal metronome. Bobby had found the cemetery.

A wind blew across the graveyard, rustling the tree limbs and dappling shadows among the slate and granite headstones. Some were weathered and indecipherable, as old as the city itself. Others were newer.

He looked at the rows of graves and knew that one of the neglected, knee-high monuments belonged to his grandfather.

Still coughing up his lungs from the run, Bobby leaned against the chain-link fence and gazed at the cemetery. Again he heard the voice. It was clearer now. It was a human's voice, but spoken in a language that he could not understand. Bobby scanned the headstones for its source and a pale silhouette dashed between the graves. A gust of wind kicked up a blanket of dead leaves and caused dim shapes to dance in the gloom. Although he could scarcely breathe, Bobby ran on.

He left the cemetery behind him, but he could not escape the voice. He wagged his head violently as though he could physically expel the sound from his ears. He muttered angrily. Whether he spoke to himself or in answer to the voice was unclear. In either case, as he dashed through the night, ranting, cursing, and slightly frothing, Bobby composed the picture of a perfect maniac.

As he stumbled on, Bobby encountered a smart couple coming home at the end of the evening. With one look at Bobby, they expeditiously crossed to the other side of the street. As Bobby careened down a block of renovated row homes, he came upon a man taking his dog for a midnight walk. Bobby's approach caused the dog significant alarm. It bared its fangs and barked. Its owner, also justifiably wary, reached into his pocket and fingered a can of pepper spray until Bobby raved past and disappeared down a dim alley.

After numerous, untraceable circuits through Fishtown, Bobby reached Belgrade and followed the street home. When he saw the cross atop St. Stephen's rising above the row homes, he was filled with ecstasy. His eyes glowed like a child's and he let out a little whimper. He dashed around the corner and ran up his sidewalk, anticipating the joy that he would experience when he threw open the door, sprinted up the stairs, and burrowed his face into his pillow. A simpering grin tugged at his lips, thankful that his long night was almost over.

But as he ran up his porch steps, something caught his ankle and he fell to the landing where his head thwacked hollowly against the concrete. Despite the violence of the impact, he remained conscious. Grasping his broad, bruised brow, Bobby looked down at the bottom of the steps for what had tripped him. Just beyond his feet, something twinkled in the moonlight. Screwing his eyes into woozy focus, he made out a bit of fishing line strung between the railings on his porch. He leaned closer and fingered it without comprehension, like an aborigine might regard a cuckoo clock.

Suddenly his attention was diverted from the curious line by the sinister laughter of children coming from a dark alley at the far end of the street. Bobby glared in the direction of the cackles. The fishing line was no longer a mystery.

Bobby crawled into his house and kicked the door closed behind him. As he moved towards the stairs on all fours, he knocked over a pile of shirts. He picked up one of the shirts and wiped his face. It came away stained with blood. He dropped it on the floor where it was framed by a shaft of moonlight. It was the "Fishtown" shirt with its rows of regimented fish, standing tail to tail across the Philadelphia cityscape.

Bobby struggled to his feet and climbed the stairs. But instead of going to his bedroom, he staggered to his grandfather's room and opened the door for the first time in years. He went to the closet and reached under the blanket on the top shelf. His hands happened across a long, blunt object. It was cool to the touch and reassuring. He took the double-barreled shotgun from the closet.

Chapter Twenty-One: Bobby Spends an Uneventful Afternoon on the Couch

Bobby slept for a long time. He was comatose through the remainder of the night and lifeless the next day. Only when evening came did he stir. He awoke slowly. His consciousness emerged from beneath a murky tide that only receded bit by bit, wave by wave.

He was dimly aware of being on the couch. With his eyes still closed, he lifted his right hand and fingered his brow. He moaned softly. After a minute of painful prodding, he finally opened his eyes and surveyed the living room, dim in the creeping twilight.

Almost everything seemed just as it usually was. The scene was totally unremarkable except for two details. First, on the coffee table sat a corduroy cat's severed head, watching over him as he slept. Second, he held a shotgun, quite affectionately, with its butt between his legs and his cheek nestled against its barrel. Bobby did not think much of the cat head, the shotgun, or anything else for that matter. He pushed himself upright, picked up the remote, and tuned the television to the History Channel.

Propping his contused head against a cushion, Bobby looked in the direction of the television. But he did not pay attention to the grainy figures on the screen, variously touting machine guns, driving tanks across desert fields, or plugging their ears as they fired artillery pieces. His eyes bobbled distractedly around the room in less than synchronous circuits, moving from the floor to the ceiling and skirting past everything in between. After much drifting, they settled on a dusty corner by the ceiling. This space, where three planes of dull white wall sheltered the wisp of a cobweb, was an appropriate analog for Bobby's vacant state of mind.

With all the self-awareness of a jellyfish, Bobby lay on the couch next to the gun. The sun disappeared entirely and the only light in the room was the cold reflection of the television. Still he did not stir. It is unclear how long he would have stayed like that, his arm draped affectionately around the gun. But sometime around seven, just as a documentary about the sexual escapades of the SS began, there were noises.

From outside his front door, Bobby heard voices punctuated by gurgles of laughter. Bobby tried to stand up and found the act unexpectedly difficult. His body ached all over. His neck was stiff and immobile. His whole person, from bruised head to twisted ankle, was drained of energy. When he finally got to his feet, he was broadsided by dizziness. Bobby leaned back against the couch and closed his eyes, waiting for the spell to pass. He placed the shotgun on the floor and, using it as a twelve-gauge crutch, hobbled to the door.

Deviating from his usual apprehension of the wider world, he pushed the door open, indifferent to what might be on the other side. Bobby boldly poked his head outside.

There were three boys sitting in a row on his stoop – one blonde-topped, one brown-mopped, and one with ginger bangles. The boys' backs were to him and they were unaware of his presence. The larger boys on either end pulled deliberately on cigarettes. In the center, the little blond child removed a cigarette from a pack of Marlboros and attempted to light it. Bobby stared as the boy lit a match and hurried to bring it to his cigarette, only to have the match go out, sputter, and bend beneath the weight of its charred-black head.

The blond boy tried again and again in automatic repetition, each time failing to light the cigarette. He did not ask for help, and the larger boys did not offer it. They were too occupied with their own cigarettes, which they puffed in silence. In ensemble, they projected an air of fantastic indifference, a look of bored insouciance that was only rivaled by toll booth collectors and postal workers. Bobby, however, was anything but

227

disinterested. He concentrated wholly on the matches, his pupils flaring with every flicker and fade of the flame.

Just as he was about to strike another match, the blond boy suddenly paused. Whether it was because he heard something or felt Bobby's eyes boring into the back of his skull, he turned around. Understandably alarmed to have a grown man staring at him, the small boy dropped his matches and leapt from the steps. The larger boys turned to see what all the fright was about. With one look at Bobby's monstrously welted forehead, they joined the blonde boy on the sidewalk, their cigarettes dangling from their slack mouths.

It did not take long for their initial shock to pass though. Conferring through a series of quick glances, the boys squared their thin shoulders and crossed their arms, smoking defiantly at Bobby, who remained half-concealed behind the door.

Bobby did not respond to the boys' impudent posturing. He regarded them blankly, his eyes expressing nothing. This aloofness unnerved them all the more. For a second time, they looked at each other uncertainly.

"Got a problem, man?" the largest boy with the brown hair said.

"Yeah, got a problem with us sitting on your stoop?" the red-head elaborated.

"Asshole!" the little blond peeped nastily.

Bobby said nothing. He chewed his lower lip like a wad of tobacco.

Emboldened by his silence, the boys grinned at one another with conspiratorial menace.

"What's your deal?" the brown-haired boy sneered. "What are you looking at?"

"Maybe he's a retard?" the redhead suggested.

228

"Maybe," the brown-haired boy supposed. "He could be a pervert though."

"Are you a pervert?" the redhead asked.

"We don't like perverts," the brown-haired boy told him.

"We'll kick your ass!" the little blonde boy exclaimed.

Bobby had nothing to say to these taunts. But what he did have was better than any words. Casually pushing the door open, he stepped onto the stoop with the shotgun nestled under his right arm.

When the boys saw the weapon, the smiles disappeared from their faces. In terrified synchronicity, their jaws dropped, the cigarettes fell from their mouths, and they fled, screaming holy terror. They covered half the block before their Marlboros touched the sidewalk.

Bobby watched as they disappeared around the corner. Once they were gone, he stumbled down the steps and picked up the matches and the cigarette pack that they had left behind.

Bobby went inside. Leaning against the window frame, he pushed the curtain back and watched the street with the abstract preoccupation of a housebound calico. With one hand resting on his gun, he meditated on the cracked pavement by his stoop. He gave more consideration to how the road abutted the uneven sidewalk than even the most engaged city planner. He studied the row homes across the street, squinting at them as though they were a familiar face of an old acquaintance whose name he could not quite recall. But, as always, it was upon St. Stephen's that his attention inevitably settled.

Unlike the rest of the block, which appeared jaundiced in the sodium vapor street lights, the church's stained glass windows glowed with salutary warmth. Bobby gazed at their ornamental designs, the depictions of saints, and the calls to virtue inscribed upon them. Broadening his perspective, he focused on the dark outline of the church. It dwarfed every

229

other building around it. The stone edifice was at once overwhelming and comforting. As Bobby beheld the church, peacefulness settled over him and his haggard features rallied into a smile.

Bobby stood by the window for a very long time, basking in the proportions of the church. He gradually became aware that his block had become very crowded. Cars filled the one-way street outside the house, taking every available space. From around the corner, he saw discreet groups of people moving towards the church. This trickle soon built into a steady stream. Bobby watched the congregation. He watched for a very long time.

With the aid of his shotgun, Bobby hobbled up the stairs to his bedroom. With only the hallway light to see, he flicked through the clothes in his closet and pulled out a plain white shirt and some pleated black slacks. From the dresser he selected a pair of threadbare argyle socks. Beneath the bed he found his black leather shoes. He dressed in the dark.

Bobby emerged from his bedroom in a modest ensemble that approximated the outfit that he had worn as an altar boy. Of course he was a little long in the tooth for an acolyte and the stubble on his chin did much to undermine the image of child-like purity. Still, the resemblance was there.

He started gingerly down the stairs, but with each step, his fatigue and discomfort evaporated. By the time he reached the ground floor, he no longer needed the shotgun for support and carried it at his side. With renewed pep he walked to the door and threw it open.

But there he paused. He looked down at the shotgun. He lifted it with both hands as though he were trying to guess its weight. After a minute of deliberation, he leaned it against the wall and stepped outside.

Bobby didn't close the door behind him. From his stoop, he looked at the church. From both directions on Belgrade, people streamed towards it, sucked inside it like rainwater down a gutter.

Bobby had no thoughts. He did not speak. He thrust his hands into his pockets and his fingers brushed against a soft box he no longer recognized. He descended his stoop and joined the stream flowing towards St. Stephen's. His feet and their feet moved as one. There was nothing except his feet.

Chapter Twenty-Two: A Conclusion

Bobby passed into the church unnoticed. As he crossed the street, he had insinuated himself into a group whose fashionable black dress obscured the weirdness of his own conservatively two-tone outfit. While he walked, he stared up at the peak of St. Stephen's like a zombie Jehovah's Witness. With each step closer to the church, he lifted his chin higher, craned his neck, and leaned back farther as he tried to keep the old stone cross on top of the building in sight. It was not until he mounted the wide step by the entrance, his contorted body worthy of a limbo champion, that it finally disappeared from view.

The heavy wooden door clapped shut behind him. The group merged into a large crowd at the center of the sanctuary. Bobby remained alone by the entrance, blinking in the brightly lit interior. When his eyes focused, he was stunned by the church's transformation. The renovations, which had been a work in progress on New Year's Eve, were now complete. The new walls were gleaming white and illuminated by long rows of track lighting on the vaulted ceiling high above. Beneath his feet the floors were polished hardwood. At the far end of the sanctuary where the apse had been, there was a raised living area decorated in a mid-century fashion that was short on Christ and long on Corbusier.

The altars along the walls were all gone. Replacing the saints and the candles that had filled them was photography: photos of architecture, interiors, landscapes, portraits, and commercial stills that ranged from advertising for cars and vodka to fitness centers and airlines. The congregants of the church milled from picture to picture as they would in a gallery, chatting and sipping cocktails. As Bobby took in the scene, he felt confused and dislocated. His anxiety condensed and seeped through his pores. He sweat like a hog in the know passing an abattoir.

Yet, when Bobby looked beyond the crowd, he realized that not everything was different. In the back of the church, rising above the apse's chaise lounge chairs and teak credenzas, was the old pipe organ, polished and towering over the sanctuary. The instrument reassured Bobby and he gazed up on it with devotion as though it was a three-story fetish. In its presence his shoulders slumped, his mouth yawned just-so, and his face conveyed the simple serenity most often found in Buddhists and the brain-damaged.

With his mind keen on the organ, holy impulses marched through his brain, filling him with happy thoughts and an enormous sense of well-being. The longer he gazed up at the organ's brass pipes climbing towards heaven, the brighter his elation glowed, the more rapidly these feelings of connection, belonging, and identity cycled through him, grounding him to a particular place and suggesting that the world was not all change and chaos and decay.

But before Bobby could reach a new plane of understanding, his sublime train of thought was derailed. The organ disappeared behind an enormous camera that was thrust in his face. It its black lens he saw a convex reflection of himself: a cold, gray image with his bruised head disproportionate atop his foreshortened body. Bobby frowned at this vision and all of his hopes drifted away like spent vespers in the night.

There was a blinding flash.

When Bobby recovered his sight, the camera had been replaced by a ruggedly handsome face with red cheeks and masculine lips.

"Cheese, I say!" Jeff cried out. "Hmm. I should have said that first. I got things a little backward. But to tell you the truth," Jeff added in a stage whisper, "I'm a little backward myself just now." He laughed with good-natured ham. Bobby eyes were desolate.

233

"Well, I suppose this is the part where I say 'welcome to the party!' I'm glad to see that you made it. It's always great to have the neighborhood stop in for a visit."

As Jeff spoke, Bobby didn't look him in the eye. His gaze settled on the camera his host held.

Jeff noticed Bobby's interest with evident pleasure.

"Nice camera, right? I just got it. It's a Hasselblad. Medium format. I bought it for a shoot I'll be doing in the Andes next month. Patagonia, you know." He lifted the bulky camera and beamed at the instrument with almost paternal pride. Looking back at Bobby, the smile fell from his face.

"Jesus!" Jeff declared. "What happened to you?"

Bobby shrank from the exclamation. He lifted his hand to cover the welt on his forehead, which looked as if an eggplant had taken root on his forehead.

"That looks like it hurts," Jeff said, brushing away Bobby's hand. "Do you need to go to the hospital or something?"

Instinctively seeking escape, Bobby scrunched his neck like a tortoise trying to hide in its shell. Jeff understood this gesture as a shrug meant to communicate all was well.

"Okay, then. If you're sure you're alright," he said. "It looks like hell though. That's the worst bruise I've ever seen." He paused as an idea dawned. "Would you mind?" he asked and lifted his camera hopefully.

Bobby did not reply. Taking silence as acquiescence, Jeff stepped to Bobby's side and snapped a photograph of his profile.

"That's one hell of a shiner!" he said.

A voice called to Jeff, diverting his attention. He waved across the room and laughed before turning back to Bobby. "It's good to see you. Get yourself a drink. You earned it. We can call it your modeling fee!"

Failing to notice that his guest had not said a word during their overwhelmingly one-sided conversation, Jeff departed, navigating through the crowd with the aid of his Hasselblad's viewfinder.

Once the host was gone, Bobby turned his attention back to the organ. He ran his eyes down the pipes, past octaves and valves, to the antique keyboard. The organ had not changed, but the bliss that he had experienced before was gone. The instrument was nothing more than three stories of brass, wood, and disuse.

With the spell undone, Bobby became hyper-aware of the roar of the party, its guests, and their nattering conversations. The desire to flee seized him and he longed to find a quiet, empty place. He looked to the exit, but the party had grown, clogging the room and blocking his path of egress. He jerked his head from side to side, desperate to escape. Towards the back of the church, it was relatively deserted beside the apse. Bobby pushed through the crowd. Reaching the fringe of the guests, he saw a nondescript door that led to what had once been the sacristy. He hurried inside.

The door closed behind him, blocking out the light and muffling the noise of the party. Bobby searched for the light switch, sliding his palm over the wall until it collided with a ridge of plastic. His vision flooded with red light and the room revealed itself in contrasting shades of black and suffocating crimson. It was like he had stumbled into a waiting room for a lesser level of hell. Reacting spastically to the sense of damnation, Bobby slapped his hand back at the switch. The red hue of the room disappeared, replaced by the sharp incandescence of 100-watt bulbs and the ambient hum of a ventilation fan.

Bobby leaned back against the wall and closed his eyes, taking a moment to still his racing heart. When he looked again, he did so reluctantly, barely opening his eyes, afraid that the infernal tint to the room might have returned. He peered through the blurry lattice of his eyelashes and was reassured to see that the light was normal and in no way infernal.

The sacristy, like the rest of the church, had changed. Gone was the sacristycredens that stored the cloaks, stoles, and chasubles. Gone were the cabinets where Bobby would gather the candles and hangings for services. Gone was the stained-glass window, which was replaced by a plain white wall. Even the stone basin where the priests would do their righteous washing up had been swapped for a stainless steel sink.

Bobby walked to the center of the room. Along the wall to his right were stacks of boxes of industrial developers and toners. To his left, where the candles were once stored, there was metal shelving burdened with photographic equipment. But what grabbed Bobby's attention was a computer on the far wall cycling through a screensaver of photographs. Like a bug to a zapper, he was drawn to the pulsing light. He sat in the computer chair and noticed a large, expensive-looking printer on the desk. A stack of photographic prints were in the tray.

Bobby picked up the photographs. The first was a study of a building in Center City. Objectively, it was a very nice picture. But he wasn't interested in the formal elements of its composition or the subtle play of light and shadow reflected in the building's windows. Bobby let the print go and it glided to the floor like a dead leaf.

The next photo was in much the same spirit. It was a generic, competent photograph of a street scene with children playing in a broken water hydrant. Bobby set the print aside. He studied and discarded a third and then a fourth picture. But as he looked at the fifth picture, his eyes opened wide. He held the picture up to the light, moving it closer and farther away as though he could not make out the image. But this was unnecessary. Bobby saw it perfectly. He was looking at a picture of himself.

236

It was a photograph from the Eagles game the previous fall, taken just as the security guard had shredded his tickets into confetti. The photograph immortalized Bobby's horror as the tickets blew in the autumn wind while the crowd around him heckled with the unsportsmanlike gusto that Philadelphia fans were known and loathed for.

Bobby's face blanched like an almond. He grabbed another photo from the printer tray and hiccupped unhappily.

In a room lit whorehouse-red, Bobby saw an image of himself slouched at a seedy bar, perfectly A-framed between the fleshy thighs of a stripper years past her expiration date. Just beyond his right shoulder, Ronnie was visible, making an unseemly stroking motion with his hand.

Bobby looked at the next photo. And the next one. And the one after that. To his awful amazement, each photograph was a moment in his life. He saw himself leaving his house. Skulking on his front step. Shame-eating a scrapple sandwich. Thrusting his fist like a madman and hollering in empty triumph at a trio of scattering children. And there he was, standing in the bay window, looking out onto what he assumed was an empty street.

Bobby took the last picture from the printer tray. It was from the New Year's party several months before. He was standing in the church by what had been the altar. Like the previous photographs, his image was captured at an unfortunate time and an unflattering angle. His arms gestured wildly, extended like broken bicycle spokes, and his face was flushed with anger. But unlike the other photographs in the pile, Bobby was not the sole subject. Suzie faced him, toting her breasts like a machine gun, declaiming drunkenly. The composition was like a tasteless parody of a wedding with them at the bygone altar, slinging angry oaths while the party around them carried on with raucous indifference.

Bobby gazed at Suzie's picture. He looked into her eyes and it seemed, for a fleeting, impossible second, she looked back at him. His lips

237

parted and he breathed a shallow breath. He whispered, just audibly, "Snooze . . ."

His heart thumped hollowly in his chest. But this pang of love lost soon percussed to a more violent beat. Unable to bear the image, he ripped the photograph in two. But this act of destruction did not quell the pain in his heart. The image, although torn, was still discernible. Even if he tore it into four, eight, or one hundred little pieces, the photograph would still exist in jigsaw form. He needed a way to destroy it absolutely and irredeemably. He searched the room for some means to annihilate the picture and the memories it recalled. He wanted to beat it. He wanted to smash it. He wanted to push it in front of a subway train. He wanted to quarter it with horses and bathe it in acid. He wanted to . . . He paused as the words came to him like a distant peal of thunder . . . He wanted to *burn* it.

Bobby fumbled in his pockets. His thumb brushed against the pack of matches. With his hand trembling, he lit a match, watching the sulfur flare. He lit the first half of the photograph and then the other.

He held the halves of the photograph, one in each hand. As celluloid paper spit and smoldered, Bobby watched the flame grow. Suzie's half burned first. The flame raced up the side of the print and her image faded and bubbled. He held the print until the flame licked his fingers. He released it and let it drift to the floor.

Bobby watched it burn on the ground, mesmerized. He was so engrossed that he forgot that the other half was burning in his other hand. A searing pain served as a reminder. He cried out and threw the torn photograph, which was now completely on fire. It pitched clumsily through the air. Bobby recalled the burning planes that he had seen in his war documentaries. A grin twitched at his lips. Messerschmitts flaming over Stalingrad. Japanese Zeros plunging into the sea at Midway. The photograph rained ashes as it wafted across the room and landed on a box filled with photographic chemicals.

Bobby watched it smolder. He saw a flicker.

Suddenly the box erupted in flames. The fire spread to neighboring boxes. For a moment, Bobby was seized with an orgiastic glee as the fire carried out the destructive impulses that raged in him. But this fraternity with the flames was soon replaced by terror as the room became like a furnace and the pyre that had consumed the boxes exceeded by several hundred degrees the conflagration in his heart.

Bobby's senses returned to him. The realization of what he'd done hit him like a haymaker in the gut. He fumbled for something to put out the fire. As he rushed around the room, he stumbled, quite literally, onto the sink where the sacrarium had been. He turned on the spigot. A stream of water hissed and dribbled out. He experienced a flash of hope that just as abruptly disappeared when he realized there was nothing to collect the water. But it was too late anyway. The fire was already climbing the walls, lapping at the ceiling and filling the room with smoke. Bobby choked when he breathed. Covering his mouth and wiping the tears from his eyes, he fled from the room.

Bobby slammed the door behind him and pressed his back against it as though he could physically contain the fire. He stretched out his neck and looked onto the sanctuary. The party had no suspicion of flames raging in the church. Bobby opened his mouth to scream, but no words came. He was dumb with fear. From the sill, hot air hissed on the back of his ankles. The door burned against his shoulders. He gripped the door knob and yelped as the metal bit into his palm.

The pain freed Bobby's voice and, like a dam unblocked, a torrent issued from his lips. He belted out a garbled alarm. His cry was lost in the noise of the party. Overpowered by loud music and a multitude of voices, his warning was only noticed by a drunk and feisty someone who shouted back in sarcastic reply.

His face twisted with horror. Bobby looked back at the sacristy. A bright orange border blazed around the door frame. The door began to buckle and beat like a living heart. Bobby felt his stomach wrench and his mouth fill with bile.

Fighting back the urge to vomit, he rushed into the sanctuary, pushing his way through the crowd and struggling towards the exit. He saw Jeff across the room, composing a photograph. Bobby screamed, but Jeff did not hear him.

Bobby ran.

The exit was just ahead. Each step through the crowd was a struggle. With one final push he reached the door. He heaved it open. The cold night air tickled his face and he laughed witlessly. As he ran out onto Belgrade Street, he coughed and quaked in idiot rapture.

Only moments after Bobby fled St. Stephen's, the voices inside abruptly fell silent before rising again, louder than before, clamoring in alarm. The great wood door was flung open and the crowd mobbed the exit, trying to escape the church, which was now universally known to be on fire. Giving sound to great lamentation, the guests scratched and clawed at one another as they fought to escape. Some spilled out onto the sidewalk. Others were pulled down and trampled by those behind them. Those that had escaped scrambled down the street before looking back. A hellish glow illuminated the stained-glass windows and swirls of smoke rose from the roof.

The fire consumed St. Stephen's with terrific speed. The roof was crowned with wild red flames and smoke blocked out the stars. The church windows exploded in a shower of bright glass. The front door, now fully aflame, groaned and hissed, giving voice to the inferno.

Every eye was fixed on the ruined church. The bloodied and soot-stained guests stared in petrified silence. No one moved. Well, almost no one. One witness dutifully raised a large and exquisitely designed German camera and snapped a photograph as the skeleton of the steeple collapsed into the blaze.

Inside the church, wooden timbers burst and crackled like gunfire. From the four corners of the city, sirens sounded as they converged on the scene. Among this chorus of destruction, another voice was heard. Somewhere, some blocks away, a poor soul howled with mad laughter. Terrible cries echoed through the streets. Those in the crowd shivered at the ghastly voice. They strained to locate its source, but it seemed to come from every direction, to be everywhere and nowhere as it traveled deeper into the neglected reaches of the city.

These howls were accompanied by a deafening blare as the superheated air convected through the brass pipes of the church organ, which wailed across the city in agony, sounding a shrill alarm in the night.

www.ingramcontent.com/pod-product-compliance
Lightning Source LLC
Chambersburg PA
CBHW060924120626

46557CB00003B/865